The year is 1943 . . .

A GI earns $21 a month, pastes photos of Rita Hayworth on his footlocker and posts letters to his sweetheart on Victory mail. Broadcasting from London, Edward R. Murrow is as familiar a voice as Roosevelt's.... The world is again at war.

On the home front, fuel oil shortages compound a harsh winter. Meat, sugar and gas are rationed. Silk stockings and tires can't be had for love or money.

"Rosie the Riveter" mirrors reality as women take to the factories, lending their talents to the war effort. After hours, "the fundamental things apply" as *Casablanca* wins the Oscar, couples jitterbug to Tommy Dorsey and the Andrews Sisters, and Cary Grant sets hearts afluttering.

It is a time of purpose, of a nation united in a common cause.

It is a time of pride, as men and women tap newfound strengths.

It is the time of Catherine Wilson and Johnny Danza....

Dear Reader,

We hope you are enjoying A Century of American Romance, a nostalgic look back at the lives and loves of American men and women from the turn of the century to the dawn of the year 2000. These stories give us all a chance to relive the memories of a time gone by and sneak a peek at romance in an exciting future.

We've traveled from the 1899 immigrant experience to 1906 San Francisco's tumultuous quake to the muddy trenches of France's Western Front in World War I, to the carefree, decadent Roaring Twenties, and to the Thirties, the era of lost fortune and indomitable spirit. Now Barbara Bretton recalls all the memories of the fabulous forties, a time when life on the home front meant the Stage Door Canteen, war bonds, Victory gardens, and the Andrews Sisters.

In the months ahead watch for all the titles—one per month—in A Century of American Romance, including next month's book, a spinoff book of *Sentimental Journey* by Barbara Bretton.

We hope you continue to enjoy these special stories of nostalgia and romance, written by some of your favorite novelists. As always, we welcome your comments. Please take the time to write to us at the address below.

Here's hoping A Century of American Romance will become part of your most cherished memories....

Sincerely,
Debra Matteucci
Senior Editor & Editorial Coordinator
300 East 42nd St
6th floor
New York, New York
10017

BARBARA BRETTON

1940s
SENTIMENTAL
JOURNEY

Harlequin Books

TORONTO • NEW YORK • LONDON
AMSTERDAM • PARIS • SYDNEY • HAMBURG
STOCKHOLM • ATHENS • TOKYO • MILAN

For my husband,
who spent even more time in the library
than I did.
Thanks for giving me your Christmas vacation.

Much appreciation to DM (of ATH fame)
who inspired,
and to DS (aka That Woman)
who encouraged.

Published November 1990

ISBN 0-373-16365-7

PART I

SAYING GOODBYE

American women are learning how to put planes and tanks together, how to read blueprints, how to weld and rivet and make the great machinery of war production hum under skillful eyes and hands. But they're also learning how to look smart in overalls and how to be glamorous after work. They are learning to fulfill both the useful and the beautiful ideal.
—*Woman's Home Companion*, 1943

Chapter One

Catherine Anne Wilson was no different from a million other young women on that warm June evening in 1943. She was twenty-one years old, engaged to be married, and impatient to get on with the rest of her life. If the war hadn't come along, she and Douglas Weaver would be married by now, snug and safe in their own little apartment with a baby in the cradle and one on the way.

Instead, there she was, still in her parents' house in Forest Hills, curled up on the window seat in the pastel-pink room where she'd played with dolls and learned how to curl her hair and dreamed of how wonderful it would be to be grown-up and married.

Now, years later, she was still waiting to find out. She was a grown woman living the life of a dutiful daughter. Each morning she arose at seven, gulped down oatmeal and a cup of cocoa, then kissed her mother goodbye, in the same routine she'd followed for four years at Forest Hills High School when she was counting the days until she was grown-up. The only difference was she no longer headed for the classroom; she headed for work, where she spent nine hours a day posting numbers at her father's manufacturing firm. She came home at night to her mom's meat loaf and her sister's Sinatra recordings and an abiding emptiness inside her heart that almost took her breath away.

Even the songs matched her mood. "Don't Get Around Much Anymore" and the painfully beautiful "As Time Goes By" only served to point out how different this world was from the one she'd imagined when she was a foolish girl.

It wasn't as if she wanted very much out of life. All she wanted was the same things women had wanted for hundreds and hundreds of years. Her own house and her own husband. Children to care for and a life that was her very own. *Woman's Home Companion* said that these should be the happiest years of her life, a time when childbirth was easier and housework more satisfying. They even hinted that the love between a man and a woman could prove that sometimes heaven was found right there on earth. Instead, Catherine felt like a hungry child with her nose pressed against the window of a bakery, longing for something as simple and natural as a loaf of bread fresh from the oven. Something that was as impossible as flying to the moon.

When her mother was twenty-one, Dot had already given birth to Catherine and was pregnant again with Nancy. She'd had a husband and a home and the happiness Catherine dreamed about every single night.

"Don't you worry," everyone said, their tones jovial and reassuring. "Things will be back to normal before you know it." The tide was about to turn any day. Hitler and Tōjō and Mussolini were on the run, and any minute the Allies would strike the blow that would put an end to this insanity.

Like most other Americans, Catherine had been raised on happy Hollywood endings, firm in the belief that the good guys always won. Lately, however, she'd been finding it harder to hold on to the notion that everything would work out the way it did in Betty Grable movies. Instead of coming to an end, the war grew larger and more frightening with each day that passed. The headlines in the *New York Daily News* and the *Herald Tribune* talked of massive troop movements and losses that brought a chill to the blood.

Six million Americans were in the military, and each day the ranks swelled as eager men signed up to defend their country. The Allies had suffered badly in Corregidor and the Bataan death march was all too real. The *Movietone News* put a good face on the truth, but it wasn't until Guadalcanal, just a few months ago, that the Allies had scored their first victory.

None of it, however, seemed to register with her sister, Nancy. The girl's voice floated up to Catherine's window from the front stoop, where the high-school senior sat chatting with her pals. Had it only been four years since Catherine herself had sat on the stoop with Douglas and made plans for the senior prom? She felt like an old woman sitting in her rocker watching the youngsters have all the fun.

Nancy's voice was high and excited—after all, it wasn't every day you got to go into Manhattan and see the real-life Stage Door Canteen. Their father had pulled a few strings and made special arrangements to take the family into the city to meet some of his squadron members. They would have a good old-fashioned celebration before he boarded a troop ship the next morning to Europe. "We're not going to sit here watching the clock tick," he had said to Dot and his daughters at the breakfast table that morning. "Let's meet the fellows and make an evening of it."

Nancy had been beside herself. It seemed to Catherine that her little sister had been baptized with stardust and blessed by Max Factor. Nancy pored over her stacks of *Photoplay* and *Modern Screen* as if they held the secret of life. Nancy believed in love at first sight, that Clark Gable was the most handsome man in the whole world, and that if she only had Betty Grable's legs, Rita Hayworth's hair and Lana Turner's smile, her happiness would be assured.

"Do you know that little girl is positive she'll meet Van Johnson and Tyrone Power tonight?"

Catherine turned away from the window at the sound of her mother's voice in the doorway. "What's worse," she said, summoning up a smile, "is that she believes they'll both fall in love with her."

"The child is starstruck," said Dot as she entered the room. Her slender figure was hidden inside the lavender housecoat Grandma Wilson had made for her birthday present, and her thick light brown hair was tightly wound into curls crisscrossed with bobby pins and dampened with Wave-Set.

Her mother's familiar scent of Cashmere-Bouquet and Pacquin's hand cream was a balm to Catherine's troubled soul. She made room for her mom on the window seat. "I'm glad Nancy's the way she is," Catherine said. "One serious daughter is enough, don't you think?"

Dot glanced at the alarm clock ticking away on Catherine's nightstand, then leaned over and poked her head out the bedroom window. "You have one hour to get yourself ready, young lady. Daddy expects us dressed and on our way to the subway at six o'clock sharp."

Dot and Catherine both laughed at Nancy's shriek of "I don't know what to wear!" followed by the sound of her black-and-white saddle shoes pounding up the front steps. Lucky Nancy, with nothing more to worry about than choosing between her red blouse and her white one.

"Are you going to wear your green dress?" Catherine asked her mother.

Dot's cheeks colored prettily. "I wouldn't dare wear anything else. It's your father's favorite."

"If you like, I'll help you pin your hair into an upsweep. Mary Clare, down the block, showed me how to roll the most adorable pompadour. With that gold mesh snood Aunt Mona gave you, you could—"

Dot gave her eldest daughter a long look that stopped Catherine cold. "What's wrong?"

Catherine glanced out the window. "Nothing."

Dot inclined her head toward the pale blue letter on her daughter's lap. "Did something in Douglas's letter upset you?"

"He's fine." A sigh escaped her lips. "At least, I think so." She held up the heavily censored letter for her mother to see. "There wasn't much left to read after Uncle Sam got through with it."

Dot's smile wavered. "I guess your dad and I will have to invent a secret code for our sweet nothings."

Catherine wanted to say something reassuring, but the lump in her throat made speech impossible. Her cheerful, upbeat mother—the woman Catherine had leaned upon for twenty-one years—suddenly looked like a frightened child. The war seemed closer to Forest Hills than ever before.

Dot looked away for an instant, and when she met her daughter's eyes again she was once more her ebullient self. "You get yourself ready now, honey. You know how Daddy hates to be kept waiting."

Catherine blinked away sudden, embarrassing tears as Dot headed toward the door. "Mom?"

Dot paused in the doorway and looked back. "Yes?"

The moment passed. "Nothing. I...I'd better get ready." Catherine longed to throw herself into her arms and cry her heart out, but Dot had her husband to worry about now. It wouldn't be fair to add her daughter's fears to her burden.

"You know you can tell me anything, don't you, Cathy?"

Catherine nodded and her mother turned, then disappeared down the long hallway to her bedroom.

You know exactly what I'm thinking, don't you, Mom? I've never been able to fool you about anything. You can see that I'm scared to death that something terrible is going to happen to Douglas, that this dark cloud I've felt hovering over me for days means something.

Catherine shivered despite the balmy June weather, and wrapped her arms around her knees as she looked out the window at the street she knew so well. Hansen Street, a narrow road lined with powerful oaks and graceful maples, was her whole world. She'd been conceived right there in the Tudor-style house three months after her parents' marriage. She'd taken her first steps in the front yard while Mrs. Bellamy and old Mr. Conlan called out encouragement.

And at twelve she'd fallen in love with Douglas Weaver, her very best friend, as they'd sat beneath his father's crab-apple tree under the star-spangled sky.

Fifteen months ago she had kissed Douglas goodbye at Grand Central Station. He had looked so handsome in his uniform, so tall and strong and painfully young, that her heart had ached with love for him.

"I'll wait for you forever," she'd said, her tears staining the shoulder of his khaki jacket. "I'll never love anyone but you."

"I'm coming back, Cathy," he'd said. "I'll be back before you have time to miss me."

A thousand other soldiers whispered the same words into the ears of a thousand other sweethearts, who also stood on the dock that snowy morning. The boys' promises were heartfelt. The girls knew the war would be over before they could dry their tears.

How wrong they all had been. The days turned into weeks, then the weeks passed into months, and finally Catherine realized the war wasn't going to end simply because she and Douglas Weaver wanted a chance at happiness.

Across the street Edna Weaver waved to Catherine's father, Tom, who strolled toward home with his *Daily News* neatly rolled under his arm.

"You shake Bing Crosby's hand for me tonight, Tommy!" Edna called out, waving her pruning shears in greeting.

Tom tipped his cap. "Come with us, Edna, and shake his hand yourself, why don't you?"

Edna laughed and pointed to her gardening costume, which consisted of her husband's cast-off trousers and her long-sleeved smock. "Movie stars will just have to wait until my rosebushes are in shape, but you and Dot dance a waltz for me."

Catherine's father promised he would do exactly that, then turned up the path to the Wilson house.

Edna resumed her gardening chores, maintaining the dazzling display of scarlet, cream and blush-pink roses, which were her pride and joy and the talk of the neighborhood. Douglas had always teased his mother that she cared for her rosebushes more than she cared for her husband and sons, but everyone knew Edna Weaver's big heart knew no bounds.

"Just you wait until Douglas comes home, Cathy," her future mother-in-law liked to say over a cup of cocoa in the front room of her red-brick house. "We'll take your wedding picture right here in front of the roses and everyone will say you're the real American beauty."

Edna Weaver tended toward exaggeration in everything she said and did. Her roses were the most beautiful; her sons and her husband, the most brilliant of men; and her almost daughter-in-law, the most perfect girl in the world. Edna Weaver also believed in happy endings, and these days that kind of cockeyed optimism was what Catherine sorely needed.

This sense of foreboding unnerved Catherine greatly. Although she had a serious nature, she invariably saw the best in others and believed that good things happened to good people. But ever since her dad had enlisted last December, she'd had the terrible sensation that nothing would ever be the same again. She did her best to push such dark thoughts aside, but they refused to be ignored, overtaking her late at night when her guard was down and her heart most vulnerable. It wasn't right that the man she loved was so far away, that the plans they'd made for the future had to be stored away for the time being like winter blankets come springtime. Douglas was her love and her friend, and she missed him more than she'd ever imagined possible.

She wrote to him every night, long letters on her pastel stationery, letters filled with her hopes and dreams for the future still ahead of them. Dreams she shared with no one but him. Even the everyday happenings took on new importance. She told him that Count Fleet won the Kentucky Derby and that she went to see *White Christmas* for the third time and loved it more than she had the first. She memorized every word of his government-censored letters and spent endless hours trying to reconstruct the missing phrases. She drew funny pictures of their neighbors and wrote out the words to "As Time Goes By" in her most elegant hand.

And she promised him a life of sunshine and beer and little Weavers if he would just win the war and come back to her.

Late at night in the darkness of her room she tried to imagine their future. She could see their children, as blue eyed as she; as blond as the man she loved. A little girl with rosy cheeks and a lopsided smile sat on her big brother's lap as he peered out from beneath the bill of his Brooklyn Dodgers baseball cap. She could picture the tiny white house with crisp black shutters they would live in, and the smart striped wallpaper and even the Philco radio that would stand majestic and proud in the corner, but she couldn't picture Douglas. Heart pounding, she would squeeze her eyes shut, trying to conjure him up in the darkness. A thick wheat-colored brow...a flash of sparkling eyes...but no more. He faded away each time like a dream come morning, leaving her alone and terrified.

She remembered his words, but the sound of his voice eluded her, also. The man she loved, the boy she'd grown up with, the one person she thought would be with her always, and she couldn't recall the timbre of his voice or the way his hair looked in the sunshine.

Would that happen to her mother? Six months from now would Dot cry into her pillow as Tom Wilson's face stubbornly refused to appear before her eyes? It seemed to Catherine that all across the country it was happening to women who waited. Somewhere in Kansas a farmer's wife sat on her front porch and listened for her husband's voice in the summer wind, then shivered as she heard nothing but the beating of her solitary heart.

The men were disappearing, all of them. The Robertson twins, Arnie from around the block, and the man who ran the hardware store on Continental Avenue had all left for boot camp in the past week. Douglas's big brother, Mac, had gone to Europe as a correspondent, but it looked like he'd be enlisting any day, too.

And now tomorrow her own father was off to war, leaving her mother alone with Wilson Manufacturing and the house and two daughters to care for. Not that either Catherine or Nancy needed full-time mothering any longer, but there was something scary about being a family of women without a man's strength to lean upon.

Their lives were changing and there wasn't anything Catherine or Dot or Nancy could do to stop it, and that fact scared Catherine more than anything else. She could write a thousand letters, knit sweaters and gloves for the soldiers, collect tin cans and rubber tires, buy war stamps and save up for bonds. She could become a Rosie the Riveter and take a man's job for the duration, but there was nothing she could do that would erase the past fifteen months of loneliness.

Men went to war.

Women waited.

That was the way things were and, as far as Catherine could tell, it was the way things would always be.

TEDDY BEARS MARCHED across the faded quilt tossed haphazardly across the bed in Nancy Wilson's room, their plump brown legs resting atop an array of bright cotton sundresses. Saddle oxfords sat on the rag rug next to her best dress shoes, with the one-inch heels that made her sturdy legs look almost elegant. Her schoolbooks, carefully covered with brown paper so they could be resold as soon as the school year was over, were buried beneath a stack of *Pho-*

*toplay*s and *Modern Screen*s that were her prized possessions.

At seventeen Nancy was both little girl and woman, and it seemed she spent half her life wanting to grow up and the other half wishing she could stay a child. She liked having an older sister like Catherine to look up to, and parents who made her feel safe and secure, but in her dreams she longed to fly away from the house on Hansen Street and try her wings.

She glanced at her reflection in the dressing-table mirror, then looked across the room at the big color picture of Lana Turner that smiled at her from its place of honor next to Clark Gable on her bulletin board. Yesterday she had tried to muster the courage to ask for a bottle of peroxide from Mr. Kravitz at the pharmacy, but the memory of how everyone had laughed at poor Marie Finestra when she'd bleached her black hair blond still lingered in Nancy's ears. "Nice girls" accepted the hair color God gave them and did nothing more than keep their tresses clean and curled.

Nancy sighed and looked back at her own round and fresh-scrubbed face. That was definitely the face of a nice girl. Her cheeks were full and rosy. Her nose was just the slightest bit pug and dusted with a sprinkling of cinnamon-colored freckles that not even Lady Esther face powder could hide. Unfortunately God had chosen to give her hair the color of a rusty drainpipe, and it was curly and unruly and thick as a pony's tail in the bargain!

Life just wasn't fair.

And that was exactly what she told Catherine as she marched boldly into her older sister's bedroom across the hall and flopped onto the pristine white bedspread with the embroidered sweetheart roses.

"What did I do to deserve a fate like this?" she moaned, burying her face against a pink satin toss pillow as the scent of lavender sachet tickled her nostrils. "I look like one of those terrible monkeys in *The Wizard of Oz*. All I need is a knitted cap."

Catherine, who was combing her hair near the window, laughed out loud. "If you're looking for sympathy, Nance, you're not going to find any here. You're cute as a bug and you know it."

"I don't want to be cute," Nancy said, peering up at her beautiful sister. "I want to look like you."

"I thought you wanted to look like Lana Turner."

"I'd settle for looking like you."

"Gee, thanks." Her sister's honey-colored hair drifted down in a graceful curve that brushed her shoulders and stopped just short of her collarbone. "Shouldn't you be getting dressed?" Catherine looked at the Hamilton watch their parents had given her when she'd graduated from high school. Nancy was due to get her own watch in a few short weeks. "Daddy wants us ready at six on the dot."

Nancy's spirits plummeted even lower as Catherine touched her already thick eyelashes with a dab of Maybelline from a tiny red matchbox container, then rouged her mouth with a tube of Tangee. Who would ever even notice she was alive with Catherine around?

Catherine was better than pretty; she was beautiful. Not flashy like Rita Hayworth or cheap like Betty Hutton, but possessing something more like Carole Lombard's smart good looks mixed with Linda Darnell's cameo perfection.

Nancy raised herself on her elbows and watched as her sister slipped into a plain blue short-sleeved dress with white collar and buttons and a narrow fabric belt at the waist. "You're not wearing *that*, are you?" she asked, unable to mask her horror.

"This is a perfectly fine dress," said Catherine, buttoning up the front, then adjusting the belt. "This isn't a high-school dance we're gong to, Nance."

"Of course it's not! This is the Stage Door Canteen, Cathy! Every famous star in New York City will be there. Don't you want to look your best?"

"I look just fine," said her cool and calm sister. "Believe it or not, not everyone wants to look like a movie star."

"I liked you better before you and Doug got engaged."
Nancy swung her legs off the bed and stood up. "You're an
old stick-in-the-mud now. I remember when you thought
Errol Flynn was dreamy."

A patch of color appeared on Catherine's high cheekbones, and her blue eyes twinkled with mischief. "I still
think he's dreamy, and if you tell anybody I said that, I'll
write to Gerry Sturdevant and send him your yearbook
photo."

"You wouldn't!"

"Oh, yes, I would." She waggled her left hand in Nancy's direction so that the tiny diamond sparkled in the afternoon sunlight. "I'm spoken for. Douglas would be so
jealous if he knew I'd seen *The Adventures of Robin Hood*
six times."

Nancy completely ignored that juicy piece of information. All she could think of was Gerry Sturdevant's face if
he ever saw that absolutely horrid photograph taken last
year when she was just a dumb kid of sixteen. "You
wouldn't send Gerry my yearbook photo, would you?"
Nancy hated it when her voice went all small and childlike,
but there was nothing she could do about it. This was too
important.

Catherine ruffled her curls with a slender, graceful hand.
"And ruin our servicemen's morale? Not on your life. Your
secret's safe with me." Catherine disappeared into the hallway and Nancy heard the bathroom door swing shut.

Nancy was tempted to read the stack of blue letters from
Douglas that rested atop the window seat, but decided
against it. A few years ago, when she was young and didn't
know any better, she would have dived right into the stack,
giggling over the mushy parts and laughing at their silly romantic daydreams. Not anymore. To her surprise, she had
her own romantic daydreams these days, and the thought of
someone violating her privacy was enough to make her bury
her head in the sand and never come out.

She went back into her room across the hall and sat down on the edge of her bed, bare feet dangling. She'd rather work in Macy's Basement than ever let Gerry see that embarrassing photo.

Nancy's high-school graduating class had been writing to servicemen for the past year. Doug's brother, Mac, a foreign correspondent, had set up the morale-boosting program after his first trip to the Pacific theater the previous year when he realized the effect loneliness had on the boys. Mac was one of Nancy's absolutely favorite people. A few years older than Catherine, he'd been the idol of all the kids on Hansen Street. Strong, opinionated and funny, everyone knew Mac was destined for bigger and better things. Mrs. Weaver had said he was in Europe now and getting itchy to join the fighting. Nancy wouldn't be surprised if one day he gave Ernie Pyle a run for his money.

But the most important thing Mac had ever done, in Nancy's considered opinion, was bring Seaman Gerald Francis Sturdevant into her life. Her freckles and pug nose didn't matter a bit to Gerry. All that mattered was that her letters kept him in touch with home and all the reasons why winning the war was so very important to Americans. And, as if that wasn't enough, he thought she was funny and friendly and much more sophisticated than she really was. Why was it that the easy humor and lighthearted conversation that came so easily for her on paper never seemed to materialize when she was face-to-face with a boy? Oh sure, she had plenty of boys as *friends*, but that special boy-girl kind of magic always seemed just out of reach.

Except with Gerry. With him she'd shared some of her biggest secrets, secrets she'd never even told her mother or Catherine.

Maybe she was just a silly kid, as foolish now at seventeen as she'd been at seven. Living in a dreamworld filled with movie stars and crooners and thick onionskin letters from a sailor she'd never meet.

She started at the touch of Catherine's hand on her shoulder. "You'd better get dressed, kiddo. Daddy expects us downstairs in twenty minutes."

Nancy jumped off the bed with a shriek. How on earth could she have forgotten to get dressed? "I'll never be ready in time!"

"Sure you will." Catherine scooped up the white peasant blouse with the embroidered trim that rested on the dressing-table chair, then pulled a wide black cinch belt from the top drawer. "This would look adorable on you."

Nancy, clad only in her white cotton panties and bra, giggled. "I'd look pretty funny, Cathy. I don't have a skirt to go with it. My green pique would look silly."

"I've already thought of that," said her older sister. "My black taffeta."

Nancy's eyes widened. "The full one with the crinolines?" Since the war had started, skirts had become shorter and tighter; a luxurious full skirt complete with crinolines was almost as exciting as meeting Tyrone Power.

Catherine eyed Nancy critically. "I think it'll fit you. You're a few years away from needing a panty girdle."

"You mean . . . ?"

"Of course I do. You'll be the belle of the Stage Door Canteen tonight."

Fifteen minutes later Nancy did a pirouette in front of the mirror, then faced her sister. "What do you think?"

"I was right," said Catherine with a big smile. "You'll break their hearts tonight."

Oh, Gerry, she thought as Catherine performed some last-minute magic on her unruly red curls, *I wish you could see me now . . .*

IN THE BIG BEDROOM at the end of the hall, Dot Wilson sat at her dressing table and watched her husband get ready for their night on the town.

"Did you get my shirts from the Chinese laundry?" he asked as he stepped into a pair of boxer shorts.

Dot nodded and tried to swallow around the painful lump in her throat. "Of course," she said, forcing her voice to sound airy and cheerful. "Twenty-two years and I've never once forgotten." Twenty-two years of cooking and cleaning and caring for him. Twenty-two years of raising both his children and his spirits, of lying down beside him each night and awakening each morning in his arms. The only life she'd ever known.

The only man she'd ever wanted.

"Oh, Tom." Her voice broke on his name. "What am I going to do without you?"

He was next to her in an instant. His chest was bare and the unfamiliar dog tags were cold and hard against her breast as he pulled her to him. "You're going to wait for me, Doro. You're going to keep the bed warm for me."

She'd promised herself she wouldn't cry, that she'd do nothing to make him any more unhappy than he already was, but her tears spilled hot and fast onto his naked shoulder. "I'm scared, Tommy," she whispered. "I don't know if I can do it alone."

"You're not alone, baby. You've got the girls with you."

She smiled despite her terror. Catherine and Nancy were her crowning achievements. Raising them was the most important thing in her life—second only to her devotion to Tom.

"I know," she said, "but I never imagined a time when you wouldn't be here with me." Even though it seemed as if every man in the country wanted to go head-to-head with the Nazis and the Japanese, it had never occurred to her that her very own husband would feel the same way.

"Is there something you're not telling me?" He gave her a playful swat on the bottom. "I'm coming home, Doro, as fast as I possibly can. Before you know it, you'll be so busy taking care of me again that you'll wonder why you wanted me back."

"Never." She covered his neck and chin with swift sweet kisses born of love and fear. She closed her eyes and tried to memorize the feel and smell of his skin as if to fortify herself for the long months when he would no longer be there with her.

Tom hadn't been drafted. As a forty-year-old married man and the father of two daughters, he was an unlikely candidate for military service. But Tom Wilson was not just a married man with children; he was also a patriotic American who could no more stay there in New York City while his countrymen fought for freedom than he could turn away from the scene of an accident.

She'd shamed herself the day he'd come home with the news of his enlistment.

"How could you!" she'd cried, thinking only of her own fears and the safety of their family. "We need you here, Tom Wilson. The company needs you." In over two decades of marriage, Dot Wilson had never opposed her husband in anything, but that day she had asked him to choose between his country and his family.

His words still echoed in her memory. "There's no choice, Doro," he'd said. "If we don't win the war, we'll lose the freedom that makes our family possible."

And so there they were in the bedroom they'd shared for the first time on their wedding night and every night since. She could still see herself standing there, so young and scared in her white peignoir set, staring at the handsome boy who was now her husband.

The terrible thought that this might be the very last time she felt his arms around her as they dressed for a Saturday night outing made her feel as if her heart would break.

His caresses grew more ardent, and she laughed softly and placed a hand on his chest. "We'll be late, Tommy."

He cupped her breast and she swayed toward him. "The Canteen will still be there."

"And after you told the girls to be ready at six o'clock sharp or you'd have them court-martialed! How on earth would we explain this?"

"Do them good to know their old folks still love each other."

She longed to stay right there in his embrace, but making love in broad daylight with the girls waiting for them downstairs was too scandalous to consider.

"Get dressed, Tommy." She kissed him soundly.

The look he gave her was so thrilling that her breath caught for an instant. "Tonight, Doro," he said as he reached for his army-issue shirt. "When we close the door behind us tonight, I don't intend to let you go."

Chapter Two

Although she had grown up right there in New York City, smack in Forest Hills in the borough of Queens, Catherine still felt a thrill each time she boarded the IND subway bound for Manhattan. Manhattan was another world, a fairy-tale land straight from the dreams of a Hollywood director.

Only who needed Hollywood when you had Manhattan right there on your doorstep! From the splendor of Central Park to the broad expanse of Park Avenue, to the electric excitement of Broadway with its neon signs and palatial theaters that housed everything from Shakespeare to Shaw to Rodgers and Hammerstein, all of it was real and only twenty minutes—and one five-cent subway fare—away.

Where else could you see the Camel cigarette man, who presided over a billboard poster that blew giant smoke rings over Times Square, or the mighty Prometheus of Rockefeller Center with the weight of the earth on his shoulders? They said that Henry Ford had worried that the excavating necessary for the Empire State Building would affect the earth's rotation on its axis, but the spectacular 101-story structure had only added to the city's grandeur. And who hadn't met a friend or loved one beneath the golden clock that hung over the information desk at Grand Central Station?

How glad Catherine was to escape her bedroom and get out!

It had been a long time since she had fussed with her hair and her lipstick or worn a dress as pretty as the tight-waisted cornflower blue that just skimmed her knees. War restrictions on clothing had taken much of the fun out of dressing up. No more full skirts. Pleats were outlawed, as were cuffs on men's pants. Even double-breasted coats were gone for the duration. Nancy had appealed to her sense of family loyalty. "All of Daddy's friends from the squadron are going to be there, Cathy. Don't you want him to be proud of you?" her little sister had asked, sending Catherine back into her closet in search of something more special than her sober workaday dress.

The rediscovery of her femininity came as a powerful surprise. She'd forgotten how wonderful it felt to primp before the mirror and actually smile at the reflection she saw there. The sweetheart neckline bared her collarbone and each time she turned her head, her hair brushed against her skin. She remembered the time that Douglas daringly pressed his lips to the hollow of her throat and—

"Will you look at them?" Nancy asked over the rumble of the subway train. "Acting like newlyweds!"

Catherine looked at her parents who were sitting together on a bench a few feet from where she and Nancy stood clutching the leather straps overhead. Her father looked handsome in his army uniform and the strange new haircut; her mother, lovely in a filmy dress of sea green, looked as proud of him as if he were a four-star general.

Suddenly she didn't want to think of goodbyes, of the war and the dangers lurking everywhere. She definitely didn't want to think about the jittery feeling that had been haunting her the past few days. She wanted to think of music and dancing, of spending an evening with the family she loved. Impulsively she gave her little sister a quick hug, almost losing her balance as the train careened around a curve, then slowed as it neared the station.

"You look so glamorous tonight, Nance." She smiled at the cloud of Evening in Paris that fairly surrounded the girl. "Gerry Sturdevant should only see you now."

Nancy blushed as red as the roots of her hair. "Don't tease me, Cath."

"I'm not. You look grand." She glanced down. Nancy's very best shoes, a pair of white pumps, glistened with Shinola polish. "How are your stockings holding up?"

Nancy laughed out loud. "It better not rain. I'd die of embarrassment if my makeup runs."

Stockings were currently in short supply, for the government was using nylon to make powder bags for explosives. These days American women wore bobby sox and anklets and knee socks, or they went bare-legged. On special occasions like tonight, enterprising females applied Dorothy Grey's Leg Show in sheer or suntan to their legs to simulate stockings. Catherine had painstakingly sponged the thick foundation onto her sister's ankles and calves and knees, getting into the same spirit of excitement that held the teenager in thrall.

Fortunately the weather was splendid. They climbed up the concrete subway steps, laughing at the Hold Your Hats! sign in the stairwell, to find the evening sky a beautiful mixture of pink and blue and flame orange. Women in snugly fitted suits and feathered hats walked arm in arm with gentlemen whose temples were as gray as their own summer suits. Sailors lingered at the corner of Forty-second Street, whistling and calling out "Hubba, hubba!" as a trio of pretty nurses walked by. "Mairzy Doats," the nonsense song that had taken the country by storm, floated out from a radio blaring inside Tad's Steak House, while moviegoers queued up at Radio City Music Hall to see Jean Arthur in *The More The Merrier*.

"Actor dies in airborne attack!" cried the headlines on the papers being hawked on every corner. Leslie Howard, Ashley Wilkes from *Gone with the Wind*, had been en route from Lisbon to England when his airliner was attacked by an enemy plane and brought down.

No one was safe. Absolutely no one.

Catherine forced the notion from her mind. There would be plenty of time in her darkened bedroom to think about it later.

Oklahoma reigned supreme on the Great White Way, and she had to tug at Nancy's arm as the girl stopped to stare at the color posters flanking the entrance to the theater.

"Hurry up!" Catherine urged as their parents crossed to the other side of the street. "We can't get into the Canteen without Dad."

That was all Nancy had to hear, and they scurried to catch up.

"I'm so nervous," Nancy said. "If I meet a movie star I'm afraid I'll die!"

"You won't die. If you meet a movie star, you'll smile and say hello, same as you would if you met a plumber."

"My stomach hurts," moaned Nancy. "I wish I had some Bisodol."

Catherine looked at her little sister and for an instant she couldn't remember how it had felt to be seventeen and in love with life. Had she ever felt all giddy with excitement, trembling on the threshold of new experiences, new adventures? It seemed so long ago since she'd approached each new day with pure joy that she felt older than her grandmother.

Her dad kissed her mother on the cheek as he opened the door to the Stage Door Canteen. "This way, ladies."

Well, if nothing else, at least she'd have something new to write Douglas about tonight.

She sighed and followed Nancy downstairs.

MOVIE STARS! Soldiers! Sailors!

All the glamour and wonder that Nancy had dreamed about was right there in that noisy smoky room. Big band music, so loud you couldn't hear yourself think, surrounded her—and so did men in uniform, a dazzling assortment of army privates, youthful marines, sailors in their jaunty outfits, and flyboys with silver wings sparkling on their chests. The room smelled of Brylcreem and Vitalis, of Old Spice and Ivory soap. Laughter rang out from every direction, and a big smile spread across her face as she realized she was right there in the middle of things in the most exciting place on earth.

"Take a look over there, honey." Her mom directed her attention toward the stage up front. "Isn't that Bob Hope?"

"Oh, golly!" Nancy's mouth dropped open in surprise. "And that's Mary Martin with him!"

Old Ski Nose and the beautiful blond star of Broadway's musical fantasy *One Touch of Venus* took the stage to a round of enthusiastic applause. They launched into a skit that Bob Hope must have done a hundred times at bases and camps around the world, yet his enthusiasm was electric, as he and Mary Martin took an imaginary stroll, arm in arm, through Central Park.

"Nice night," said Bob.

"Nice night," said Mary.

"Nice party."

"Nice party."

"Nice moon."

"Nice moon."

"Nice bench," said Bob, waggling his eyebrows in a mock leer.

"Nice bench," said Mary, all-innocence.

"Some do."

"*I* don't!"

The crowd loved it, but no one loved it more than Nancy. Everything was as she'd imagined it would be—and even better. Bob Hope put on an apron and magically transformed himself into the world's most famous busboy, while Mary Martin perched on a high stool and sang along with Harry James and his Music Makers.

"'Scuse me," said a male voice behind Nancy. "Care to dance?"

She turned and saw a cute jug-eared sailor with even more freckles than she had. "I'm Nancy," she said, smiling at him.

"Bobby Dunn. I'm not much good at jitterbugging, but if you're game . . ."

"Sure," said Nancy, ignoring her father's knowing grin from across the room. "Why not?"

Bobby Dunn didn't lie. When it came to jitterbugging he was about as graceful as a cocker spaniel, but somehow it didn't matter. He made her laugh as he told her all about life in a small town in Illinois, and she had him guffawing with stories of her one and only attempt at milking a cow on her grandma's farm in central Pennsylvania.

Bobby Dunn gave way to Charlie, a marine from San Diego who obviously believed girls swooned over men in uniform. He was right about that, of course, but Nancy wasn't about to give him the satisfaction. She did the fox-trot with an officer from Cheyenne who said she looked like his youngest daughter, and waltzed with an elegant young lieutenant from Maine with aspirations of giving General Eisenhower some real competition.

The Andrews Sisters, Patty and Maxine and Laverne, took center stage and launched into a rousing rendition of "Boogie Woogie Bugle Boy" that had everyone dancing in the aisles.

If only the night would never end. . . .

CATHERINE GLANCED at her watch and tried not to think about how much her feet hurt.

Within the first hour she'd danced with four English sailors, three American marines and a half-score of army privates, most of whom managed to fox-trot all over her toes. Her father had introduced her to most of the members of his squadron, and she'd jitterbugged with each of them in turn for the better part of the next hour. Her dad beamed his appreciation, and the look of pride and apology on her mom's face went a long way toward easing her aching arches.

They were a nice group of guys, just a bunch of regular Joes who were looking for nothing more than a few happy moments to take with them into the unknown. It wasn't hard to talk to them, to make them laugh and to listen to stories about their sweethearts and their hopes for the future. Any one of them could have been Douglas, far away from home and scared, even though no self-respecting American boy would ever admit to such a thing.

She leaned against the railing and looked down at the couples dancing to the Andrews Sisters' rendition of "Rum and Coca Cola." The thought of an icy-cold Coke sounded wonderful. She was on her way to the bar when her dad waylaid her.

"Cathy, there's someone I want you to meet."

"I thought I met all of the fellows in your squadron."

"Not Johnny. He just got here."

"Couldn't he wait a moment, Pop? I'm so thirsty. I—"

"Have this." A huge frosty glass was thrust in front of her face.

She looked up into the clear blue eyes of a man about her age.

"You're a mind reader, Danza," said her father.

She accepted the glass from the stranger and took a long grateful sip. "I don't know if you're a mind reader," she said, "but you certainly have great timing."

"This is Johnny Danza," said her father, gesturing toward the tall man who stood before her. "Private, first class."

Johnny Danza stood a full head taller than her, his close-cropped hair blacker than jet. Thick long eyelashes framed those dazzlingly blue eyes, and she couldn't help noticing the arrogant set of his jaw, the bold thrust of his Roman nose, and his angular cheekbones.

"I'm Catherine," she said, as her father disappeared back into the crowd.

"Glad to meet you." Danza shook her hand firmly. "Your old man's told me a lot about you."

"You have me at a disadvantage," she said, noting the rough strength of his grip and the street-tough sound of his voice. "You in my dad's squadron?"

Danza's laugh was short and husky. "You bet. We met up in signal-corps school. Us New Yorkers had to stick together down there in Georgia."

Her dad had been away an extra few months for specialized training after boot camp. "Were there many New Yorkers?"

"Enough. Looks like we'll be going the whole way together."

Her heart did a funny kind of skip at the thought of the unknown that stretched before her father. "Wh-where do you think you'll be stationed?"

"Hey! What's with you?" He put an index finger against her mouth. "Loose lips sink ships, Cathy. Didn't old Tom tell you that?"

She glared up at him. She wasn't used to men like this brash young Italian American from Brooklyn. "'Old Tom,' as you put it, has been busy taking care of his business and his family, Johnny. It was just an innocent question."

"Yeah, well, questions like that can get a whole lot of people in trouble."

"I don't think it's the questions that are the problem," she observed. "It's the answers."

He grinned at her. "You won't be getting any from me."

"Somehow I didn't think so."

Catherine couldn't imagine two more different human beings than her taciturn father and this fiery young man, but apparently war made for strange friendships. Besides, who was she to question an allegiance that might help her father weather the storm ahead?

Johnny had that lean and hungry look Catherine had come to associate with soldiers on their way to war. Even her own father now had that taut sinewy look about him, but with Johnny the look seemed an extension of personality, not just circumstances. He couldn't possibly be that much older than she was, but something about his demeanor made her feel terribly young and painfully inexperienced.

Casual conversation became a struggle.

"So how do you like the army?" she managed at last. "It must take some getting used to."

He shrugged and took a drag on his Lucky Strike. "I've been in since I was nineteen. Hard to remember anything else."

"You make it sound like you're forty years old," she said with an amused laugh. "You can't be more than twenty-two."

"Twenty-five." He glanced down at her. "Last month."

She grew silent. He wasn't anything like the boys she had grown up with. Even after boot camp, Douglas hadn't had this sharp edge, an edge that went beyond anything the army taught its men. With Johnny you had the feeling he actually looked forward to battle, as if he had something to prove. Something that couldn't be proved any other way.

She wondered if he had a girlfriend, but knew she would seem terribly rude and forward if she dared to ask such a question. But she could ask her dad later about Johnny's background—in a very casual way, of course. Not that she was interested for herself, naturally, but try as she might she couldn't quite conjure up an image of the type of girl he would keep company with. A brash and overbleached blond? A flamboyant redhead? Or would he go against type and favor a "girl next door"?

The image of Johnny sweeping this imaginary sweetheart into his arms popped into her mind, and she felt her cheeks redden as she tried to push the unbidden—but quite intriguing—vision from her mind.

CATHERINE WILSON was one of the prettiest girls Johnny Danza had ever seen. Tom had told him so, but Johnny knew that fathers often thought the homeliest daughters were as beautiful as Hollywood stars. In this case, however, Tom hadn't even come close to describing just how lovely his older daughter was. And she didn't seem stuck on herself, either, the way so many pretty girls were. Why, she was even blushing just because he was admiring her!

Johnny glanced down at the diamond chip sparkling on the ring finger of her left hand. Too bad some other lucky guy had already spoken for her. It would be nice to know a girl like Catherine Wilson was waiting for you to come home....

He stubbed out his cigarette in one of the sand-filled canisters lining the wall.

"That's some great music they're playing," he tossed out, doing his best not to notice the sweet smell of her perfume. He didn't believe in making a play for another guy's girl. He was a lot of things, but he wasn't a bastard.

Catherine nodded, her dark blond hair swinging gently with the movement of her head. "I can't believe I'm standing here listening to Harry James in person."

"Makes you feel like dancing, doesn't it?"

She gave him a sideways look, her clear blue eyes sharp and questioning.

He felt a rush of blood redden his throat and cheeks. It was a safe bet he hadn't blushed since he was eight years old, when the head of the orphanage caught him lobbing spitballs in church. "I'm pretty good at jitterbugging."

She grinned. "So am I."

He reached for her hand. "Let's cut a rug then, Cathy."

What he really wanted was to hold her in his arms, but the music was jumping, and before long so were they. He loved the way her skirt twisted about her knees when he spun her out. He also loved the way her eyes sparkled as the tempo increased and they were almost flying with the music. He'd picked up a few tricky moves when he was down in Georgia, and Tom's daughter managed to keep up with all of them—and show him a few in the bargain.

"You *are* good," she said, panting, as the music faded.

He tugged his uniform jacket back into place. "So're you." The lights dimmed and a smoky romantic ballad swelled around them. "Want to go back on the floor?"

She shook her head. "Thanks, anyway, but I think I'll sit this one out."

"'Moonlight Serenade,'" he said. "It doesn't get much better than that."

"I know it doesn't, Johnny, but I should see what my sister is up to."

He watched as she drifted back into the crowd. She was taller than many of the women there, and it wasn't hard to keep her in sight as she threaded her way through the knots of servicemen and dancing couples jammed into the Canteen. She carried herself straight and proud, her bearing almost military.

Shaking his head, he lit up another cigarette. Both of them were New York born and bred, but you'd never know it. The rough sound of his Brooklyn neighborhood flavored every word he uttered, while Catherine sounded as if she'd been brought up in some fancy Park Avenue apartment instead of a house in Queens.

Class was a funny thing, he thought. You either had it or you didn't. No doubt about it: Tom's daughter Catherine had it in spades.

Johnny grabbed himself a beer and raised it high in salute to her absent fiancé. Maybe he didn't know the guy's name, rank and serial number, but he knew something even more important: Catherine's fiancé was one lucky man.

BACK IN FOREST HILLS, in a storefront on Continental Avenue, Catherine's future was being decided.

Stuart Froelich, Western Union supervisor, took off his wire glasses and rubbed the bridge of his nose, then continued to paste the message together.

We regret to inform you that your son, Private Douglas Weaver, died in battle 29 May 1943 in the Aleutian Islands.

Being the bearer of bad news was rotten enough; bringing bad news to friends was more than he thought he could stand. His own daughter, Susan, had gone through school with Doug and his girlfriend Cathy Wilson. His photo albums were filled with snapshots of the three of them in school plays, at the junior prom, on graduation night.

Dear God, he thought as he folded the telegram into an envelope. *Give Edna and Les the strength they need to accept this.*

And help Cathy to get on with her life.

TOM'S FRIENDS WERE really a swell group. Dot thoroughly enjoyed listening to their stories about boot camp and how her husband had withstood their merciless teasing with remarkable good grace. It helped, this putting faces to the names of the men who would go into battle with the man she loved.

"Gotta hand it to Tom," said Johnny Danza as he waltzed her around the crowded dance floor. "We razzed him pretty bad about being the oldest recruit around, but he laughed along with the rest of us."

"That's my Tom," she said, tears welling up despite her easy laughter. "He can take it, as well as dish it out."

"A real nice guy," said Johnny, shaking his head. "Don't meet too many guys as nice as him these days."

I won't cry! There will be plenty of time for tears once Tom leaves tomorrow. She swallowed hard and gently steered the conversation in a less emotionally dangerous direction. "I'm glad you and Tom will be together...." She hesitated. "Well, wherever it is you'll be out there."

He nodded but said nothing, simply swept her into a more intricate pattern of dance on the floor. She could see the raw emotion on his strong-boned face, and she averted her gaze to afford him a private moment to recover himself. For all his toughness, Johnny Danza had a soft quality. It pleased her to see that, to know that her husband would be there with this young man, who perhaps would ease his way along the rough road ahead.

"We will be seeing you at breakfast tomorrow morning, won't we?" she asked as he twirled her around the crowded floor.

He had a wonderful, boyish smile that made her maternal instincts leap to life. "I, uh, Tom told me about it but I, uh, I wasn't sure you'd want a stranger there...." His words drifted off with an embarrassed shrug.

"You listen to me, Johnny Danza! I make the best pancakes in New York City and you're expected to be at the table at 8 a.m. sharp. Do you understand?"

"Yes, ma'am!" He gave a quick salute. "You're tougher than our drill instructor."

"And don't you forget it!"

The waltz came to an end, and Harry James announced a fifteen-minute break to a chorus of good-natured boos from the crowd.

Johnny saw Dot back to the table where her husband sat, still talking with a group of soldiers, each of whom had the wide-eyed look of a visitor on his first trip to New York. For a moment she considered asking each and every one of them over for a pancake breakfast, but because of shortages due to the War effort, she knew neither her pantry nor icebox held enough food to accommodate them all. She would, however, give Private John Danza a breakfast to remember.

HE WAS WATCHING HER, Johnny Danza was. Catherine was acutely aware of his gaze on her as she danced with soldiers and sailors. Time and again pretty hostesses with bright smiles would try to engage him in conversation, but he turned each one away with a shake of his head. How could she listen to the GIs' stories and laugh at their jokes when her attention was drawn back time and again to the darkly handsome soldier standing near the bar, his deep blue gaze firmly locked on her?

Why on earth had she ever listened to Nancy and worn this ridiculous powder-blue dress? Every movement she made sent the skirts twirling up over her knees, brushing against her thighs in a most disconcerting fashion. And he noticed—she *knew* that he noticed. She grew conscious of the way her hair swung over her shoulder as she danced, of the sound of her own laughter, the warm air heating the skin bared by the sweetheart neckline. And all because a man was watching her dance....

Ridiculous! she thought as Johnny flashed her a grin from across the room. She was acting like Nancy, getting all flustered because a man was looking at her. If he wanted to be so bold, she'd simply pay no attention to him. No attention at all.

NANCY COULDN'T HELP but notice the way her dad's friend Johnny watched Catherine. It didn't matter if her older sister was on the dance floor doing the lindy hop with a marine from San Diego or chatting in a corner with a group of British sailors, the dark-haired private from Brooklyn never took his eyes off her.

Nancy sighed and reached for her third—or was it her fourth?—7-Up. Oh sure, she'd had her share of attention from homesick GIs that night. Her friends would be pea green with envy when she told them tomorrow about the cute fellows she'd met and danced with. Of course, any girl who was younger than Edna Mae Oliver or skinnier than Kate Smith was a star in the eyes of these frightened young men. But with Catherine it was different and always would be.

Old ladies talked to Cathy while they waited for a bus. Elderly men tipped their hats when she walked by. Nancy's

GI pen pal Gerry would probably be just like the rest of them, falling all over himself for one of her sister's smiles.

She watched as Private Danza threaded his way through the crowd, his sights set squarely on Cathy. Nancy wondered if anyone would ever look at *her* that way, as if she were the center of the universe?

It was so unfair! Cathy already had a beau. Douglas loved her more than anything, and that diamond on Cathy's finger was proof positive that, after the war was over, their future would be just so much velvet. Boys tended to think of Nancy as a pal. Someone to go ice-skating with or take to a ball game, but very few boys looked at freckled redheads the way Johnny was looking at Catherine right now.

Nancy had felt so excited just an hour ago, filled with the sense that anything at all could happen in a magical place like the Stage Door Canteen. Somehow she had believed that talking to movie stars would change her life forever. Now she knew that the place might be magical, but she was still the same old Nancy she was back on Hansen Street, and not even Tyrone Power could change that. Maybe having a paper-and-pen romance was the best possible world for someone like her.

When she sat down later to write to Gerry Sturdevant, she would describe the music and the laughter, the movie stars and the sense of excitement in the air, and through her words she'd make it all come alive for Gerry there on the other side of the world.

"How 'bout a dance?"

She looked up into the big brown eyes of the dreamiest fly-boy she'd ever seen. "Me?"

He made a show of looking around the room. "Don't see anybody else sitting there with you." He held out his hand. "Come on. The music ain't gonna last all night."

"You're right." She stood up and took his hand, her melancholy mood falling away from her like an old coat. The music wouldn't last all night, but the memories of her evening would be with her forever. "Let's dance!"

THE TEN STEPS to the Weavers' front door seemed like a hundred to Stuart Froelich as he trudged up to ring the bell. His right arm hung limply at his side, the telegram dangling from his fingers like a lowered flag of surrender.

Laughter floated out through the open window, laughter and the sweet sound of Dorothy Collins's voice as she sang "Don't Get Around Much Anymore."

"Let's have a hand for the little lady," said Snooky Lanson. The audience applauded.

Stuart rang the doorbell.

Chapter Three

Catherine did her best to enter into the spirit of things. She joined her mother and father at the big table they shared with myriad boys and men who would be sailing away with her dad come tomorrow morning. A guy from a potato farm way out on the eastern end of Long Island told a funny story about his first trip to the big city, and Catherine found herself laughing heartily along with everyone else at the soldier's wide-eyed tales of his adventures on the subway.

"Mind?"

She looked up to see Johnny Danza standing next to her. He motioned toward the empty space on her bench.

"Not at all," she said, scooting over to make room for him. "Please sit down."

"Danny telling his subway story again?" Danza asked, pouring himself a beer from the pitcher on the table. "I must've heard about the A train fifty times in boot camp."

"It's a funny story," she said, defending the young recruit. "Just because we grew up riding the subways doesn't mean they're not confusing to a country kid."

Danza took a large swig of beer. "I'm not making fun of the kid, Cathy. You don't have to get so defensive."

She grew aware of heat flooding her cheeks. "I'm not getting defensive."

He arched a brow and grinned. "Sure you are."

She laughed despite herself. "Well, maybe," she said after a moment. She'd been off balance all day, as if her feelings were running one step ahead of her mind. Listening to Danny's story, she'd found her emotions careening like a roller coaster. Laughing one moment, verging on tears the next. Was she the only one in the room who understood how terrifying the world out there was?

One of the soldiers, a fellow from Nebraska named Harold, launched into a gory tale about his cousin who was killed at Pearl Harbor while playing tennis with his fiancée. Beads of sweat broke out behind her neck and along her temples, and she shivered.

"Cold?"

She looked at Danza and shook her head. "Someone must have walked on my grave."

"So you're as superstitious as your old man?"

"Not quite as bad as Daddy, but close." The Pearl Harbor story was awful, but the one about Guadalcanal was even worse.

"What a gloomy conversation," Dot said, her voice painfully cheerful. "Can't we talk about something else?"

Catherine thanked her mother silently. The men gamely tried to steer their talk away from blood and guts, but in moments they were speculating about what dangers awaited them at the front. Danza rested a hand on her shoulder and she turned back toward him.

"That's my favorite song they're playing," he said, his tone easy. "Dance with me?"

She hesitated. Jitterbugging with a handsome soldier was one thing; dancing close as the strains of "Moonlight Becomes You" tugged at her heart was something else entirely. "I—I don't know if..."

But he wasn't waiting for an answer. He was on his feet and reaching for her.

"...lambs to the slaughter..." she heard her father say as she took Johnny's hand. "Those poor GIs didn't stand a chance."

No, she thought, escaping with Johnny onto the dance floor. *I'm not going to think about anything but the music.*

Danza threaded his way through the couples jamming the floor until he found a secluded spot to the right of the band. He stopped, then opened his arms to her, and for an instant Catherine hesitated. She had danced with a score of soldiers that evening and not given it a second thought. Why on earth did she find the notion of stepping into Danza's embrace so difficult?

The moment he drew her close and they began to sway to the music, she knew. How long had it been since she'd been held this way, her cheek nestled against a muscular shoulder, her skin registering the warmth of another body? Her hand felt natural in his; the way he held her was both comfortable and exciting. It wasn't hard to imagine away the dozens of couples who shared the floor with them. It wasn't hard to imagine away the brash kid from Brooklyn. Douglas had held her like this once, a very long time ago. She'd felt his strength and sensed his power, just like now. That wonderful feeling of being close to a man—

No! She wouldn't think like that. It was disloyal and unfair to the man she loved. She willed herself back to reality and favored Johnny with her brightest smile. "Where did you learn to dance like—"

"Quiet," he said, his voice gruff but warm. "Just dance."

MUCH AS JOHNNY WANTED to take credit for the way Catherine Wilson melted into his arms, he knew exactly what was going on. She wasn't dancing with him; she was dancing with her fiancé, the lucky SOB who'd one day make her his wife.

He'd had a lot of experience playing second fiddle in his life, fighting against a world that had little time for him—an abandoned kid who'd spent his childhood being kicked out of one orphanage after another.

Funny thing, though. This time he didn't mind coming second to the man she loved. He didn't stand a chance with her and he knew it. Even if her guy was out of the picture, Johnny knew the chance of someone like Catherine Wilson giving him more than the time of day were about as good as his chances of spending the war Stateside.

Girls like Catherine were special. Their hair always smelled like apple blossoms in the spring. Their laughter sounded like silver bells. And the guys they loved never got their hands dirty earning a living. Hell, if he hadn't joined the army, Johnny was hard-pressed to figure what he would be doing right now. He was smart but uneducated. He understood business and the way things operated, but no one was likely to give a chance to a guy who'd barely made it out of eighth grade. Guys like him worked with their hands and were grateful for the chance.

But the army—and then the war—made everything different. He had a place in the world, for however long it lasted. He was young and healthy and strong, and that counted for something these days. The uniform gave him respect, something he'd never known before. Maybe when the war was over he'd go back to being a nobody on his way to no place, but for now he was important and that was all that mattered.

Like right now on the dance floor. It didn't matter that this time tomorrow he'd be on a troop ship somewhere in the Atlantic. It didn't matter that her heart belonged to someone else. For as long as the music played he could hold Catherine in his arms and pretend the world was his for the taking. And if she wanted to pretend he was the man she loved, well, Johnny was smart enough to know a good thing when he saw it. He only wished it never had to end.

THE PARTY MOVED from the Stage Door Canteen to the Oyster Bar at Grand Central Station. Dot, Catherine and Nancy begged off on trying the slippery sea creatures, but Tom and Johnny and a few of the other guys manfully did their bit to deplete the oyster population.

From the Oyster Bar they trooped over to the Automat, where they fed nickels and dimes into the appropriate slots and ate their fill of apple pie and hot coffee. Even there at the lowly Automat, handsome men in uniform squired beautiful women in silks and satins. They helped themselves to plates of macaroni and cheese as if they were fancy steak dinners with all the trimmings, and not one of them seemed to notice they weren't at the Stork Club.

The air crackled with a reckless kind of excitement. The world was an uncertain place, fraught with danger at every turn. Some people coped with that danger by grabbing life with both hands and shaking every last drop of happiness out of it. Men like her father and Johnny Danza pursued that danger, confident in their ability to conquer the enemy and return home triumphant. Her mother pretended the danger didn't exist, while Nancy drank it up and turned it into the stuff of teenage dreams.

For Catherine it was all too real. She wished she could curl up under her covers and not wake up until the war was over and Douglas was safely back home and life was the way it used to be before names like Bataan and Corregidor became part of everyday conversation.

The Wilsons parted company with the other GIs at the subway station. The night was still young and New York was a city made for handsome bachelors in uniform. The Folies Bergères had opened just two nights ago and there wasn't a red-blooded American male who wouldn't love to watch the show girls in their skimpy costumes parade across the stage.

Nancy shook hands with her father's new friends, while Dot hugged each and every one of them. Catherine couldn't help but notice that she gave Johnny Danza an extra-big squeeze and whispered something in his ear.

The guys were a little shy with Catherine and she had to take the initiative and extend her hand to them in farewell. Johnny, however, wasn't shy at all. He caught her hand then spun her close to him as if they were back on the dance floor, and before she could protest, he executed a quick dance step that turned her indignation into laughter.

"Take care of yourself," she said, planting a sisterly kiss on his beard-roughened cheek.

"You, too." His eyes lingered briefly on her mouth, and for a moment she wondered if he was going to kiss her. A grin flashed across his lean face, then he pressed his lips quickly to her forehead.

Instantly—absurdly—her eyes filled with tears, and it was all she could do to blink them back before she embarrassed herself right there in front of everybody.

"No one's paying any attention," he said, brushing a tear from her cheek.

"My father," she managed, glancing over her shoulder to make certain nobody was watching them. "Please take care of him, Johnny." She met his eyes and saw compassion in them, and understanding. "If anything happened to him..."

"Nothing's going to happen to him," said Johnny. "I'll make sure of it."

Believe him, she thought. *Believe him or you'll go crazy.* She started to thank him, to tell him how much his words meant to her, when her dad popped up at her elbow.

"Might as well save your goodbyes, honey," he said to her. "Your mom's invited Johnny for a farewell breakfast tomorrow morning. You'll have plenty of time over pancakes to say goodbye to this wolf."

Danza's shrug was good-natured. "Can't blame a guy for trying, can you? I haven't met too many like your daughter, Tom."

"And never will again, most likely." Tom winked at the kid from Brooklyn. "Just you remember that she's taken."

Danza could have protested. He could have told Tom that his daughter was worried sick about him, that she'd asked him to look after her father, that she wasn't even his type. What he did, instead, endeared him to her forever. "Yeah, Tom," he said, "I guess some guys have all the luck."

They rode home on the subway in silence. The car was empty, save for a few shift workers on their way to factory jobs in firms like the one her father owned. Nancy dozed with her head resting lightly against Catherine's shoulder, while across the aisle their parents talked softly, voices mingling with the steady rattle of the steel wheels against the tracks.

Strange, but somehow Catherine felt sorry for Johnny. Oh, he was filled with bravado and bluster, but beneath it all, she glimpsed a real person. A person she liked. In the ladies' room at the Canteen, Nancy told her that Johnny had been a foundling, who spent his childhood being shipped from one orphanage to another until he finally kicked over the traces and worked his way west. Nancy didn't know what had happened to bring him back to New York again, but she was certain a broken heart had something to do with it.

Of course Nancy was certain a broken heart was the reason for everything she couldn't understand. It was one of the benefits that came with being seventeen. The other benefit was the ability to sleep on the subway. Catherine had to gently shake her younger sister awake when the train finally rumbled into the station at Continental Avenue, then assist the drowsy girl up the cement steps to the street.

The summer sky was a swath of black velvet sequined with stars. The afternoon's intense heat had given way, cooled by breezes blown in from the waters that surrounded Long Island. Catherine could smell the sea in the distance, that salty, briny tang that conjured up dreams of exotic ports with names impossible to pronounce. One day, she thought, Nancy would probably send her a postcard from Tahiti and Timbuktu. Wanderlust raced through Nancy's veins; Catherine wanted to set down roots. She wanted the life that her mother and Douglas's mother took for granted, a life of security and happiness and love.

Half a block ahead of their children, Dot and Tom strolled along hand in hand, looking for all the world like young lovers.

"I'm going to miss Daddy." Nancy's voice, young and tremulous, broke the stillness. "Aren't you?"

Catherine draped an arm about her sister's shoulders. "Of course I am. But remember what he said—it's up to us to be cheerful for Mom. She has enough on her mind."

They turned right onto Hansen Street. The yellow glow from the gas lamps, remnants from another, more graceful era, bathed them in light.

Nancy looked over at Catherine. "Awfully quiet tonight, isn't it?"

"I guess Saturday nights aren't what they used to be, Nance." Her words came easily enough; unfortunately, so did a burning lump of fear that settled in her chest. She and her sister had grown up on this street. On a night like tonight their neighbors would be relaxing on their respective stoops, or gathering on the Weavers' porch to argue about the Dodgers. They certainly wouldn't be locked away inside their houses as if they were afraid to be out on the street after dark.

"Maybe it's the dimout," she said, more to herself than Nancy. "Maybe everyone decided to go to a film...."

And then she saw it. The Weavers' house was ablaze with light, and through the lace curtains she could see a knot of people in the parlor. Dot and Tom stood at the curb, stiff and straight as tin soldiers. Nancy grabbed Catherine's forearm. Catherine barely registered the sharp pinch of the girl's nails on her bare skin. In some hidden part of her soul she knew the truth, had known it for days but had refused to acknowledge it. This time, however, there was no turning away.

There on the front step stood Edna Weaver. Her plain dress was covered with a gingham apron and her hair was knotted atop her head. If she lived another thousand years,

Catherine knew she would never forget the look in that gentle woman's eyes.

"Don't say it," she whispered. "If you say it, you'll make it real...."

"It's Douglas," said Edna, her voice breaking. "Our boy is gone."

The sidewalk rushed up to meet Catherine as she gave herself over to the darkness.

PART II

V-MAIL

Can you pass this mailbox with a clear conscience?

—V-Mail poster

Chapter Four

Delayed—Received June 7, 1943
May 20, 1943

Dear Cath,
Happy Birthday! You didn't think I'd forget my girl's twenty-first birthday, did you? I guess you know it's a little hard to find a decent greeting card out here in the middle of nowhere, so I hope you'll close your eyes and pretend this letter is a big fancy 25-cent card, complete with a red satin-and-lace heart right in the middle.

I guess you also know how much I wish I could be there with you. Remember your eighteenth birthday? Three years ago! Makes me feel like an old man to think about it. Do you still have that pale blue dress with the full skirt you wore to Toffenetti's? You looked so beautiful, Cath, with your hair brushed back from your face and caught up with one of those fancy clips. Sometimes when I can't sleep at night I think about that night and remember the way you looked, the way we danced, the way we talked about the future and all the wonderful things we were going to discover together.

We're still going to discover them, Cath, I promise you. It's just going to take a while before we're together again. I keep a picture of you in that blue dress with me all the time. The other guys say I'm a lucky son of a gun to have a girl like you, but they don't know the half of it.

Our time's coming, Cath! As long as you go on loving me, I know that not even the enemy can do anything to hurt me.

With all my love,
Doug

June 15, 1943

Dear Gerry,

I know you must be mad at me for not writing to you sooner. A lot has been going on here at home and I guess I just didn't know how to tell you.

I'm afraid I have some really bad news. Cathy's boyfriend, Doug, was killed on May 30. They say he died a hero's death, but that doesn't seem to make it any easier on his mom and dad, or on Cathy.

Aunt Edna and Uncle Les—our families are so close we call the Weavers that—hung a big gold star in their front window to show their son had served his country, but every time Cathy walks by I'm afraid she's going to throw a rock through the glass.

I wish she'd cry. At least if she cried, I know she'd feel better. But she's keeping it all bottled up inside and snapping at everybody who tries to help her. She didn't even cry when a letter from Douglas arrived the day of the memorial service. Yesterday she made Mom cry and I wanted to shake her as hard as I could, but I was afraid that she would— Well, I don't know exactly what I was afraid she would do, but there's something really scary about the way she's acting. It's almost as if nothing has happened. Or even worse, it's like Douglas never *was*. One minute he was the center of her life and, now that he's gone the place in her heart where he used to be has closed in on itself like a lake over a skipping stone.

As it is, I can't seem to do anything right. She says I hog the bathroom and play the radio too loud and don't do my share of chores around the house. Yesterday she threw a slipper at me like I was the Weavers' mutt, Sandy, and when I told my mom about it, she just patted me on the head and said I had to be more understanding.

I guess I just don't know *how* to be more understanding. I feel like everybody's forgotten I'm alive. Tonight is my high-school graduation, the most important event in my entire life, and I don't think anyone in my whole family even remembers. When Cathy graduated, Mom and Daddy gave her a beautiful watch complete with an inscription on the back, and a string of pearls. I'll be lucky if Mom remembers to show up at the auditorium to see me get my diploma.

Thank you very much for the pretty scarf. Mrs. Carlino down the block said it must be silk. I am going to wear it to work on Monday morning when I start my job at the bank. I bet I'm the only girl there with a present from the front! See what I mean? There you are, thousands of miles away from everything, and you remember my graduation and my very own family acts like this is just another day.

Even my friends don't understand. They're so busy with their own graduation parties that they don't even realize that I'm the only girl in school who won't be giving one of her own. I'm so glad I have you to write to, Gerry. Even though we've never met, I think you're my best friend.

Please take good care of yourself. I promise that next time I'll tell you all about the movie stars I met at the Stage Door Canteen.

Love,
Nancy

ARMY CASUALTIES INCREASED BY 875
Thirty-nine Men from New York,
11 from New Jersey, 7 from Connecticut

—*New York Times*
June 30, 1943

July 1, 1943

Dear Nance,

I can't believe how fast your letter reached me. I can't believe I got so lucky. Wish it could happen more often but I know there isn't much chance. (Troopships are slower than snails.)

I'm real sorry to hear about Cathy's boyfriend. We heard rumors about a real bad skirmish up there in the Aleutians. Guys killed and wounded, and for what? It didn't even help the war effort, at least not so far as anybody can see. I hope she's starting to feel better about things now.

Glad you liked the scarf. I can't tell you exactly where I got it (they'd probably censor it out anyway!) but Mrs. Carlino wasn't far from wrong.

Things have been real hectic around here lately. We did a bit of traveling from island to island. Rumor has it we're going to see some action any day now. About time! I've been here almost a year and I still haven't seen the enemy except in the movies. I know you like to think we're all running around like John Wayne and all those other stars you're so crazy about, but I'm afraid the truth is pretty boring.

It seems like we spend most of our time waiting for something to happen, and then once it does, we spend more time waiting to find out when it will happen again. I guess the fly-boys get most of the glory, while the rest of us hang around waiting to do what we were trained to do—kill the enemy. We spent three weeks on C rations and now I'm even skinnier than I was before. Good thing Mom can't see me! She worries enough as it is, especially since my kid brother Andy joined the marines back in May and will be shipping out any day now.

Bob Hope and his show will be coming our way around Thanksgiving. They also say Rita Hayworth will be with him!!! Most of the guys have a picture of Rita taped to their mess kits and one of Betty Grable glued to the inside of their helmets. Ever since you sent me that picture of you in your senior-prom dress, Rita doesn't stand a chance! You're real pretty, Nancy, and, yes, I do like redheads.

I don't know why you're so hard on yourself. You're smart and you're pretty and by now I bet your parents have given you your graduation watch. I wish I could give you the string of pearls.

Well, it's time to go. Please keep on writing to me, Nance. Your letters mean a lot to me!

Love,
Gerry

July 12, 1943

Dear Mrs. Wilson,
I showed up at your house that morning but a neighbor lady of yours told me what happened to Catherine's boyfriend. I'm really sorry. Please tell her that for me.

Maybe you'll give me a rain check on that big breakfast when we come home.

Sincerely,
Johnny Danza

August 2, 1943

Dear Johnny,
Thank you very much for the kind words. I hope you don't mind that my mother showed me your letter.

She also said to ask you if you want pancakes or waffles. Take care of yourself and please watch out for Daddy.

Sincerely,
Catherine Wilson

P.S. Pick the waffles! Mom makes the world's best—C.

September 8, 1943

Dear Catherine,

Waffles. Fried eggs over easy. Bacon. Fresh milk.

We haven't been over here real long and already I'm beginning to dream about good food. You're lucky to be able to eat anything you want, whenever you want it. They switched us over to K rations because they're easier for us to carry on bivouacs. Besides, those empty gold C ration cans were making it easy for the enemy planes to pick us out. I guess we're not the neatest bunch of Joes around. You learn how to eat right from the cans, don't even bother with the mess kit. Mostly you scoop up your food with a hard biscuit or spoon.

K rations give you just about everything they say you need. Only trouble is, they don't taste too good. They even put a pack of cigarettes and some crackers in there to keep the can of meat from rolling around. Some of the guys have made up a recipe for D ration fudge. You kind of mash sugar and chocolate and condensed milk with a shell fragment and cook it over a Coleman stove—if you're lucky enough to find one. They say we're the best-fed soldiers in the war, but I bet this wouldn't hold up to your mom's cooking. (Or maybe yours, too? Are you a good cook? Somehow I can't imagine you standing at the stove!)

It was good to hear from you. I hope you keep writing.

Sincerely,
Johnny

P.S. Your dad's doing real well here. He's the oldest guy in our platoon but probably the toughest. (Except for me, of course.) Do me a favor—write and tell him to shave! That is one crummy-looking mustache.—J

September 17, 1943

Dear Princess,

I've been hearing some good things about you from Lou and Victor and the others at the plant. It seems you've been shaking things up around the office. In fact, Betty Hudson told me you even managed to reorganize payroll and that things are running smoother than silk, even with the overtime they've had to put in.

You're really making me proud, Cathy. I've been worried about the business, but hearing those glowing reports has eased my mind. But don't work yourself sick. You're the owner's daughter. You don't have to put in 18-hour days. That's why I put Lou Alfano in charge in the first place. Go out to the movies with your mother and Nancy. See your friends.

Remember you're only young once. The war won't last forever. Don't spend all your time working. A pretty young woman like you has better things to do.

Last night I had to write to a guy's mother and tell her that her son had died a hero's death. Packing up his personal effects was about the hardest thing I've ever done. It made me think of Douglas. Take pride in the way he lived and died, princess. He did what he had to do to make the world safe for the rest of us.

Take good care of your mom and little sister, and extra-good care of yourself.

Much love,
Dad

September 26, 1943

Dear Pop,
I know I shouldn't be writing to you about this (and I really hope you won't tell Mom I did) but I am so unhappy that I just can't stand it anymore.

Cathy has been awful to me lately and I don't think it's fair. I feel very sorry for her—losing Douglas was awful and I miss him as much as everyone else does—but is that an excuse for treating me so mean? Nothing I do is right and she yells at me all the time. We used to be good friends. Now she acts as if I'm her worst enemy and it's making me feel terrible. I didn't make this bad thing happen to her, but she's acting as if everything was all my fault.

She won't let me talk to her about anything. She works all the time, and when she isn't at work she's at the USO or volunteering at Horace Harding Hospital. When she *is* home, she's buried up to her elbows in ledgers and reports and if I even make one teeny-tiny noise she yells loud enough to knock the walls down.

I know she's lonely and sad and I really want to help her but she just won't let anybody near her and I don't think it's fair that she's making everybody feel so bad, especially Mom. I hope you'll say something to her in your next letter. I'm getting tired of not being able to play my Frank Sinatra records or have my friends over.

Hope you're fine. Say hi to Johnny for me.

Love and kisses,
Nancy

October 8, 1943

Dear Dad,
I'm sorry Nancy found it necessary to write you about my disposition. Believe me, I am doing very well. Yes, I am working hard but there is a lot that needs to be done at the factory, and if Nancy would get her head out of the clouds, she might realize that. I've told her we could use her on Saturday mornings but she would rather spend her time at the movies.

I am sorry if her letter caused you any worry. Things are under control here. Don't give it a second thought.

Much love,
Cathy

P.S. She can play her Sinatra records all day and all night if she wants to—C.

October 11, 1943

Dear Catherine,
Al (the guy from Florida I told you about) took these snapshots of your old man on KP duty. (That's me behind him. I'm the one waving the potato peeler in the air.) Thought you'd like to see for yourself that he's doing just fine. Make sure you show your mom.

We saw some combat the other night. Sure isn't anything like it is in the movies. I can't say any more, but imagine being stuck in the middle of the worst thunderstorm you ever heard as a kid, and you'll kind of get the idea.

Haven't heard from you for a while. Is everything okay? Write when you can. I'd really like to hear from you.

If you have a picture of you and your mom and sister that you can spare, I'd really like to have one. It's nice to know what we're fighting for! Most of the guys here have someone back home waiting for them. I wouldn't mind being able to look at your picture and think about the way you looked at the Stage Door Canteen the night we met.

Best wishes,
Johnny

November 25, 1943

Dear Johnny,
Happy Thanksgiving. It's been a long time since I last heard from you. I heard Bob Hope on the radio last week and he

said the army actually roasts turkeys for the men and serves them up with all the trimmings on Thanksgiving. It doesn't feel like Thanksgiving here without Dad to carve the turkey and say grace. Nancy and I were going to take the subway into town to see the Macy's parade but it's been canceled. I guess all the rubber they'd use in their Tin Woodman and Uncle Sam balloons could go to better use in the war effort. I saw in the paper that 4,000 of their employees are in the armed forces now. They say their mechanical Christmas windows will be as spectacular as usual, but I don't know when I'll have the time between now and Christmas to go and see.

Did you ever get the photos I sent you? They really were terrible, weren't they? No wonder you stopped writing! But seriously, let me know if they got through. If they didn't, I'll ask Aunt Pat to hurry up and make more copies and we'll try again.

I've cut my hair a little since I last saw you. Maybe you should forget all about the way I looked at the Stage Door Canteen that night. (It seems like a lifetime ago, doesn't it?) There just isn't time to fuss with curlers and rouge these days. I bet if you saw me now you'd think I was as serious as a librarian! Not your type at all, I'll bet.

Things at the factory are booming. I think Dad will be very happy when the year-end financial statement is calculated. (I just sat back and reread this letter. Is that really me writing about financial statements? It's hard to believe that only a year ago I didn't even know what a financial statement was! It sure proves you can learn anything in this world if you really have to!)

I hope you and my father have a wonderful dinner. We'll say a prayer for you and thank God that both of you are well.

Sincerely,
Catherine

P.S. Enclosed is a small present. Hope it sees you through the cold winters in ??—C.

December 31, 1943

Dear Cathy,
Your letters reached me a few days before Christmas. I guess
Tom told you we've been moving around a bit. You were
right about the Thanksgiving turkey dinner, right down to
the cranberry sauce and candied sweet potatoes. That was
about the best meal I've had in years. (But I still have my
fingers crossed that I'll be having that breakfast with all of
you before too long.)

I hope you and your mom and Nancy have a Happy New
Year. Sergeant Munson got some whiskey on the black
market and we're going to toast 1944 in style.

One year ago I was in Atlanta welcoming in 1943. Boy,
did twelve months bring a lot of changes. Makes you wonder what we'll all be doing this time next year, doesn't it?

Maybe we'll be lucky and we'll welcome in 1945 together.

Who knows? Anything's possible, right? Maybe we'll
even get to dance together again. Even with your new haircut, you're probably the prettiest girl I've ever seen.

Best wishes,
Johnny

P.S. Thanks for the scarf you knitted for me. Next time
make it a blue one. I've seen enough olive drab to last me the
rest of my life!—J.

January 15, 1944

Dear Johnny,
I'm afraid we didn't have a very exciting New Year's Eve
around here. No one had much enthusiasm for noise-
makers and confetti, especially not on Hansen Street. Aunt
Edna and Uncle Les tried to put a good face on it, but it was

hard to make merry when we've lost someone so important to all of us.

This is the first year my mom has ever spent without Daddy around. Did you know they were childhood sweethearts? They grew up right next door to each other in Astoria. Mom says she knew she wanted to marry Daddy from the first second he peeked into her crib. It's so hard for her to be without him, but she never says a word. Never complains about anything. Sometimes I wonder if I'm a changeling. There are times when I just want to scream at the top of my lungs about how unfair this war is and how much I hate it, but then I think about the terrible things that are happening in this world and I feel so selfish I'm ashamed of myself.

What a terrible letter this is! And here we're supposed to be cheerful when we write to our servicemen overseas! I promise to write again tomorrow and tell you the funny things that have happened at the plant.

By the way, you said you wanted a blue scarf, right?

Hope you like it!

Keep warm,
Cathy

P.S. The traffic lights are back on at night! The dimout seems to be ending. Do you think that's a good sign??

P.P.S. I'm glad you liked my picture.

U.S. SHIPS AND PLANES HIT ATOLLS
IN SAVAGE ATTACK ON MARSHALLS:
AMERICANS BOMB GERMAN CITIES
—*New York Times*
January 31, 1944

February 14, 1944

Happy Valentine Day, darling!
I'm curled up on the window seat in our bedroom, watch-

ing the snow fall. The radio says it's the coldest day of the year so far, but I'm nice and warm under the quilt your Grandma Alice made for our wedding present. Hard to believe that was almost 25 years ago!

The girls are both at work. Nancy has been complaining about the bank a lot the past few weeks. She says her boss is a cranky old lady who hates young girls, but I think it's more than that. Nancy has many good qualities but punctuality isn't one of them. Sometimes I think if I didn't make it my business to see she got out of bed in the morning, she'd still be asleep come dinnertime. I wish you were here to give her a good talking-to.

Work has been Cathy's salvation. She is the first one in the office in the morning and the last one to leave at night. She has put her heart and soul into helping out at the factory and I'm certain the men all appreciate her efforts.

She's become best friends with Eddie Martin (remember him?—you hired Eddie just before you left to handle the shipping department) and the job the two of them are doing would make you proud. But don't worry. We'll keep everything running smoothly at the plant. You just worry about keeping yourself safe so you can come home to us soon. More than anything in the world I want things to be the way they used to be.

The hot water pipes nearly froze last night. We had to hurry down into the basement and wrap them with blankets the way you told us to. Coal deliveries have been cut back. Mr. Russo promised me we'd be first on his list next week.

Did you get the sweater I made for you, and the cookies? Mr. Fontaine at the post office said the cookies would arrive just fine if I wrapped them up right. They're your favorite kind—chocolate chip. Sugar and butter are hard to come by these days so I may not be making cookies again for a while unless I can trade ration coupons with someone on the block. You wouldn't believe the wonderful vegetable casseroles I've concocted—we don't even miss roast beef!

I don't mean to concern you, but Nancy has been talking about finding a job out on Long Island, near your sister. She and Cathy haven't been seeing eye to eye lately. I suppose it's inevitable—how can a girl as young as Nancy understand what it's like to lose the man you love? As much as I don't want Nancy to leave home, perhaps there is something to the notion of allowing her the chance to be young and carefree. At least as long as Anna and Frank are nearby to keep their eyes on her.

I hope the army is taking good care of you. I worry that you're not eating well or getting enough sleep. In Johnny's last letter, he told me the food there is really quite good, but I'm not certain he's not saying that just to ease my mind. You ease my mind and send me a snapshot of the two of you as soon as you can so I can see for myself that you're fine.

The snow is drifting against Edna's front stoop. Last night she covered her rosebushes with newspaper and twine to keep them safe. Right now they're buried under the snow. I hope they survive. I can't imagine spring without Edna's roses.

The girls bought me a tiny heart-shaped box of Fanny Farmer chocolates and Nancy promised to make supper tonight for all of us. Macaroni and cheese. I wish so much that you were here with me, Tom, darling. The house is so empty and lonely without you.

God bless you and keep you safe from harm.

I'll write again tomorrow. I miss you and love you more than you'll ever know.

Your Doro

March 1, 1944

Dear Doro,
Hadn't heard from you in a while, but then eight letters

came from you today. Also three from Cathy and Nancy, and one each from Edna and my sister Grace. Best haul I've had in almost a year. I wish the stinking post office could spread the bounty out a little better but beggars can't be choosers. Some guys here don't get any mail at all. I almost felt embarrassed to be so lucky. (But don't stop writing!)

I'm glad you and the girls are writing to Johnny. He's a little rough around the edges but he's a damned good kid and a real friend. He has a lot going for him, but his temper keeps getting him in hot water. Nancy's Christmas poem made him laugh and I swear he only takes Cathy's green scarf off to shower. I suppose you saw that crazy-quilt blue one she made for him after Christmas? The guys laughed so hard, they cried. There must have been every shade of blue in the rainbow in that scarf. Nobody laughed harder than Johnny. Don't tell Cathy that the green scarf is glued to him. He'd probably be embarrassed if he realized I'd even noticed. Somehow I don't think anybody's ever knitted a scarf for him before. Or done much else for him, either, if you want to know the truth. I don't know what it is about that kid that gets to me—maybe he reminds me of myself at his age. (Was I really that pigheaded, Doro? You always used to tell me that my head was harder than an iron skillet!)

Have you gone down to the bank yet to talk to Paul? I told you before I left that I wanted to make sure you and the girls would be provided for. I know you don't want to hear it, but it's important. Paul has the papers. He will explain everything. If you love me, Doro, you'll take care of this.

Lately I've been thinking a lot about home. When I first came here I worried about the business and all the fellows whose jobs would be affected by my decision to enlist. I knew you and the girls could cope with anything life threw your way. You're a strong woman and you've raised strong daughters and I don't deserve any of the credit for the way they've turned out. The credit belongs to you.

If Nancy finds herself a job out in Suffolk County, maybe we should let her stretch her wings. Write or call Anna and tell her our little girl may be heading in their direction. I know she and Frank will make certain Nancy is taken care of in fine fashion.

You haven't changed anything in the house, have you? When we march, I pretend I'm walking through the house and I can see each room exactly the way it was when I left. Those chintz covers on the divan that we fought about—remember I said they looked too fussy and frilly? I can see you sitting in the wing chair by the window with your head bent over your sewing and your hair drifting across your cheek.

Don't worry if you don't hear from me for a while. I think we'll be moving camp again in the next few days. Where we're headed is anybody's guess. I keep thinking that sooner or later something has to happen, but the days and the weeks pass and still nothing. Sometimes I think this war will never end.

All my love,
Tom

GREETINGS!

Yes, it's that time of year again!

This small postcard is a reminder that it's time to plan your Victory Garden for 1944. Our boys at the front need our support once more. Don't use canned foods that can help provide nourishment for our soldiers and sailors. Plant your garden today and harvest your vegetables tomorrow. Remember: do your share for Victory now!

F. LANGELLA & SON NURSERY

March 21, 1944

Dear Johnny,

I guess it's just one of those nights. It's a little after midnight and for the life of me I can't seem to fall asleep. Maybe it's the weather. Today is the first day of spring, but instead of the promise of warmth, it is raw and cold and more than likely ready to snow.

Today I thought I saw Douglas. I had worked late and was coming up the subway steps a little after eight when it happened. A cold nasty sleet was coming down and I was struggling with my packages and trying to put up my umbrella. I wasn't watching where I was going and I stumbled on the top steps, and the next thing I knew a man was helping me up from the puddle where I was sitting. He asked me if I was okay and I looked up at him and just for an instant, Johnny, I thought Douglas had come back to me. It was as if a magician had snapped his fingers and the past nine months disappeared in a puff of smoke! All those months when Douglas was away, I couldn't remember how he looked, how he sounded. I'd close my eyes tight as could be and try so hard to remember and the more I tried, the farther he drifted away.

But you know what, Johnny? The second I heard he was dead—the *very second* Aunt Edna said those words—I saw him right there in front of me on the street and I heard his voice say my name just as if he were standing there next to me.

And that's exactly what happened tonight. For a moment that poor man who helped me up from the puddle was Douglas. He was as tall as Douglas and his hair was the same light blond and I suppose my imagination filled in the rest. For one wonderful second, he was Douglas to me and everything else dropped away and I was happy, *really happy*.

But then he asked me again if I was hurt and I shook my head. He turned and disappeared down the stairs and into the subway. I stood there, clutching my packages and my umbrella, and I started to cry. (You don't know me very well, Johnny, but I'm not a girl who cries easily.) I didn't just cry, I sobbed. An elderly lady came over to me and offered me a handkerchief, but I shook my head and just kept on crying for Douglas, and for me, and for the life together we'd lost.

I guess all along I'd been convincing myself that it had never really happened, that there had been some terrible mistake and Douglas was still alive somewhere out there, and one day he would suddenly show up and I would run into his arms and we would pick up exactly where we'd left off the day we said goodbye. Tonight I finally realized that he isn't coming back. He's dead and I have to let him rest in peace. Now comes the hard part—trying to figure out what I'm going to do with the rest of my life.

It's after two in the morning now. My mother just tapped on my door and asked if I'd like some warm milk with her. I thank God every night that I have such a terrific family. I don't know how I would have managed without them.

Thanks for listening, Johnny. It really helped to talk about this. I hope I can return the favor one day.

With gratitude,
Cathy

March 22, 1944

Dear Johnny,
Please forget my last letter. I don't know what came over me. I never should have unburdened myself on you, especially since we are almost total strangers. Please, I beg you not to worry Daddy with anything I said. Honestly, I've made my peace with losing Douglas. I guess his birthday just hit me harder than I'd expected.

Sorry for such a hurried letter—the postman is walking toward the house and I want to get this in the mail today.

Hope you're doing fine—
C.

P.S. Everything around here is changing. Nancy quit the bank and will start work next week at an aircraft factory way out on the eastern end of the Island! She is feeling quite grown-up and independent. Can you imagine how upset she'd be if she knew Aunt Anna and Uncle Frank will be watching over her? Our very own Rosie the Riveter. (I'm glad you and Daddy aren't in the air force!)—C.

May 30, 1944

Dear Cathy,

You don't have to apologize for anything. I'm really proud that you felt you could talk to me. I don't have a lot of experience giving advice to people, but it seems to me that you're going to be fine.

Who sets the rules about things like that, anyway? It takes as long as it takes to get over losing someone you love. It's nobody's damn business but yours. I lost my wife a couple of years ago. No, she didn't die—she left me—but I'll tell you it felt like somebody'd cut my heart out with a knife. I know I don't look like the kind of guy who's interested in having a family (especially since I didn't have one of my own as a kid) but I really thought Angie and I could make it work.

Maybe we could have if the war hadn't come along when it did. She met this other guy at the office she worked in and—well, you can guess the rest. It's an old story. Now I know why she didn't want to get married in the church. She got an annulment one-two-three and took off with her pal. I guess in a way I should be glad, but it's taken me a long time to figure that out.

When you've been alone all your life like me, you don't spend a whole lot of time thinking about having a future with someone. It's real hard to imagine someone being there all the time for you, someone you can rely on.

But I guess you wouldn't understand what I'm talking about, would you, Cathy? You come from a real nice family (the best) and I bet you've never had to wonder if anyone really cared about you.

Enough about that. Maybe being hungry is making me shoot my mouth off!

You asked if the war is scary. The answer is yes. I've seen a lot of buddies come and go. Some died. Some lucky dogs got to go home with a purple heart and discharge papers. You never know from one minute to the next if all hell will break loose around you until you can't even think straight.

We get a broadcast from President Roosevelt on Sundays. I used to really like listening to him but now I don't bother. What can he say that matters? The war is going to take as long as it takes. Nothing he tells us in a phony "fireside chat" will change anything.

About the factory. Why would your mom be interested in the everyday problems going on there, anyway? Most women wouldn't be. With both your dad and Lou gone, you're going to have to make the decisions. At least until the men come home and things get back to normal.

Looks to me that, like it or not, you're the head of the family.

But don't worry. It won't last forever.

Love,
Johnny

ALLIED ARMIES LAND IN FRANCE
IN THE HAVRE-CHERBOURG AREA,
GREAT INVASION IS UNDERWAY
—*New York Times*
June 6, 1944

June 21, 1944

Dear Gerry,
I'm so glad you're in the Pacific and not caught up in all the fighting in Europe!

I caught a ride home this weekend in the company delivery truck, and Mom and Cathy are beside themselves with worry. The D-day invasion is all anybody can talk about, especially since no mail has come in for weeks and weeks now. The last time they heard from Daddy was the end of May. He had said not to worry, that they would be on the move for a while, but it's hard not to when the radio broadcasts are filled with scary stories about blood on the beaches at Normandy. They're calling it the D-day invasion and they say the D is for death.

I didn't say anything to Mom, but I borrowed Aunt Edna's newspaper and checked the casualty lists with a fine-tooth comb. My heart was pounding so hard I couldn't catch my breath. "Wilson" is a long way down the list, I'll tell you that. Once I made sure Daddy's name wasn't there, I checked for his friend Johnny Danza and his name wasn't there, either. Problem was, nobody's heard from either one of them since D-day and I guess our imaginations are going crazy.

It was so good to be home again, even if everything has changed so much since last year when Daddy went away. I know I made a terrible mistake in taking the job way out on the Island, but at the time I wanted so much to be on my own. The truth is, seeing Cathy so sad scared me. I didn't want to be forced to think about what was really going on in the war. I wanted to go on thinking about USO shows and the Stage Door Canteen and how exciting it was to dance with a boy in uniform. What I didn't want to think about was that people were dying.

Now I don't know how I ever managed to forget such an important thing. I guess it took writing to you, Gerry, and what happened to Douglas to make me open my eyes.

What I want now, more than anything (well, not more than finally meeting you!) is to go back home. I hate this boarding house. I hate Old Man Winfield's talcum powder and the smell of Mrs. O'Neil's cabbage soup and the way the landlady's son looks at me when I get in at night. No one talks to me and if it weren't for Aunt Anna in Mastic Beach I'd feel so lonely I would die. I manage to get over there at least once a week. I've sworn Aunt Anna to secrecy—if Mom knew I was homesick she'd worry and she does enough worrying as it is.

Cathy didn't say anything but I could tell she's having a lot of problems at the factory. She works six days a week and sometimes she doesn't even take all of Sunday off. She's skinny and short-tempered and for the very first time I could understand how much she has on her shoulders. I wish she'd tell Daddy just how hard it is on her. Mom doesn't pay much attention to what's going on at the factory. When Cathy tried to tell her about a problem with the union organizer, Mom just said, "That's nice, dear," and continued rolling bandages for the hospital.

The men fight Cathy about everything. Back in the beginning, right after Daddy went overseas, they were real nice to her and said "Yes, Miss Wilson" and "No, Miss Wilson" and pretty much kept on their toes. Not anymore. The men who are there are either biding their time until they go to war or else they're too old or too sick to join up. Whatever the reason, they're awfully angry about something and now that Lou Alfano is gone, it seems they're taking it out on Cathy. She used to go head-to-head with them but now I think she's getting scared (those union organizers are very tough). She's hired some girls to work on the assembly line but the men kicked up such a fuss that she's been forced to assign the girls to one area and keep them all together. I guess there's safety in numbers.

She's started asking Eddie Martin (he's a clerk) to do all the talking for her and that's making her *very* mad, let me tell you. They're working around the clock at the factory and what with the union trying to come in she's worried that she'll lose control completely. I guess it's hard for a man to take orders from a girl.

One good thing—I think Cathy has finally accepted the fact that Douglas is gone. Sure she was short-tempered and tired, but I didn't see that haunted look in her eyes that used to scare me so much when I lived at home. She even went over to Aunt Edna's Saturday night for the Weavers' anniversary party and didn't come home all pale and quiet. It's hard to imagine what her future will be like—for as long as I can remember, it was always Cathy-and-Douglas, like it was one name instead of two. But at least she's smiling now.

I should be home with my mom and Cathy. I know that now. I didn't have to leave Forest Hills to work for the war effort. I could have done that right there at home at Daddy's factory. Maybe if I was in the office, I could help Cathy with her problem with the men. Right now I don't know exactly what I'm going to do—or even if my mom wants me to move back.

But I promise I'll let you know if my address changes back to the old one, okay?

In the meantime, please take care of yourself and write to me soon!

> With much love,
> Nancy

August 1, 1944

Dear Nance,

You really have me worried. What do you mean you don't like the way the landlady's son looks at you? Did you tell your mom? Did you complain to the landlady?

Pardon my language, but I think you should get the hell out of there and fast. I can't stand being so far away and not able to take care of you. How can you think your mom wouldn't want you back? Just pack your bags and go home. I bet they welcome you with open arms. (Even Cathy!)

It took a while for us to get the scoop on D-day. Newspapers take time to reach you on the other side of the world. I'm glad we're beating the hell out of the Germans but it's sure going to put the heat on us over here. They're talking about sending us more manpower and making a push on the Japanese forces in [CENSORED]. I'll bet we're here at least another year. Maybe more. Are the leaves changing yet? It's hot and steamy here. Your clothes feel wet all the time and you can't breathe without feeling like your lungs are clogged with soggy cotton wool. A USO show came through last week on some little island where we were anchored for repairs. I had a day off so I yanked a wheelbarrow into the field and set myself up with a front-row seat. It rained—natch!—the day of the show but all I had to do was cover myself with an old tarp and it was almost as good as being at Radio City Music Hall. I saw Rita Hayworth and Joan Leslie. Jack Benny and Rochester did a skit about being stuck in a bank vault, and Bing Crosby sang "Blue Skies" and "White Christmas" even though Christmas is over nine months away.

Please move back home, Nance. It's where you belong. Families should stay together. Besides, I want to know you're safe and sound.

Much love,
Gerry

September 5, 1944

Dear Johnny,
I feel as if we've gotten to know each other pretty well these past fifteen months and I believe I can trust you to help me relieve Daddy's mind.

We're having a bit of trouble at the factory. To make a long story short, morale is pretty bad and a union organizer is stirring everyone up. My father's position has always been anti-union and I am holding fast to his wishes, but it's getting harder and harder to keep the peace.

I know it isn't right, asking you to lie for me, but it's important that my father not have anything more to worry about. My mother isn't very interested in what goes on at the factory, but I know that the union organizer has written my father a three-page letter filled with demands—and unfortunately a few threats.

I have sent Daddy a letter of reassurance and am begging you, Johnny, to back me up. Tell him my letters to you have been filled with success stories about the factory. The truth is, we've never been more productive, but if the union organizer gets his way, that productivity is going to stop any time now.

Believe me, I can handle this problem. The one thing I can't handle is my father's peace of mind. Would you do that for me?

It would mean the world, Johnny.

Love,
Cathy

October 15, 1944

Dearest Tom,

How I miss your letters! It's been over two months now since I last heard from you and, as you can imagine, my imagination is running riot. The newspapers are filled with talk of Aachen and burning cities and I am terrified that you are in the midst of it all. I'm certain you must be—Cathy hasn't heard a word from Johnny, either. How we worry about the two of you.

I love you, Tom, and will wait for you forever. I said a rosary last night to pray for your safety and Johnny's—and the safety of all the men who are fighting for us so bravely. Must go now. I'm writing this from the hospital and my lunch break is over. We're having a knitting bee this afternoon—more of those long white bandages. Much more tomorrow, darling, and every day until you are home in my arms.

All my love always,
Doro

November 8, 1944

Dear Johnny,

I hardly know how to begin this letter. I am afraid I have offended you and I want to apologize if that is the case.

Looking back, I can hardly believe I sent that letter to you. Johnny, I know I had no business dragging you into a family matter—on business, no less!—and I realize I put you in a terrible position. You and Daddy are friends. Had I taken a minute to think about it, I would have understood that your loyalties are to him. (And they should be.) I was going through a difficult period then and I was desperate for support. I apologize for asking you to take sides in a family matter.

Over the last few months I've really come to count on you as a friend. Isn't that strange? I mean, I barely know you—we only saw each other that once at the Stage Door Canteen. And yet I can talk to you the way I can't talk to anybody else around here. Everyone else wants to think of me as solid, capable Catherine, when inside there are times when I wish I could just bury my head under the covers and let someone else take over. It was so much easier before the war. Now I hardly know what it is I'm supposed to do. Or who it is I'm supposed to be.

I hope you'll forgive me and drop me a note. I miss your letters, Johnny. I miss talking to you.

Love,
Cathy

November 24, 1944

Dear Gerry,

I hope you had a wonderful Thanksgiving Day yesterday— well, at least as wonderful a day as you can have so far away from home.

Cathy was in better spirits. She even lent me her copy of *Forever Amber*. She is making a real effort to be more cheerful around the house right now. We haven't heard from Daddy in a long time—a couple of months, to be exact. And it's been just as long (or longer) since any of us have heard from Johnny Danza.

I know I've gone all around the mulberry bush with this. I guess that's because I'm really afraid to say what's on my mind, almost like if I say it, it'll come true. Gerry, I think something terrible has happened. Cathy has always said she knew all that week that something had happened to Douglas but she was afraid to admit it to her herself. Well, that's exactly how I feel right now, except I'm not sure who it's happened to. (Not you! I'm certain you're fine—I couldn't live if you weren't.) Sometimes I think Daddy has been shot and other times I think it's Johnny or one of the boys we went to school with.

The only thing I'm sure about is that things are going to get a lot worse before they get better. General Eisenhower told us on the radio yesterday that the courageous troops are suffering and need "myriads" of supplies. We're bombing Tokyo and not even that is enough to end the war. But worst of all was a little article buried among the lists of wounded and dead. Up until the beginning of this month, we've had 528,795 casualties in all theaters, and 88,245 of our boys have been killed. One of them was Douglas. Now I'm scared one of them might be my father.

Please, please keep yourself safe and healthy.

I love you, Gerry.

Nancy

December 1, 1944

Dear Johnny,

I am so scared I can barely hold my fountain pen still enough to write this letter. All day long I've had this terrible feeling that the worst has happened, that you or Daddy have been injured and I just can't shake it.

I keep telling myself that maybe my letters just aren't getting through. The man at the post office says it's almost impossible to deliver mail to the European front these days, but even though I know he's telling me the truth, there's a little part of me that's so scared, Johnny, that I can hardly think.

Every night I pray to God that my father comes home safely. I can't even bear to think what would happen to my mother without him. But I also pray to God for you. Please come back hale and hearty, Johnny.

More than anything, I'd like to get the chance to know you better. You've come to mean so much to me.

With much love,
Cathy

PART III

THE HOME FRONT

I think that this is as good a time as any...to warn men that when the war is over, the going will be a lot tougher, because they will have to compete with women whose eyes have been opened to their greatest economic potentialities.

—*Saturday Evening Post*
Harold Ickes, Secretary of the Interior.

Chapter Five

No one could pinpoint exactly when it happened, but by Christmas Eve of 1944, it was clear that Catherine was in charge of Wilson Manufacturing.

No announcements were made. No papers were signed. But everyone understood that the buck stopped right there on Catherine's desk. Lou Alfano, her father's right-hand man, had retired just after Easter, but the truth was few people even noticed. Catherine had become the heart and soul of the Wilson factory, pushing them on to greater levels of production than even the most optimistic War Office officials could have hoped for.

Even the trouble with the union organizer had been resolved—at least, in a manner of speaking. Tom Wilson had been gone for eighteen long months; the situation he had left behind was not the situation Catherine dealt with on a daily basis. Despite the wartime prosperity the United States was enjoying, the Depression was still fresh in everyone's mind. It had happened once and no one doubted it could happen again—no matter what the powers-that-be had to say.

"Hey, Cathy!" She looked up and saw Eddie Martin standing in the doorway to her office. "It's time to give out the Christmas bonuses."

She rubbed her eyes and mustered up a smile. "Is it eleven already?"

Eddie looked down at his pocket watch. "Five minutes after. The natives are getting restless."

"Eggnog all gone?"

"An hour ago." His grin spread from cheekbone to cheekbone. "Bill Danneher dug up an old bottle of rum to spike the punch. You'd be surprised how quick the eggnog disappeared after that."

"No, I wouldn't." She ran a brush through her hair and reached for her lipstick in the top drawer of her father's battered desk. "With rationing the way it is, an extra pound of butter would be enough to start a riot."

Eddie struck a jaunty pose as he leaned against the doorjamb. "I guess you don't want to hear about the ton of butter cookies my mother made, do you?"

Catherine flashed him a stern look. "The black market is going to get you in a lot of trouble, Edward Martin. I'd think you, if anyone, would be smart enough to stay away from it." Eddie had been struggling for more than two years to get into the armed services. It amazed Catherine that he would bypass the limits imposed by the government.

Since rationing had taken effect, a healthy black market in butter, sugar and the other "luxuries" prized by American homemakers had sprung up in almost every city and town in the country. You could have anything you wanted— for a price.

Catherine was adamantly opposed to black-market profiteering, but she understood all too well the desires that drove men and women to take advantage of the system. Rationing made it impossible to save up coupons for a holiday baking spree; coupons came complete with expiration dates. The motto of the day was Use them or lose them. Housewives were urged to "Use it up, wear it out, make it do or do without," and for the most part, they did. Some enterprising women on Hansen Street, led by the redoubtable Edna Weaver, had pooled their resources with those of single working girls and managed to continue their baking traditions for one more Christmas.

She looked at Eddie's freckled face and sighed as she swiveled the lipstick back down into its case. "I guess a few trays of butter cookies won't hurt the war effort, will they?"

Eddie's dark brown eyes twinkled with merriment. "Especially not when they're going out with the next troop carrier leaving the pier."

She threw back her head and laughed. "I should have known better. Your mother is about the most patriotic woman in town."

"I had you going for a minute, didn't I, Cathy?"

"I wouldn't brag about it, Martin. I could still hold back your Christmas bonus." She looked at him across the desk. "Did the year-end projection come in yet?"

Eddie's smile turned into a full-fledged grin. "We're running thirty percent ahead of last year. At this rate we're providing enough metal parts to build a ship every six and a half days."

She leaned forward, fingers tapping on the scarred desk top. "Think we can up production ten percent for January?"

"Think you can help me get into the service?"

She touched his hand lightly. "Still 4-F?"

He nodded, the twinkle in his eyes dimming. "You were expecting something different?" He paced the small office, fists thrust into the pockets of his trousers. "I'm still short, half-blind, and too damned stupid for the army."

"You're not stupid, Eddie."

"Yeah, right." He glared at her as he paced. "Now tell me I'm not short and blind and I'll marry you tomorrow."

"Careful what you say, Eddie. I might take you up on it."

"Hey, look," he said, spreading his arms wide in mock appeal. "I'm desperate!" He stopped short, his round cheeks reddening. "Geez, I'm sorry. I didn't mean . . . you know I wouldn't . . . Cathy, I—"

Her laugh broke the tension in the office. "I think you need some food in your stomach. The eggnog has gone to your head."

"Yeah, right. Throw me a bone, why don't you? I don't want your sympathy, Wilson."

She stood. Even in her lowest-heeled shoes, she was able to look him right in the eye. "You're not going to get it, Martin. You're too valuable to me right here for me to be wishing you off to war."

"Thanks a lot," Eddie mumbled. "Fat lot of good that does me."

Catherine, who knew exactly how he felt, pretended she didn't hear him. "Come on," she said as she picked up the Christmas bonus checks from atop the filing cabinet. "Let's join the party."

The truth was, Eddie Martin needed Catherine's approval far more than he dared let on. They both knew it, but Catherine made certain she never acknowledged the fact. He was proud and she respected him. His job with Wilson Manufacturing was one of two things in his life that mattered.

The other was going off to war.

Both of Eddie's brothers entered military service not long after Pearl Harbor, sailing off on a tidal wave of patriotism and youthful enthusiasm. Eddie wanted to sail off with them; the thing was, the navy didn't want him. Neither did the army or the marines or the coast guard. He begged; he offered bribes; he threatened and cajoled and underwent test after test after test until his poor body was as battered and bruised as his ego.

Once a month, as regular as the phases of the moon, Eddie called in sick to Wilson so he could present himself to the powers-that-be down on Whitehall Street and offer Uncle Sam his body and soul.

And once a month they turned him down.

He'd gone his whole life not knowing he had a portion of his spine missing and he'd done just fine. He was short but not too short. His eyes were bad but passable. He could hear a pin drop three states away. He could run, swim and hike, but he couldn't do a thing about his spine.

So there Eddie was, stuck working in some factory making metal parts for the battleships and destroyers that would go out there and get the job done. There were times Catherine longed to put her arms around him and comfort him, but he was as stiff-necked as most men, and she knew he would have hated the gesture. More and more of the male employees were getting their greetings from Uncle Sam. Eddie said before long it would be just Eddie and thousands of women holding down the home front while the men—the *real* men—went out and won the war.

Just the other day Catherine had been thumbing through the newspaper and noticed a Lord & Taylor ad for an Eisenhower-style jacket that must have been a slap in his face: "Even if he's 4-F he can feel like a hero..."

But there was nothing Catherine could do to make his world seem right. Maybe one day he would understand that what he did on the home front was important, too. But judging from the set of his jaw as they made their way through the labyrinthine hallway, the prospect was unlikely.

The Christmas party was winding down when she pushed open the swinging doors to the cafeteria. A haze of cigarette smoke softened the harsh whitewashed walls of the cavernous room while the plaintive sounds of Bing Crosby's "White Christmas" added to the bittersweet mood. As usual, the men pretended she wasn't there, but some of the women waved at her and smiled.

All you had to do was look at the careworn faces of the employees of Wilson Manufacturing to see the toll the past three years of war had taken on the people at home. There was Marie Gianella standing in the corner by the big Philco radio that blared dance music every lunch hour; Marie's boy Andy had been wounded that distant morning in Pearl Harbor, and now she worked and worried about her two other sons who battled somewhere in the Pacific theater. Was it any wonder her lustrous dark hair was quickly turning gray?

And wasn't that Ella Friedman sitting at one of the lunch tables, her ubiquitous knitting basket by her side? Ella had been the first woman hired by Wilson Manufacturing—and the first employee to lose a member of her family to the war. When her husband, David, was killed in November, 1942, Ella only missed one day's work. "Sitting home won't bring my Davey back," she had said, her blue eyes wet with tears, "but coming to work might bring someone else's husband home safe and sound." It wasn't until Douglas was killed that Catherine understood the full measure of Ella's courage.

They were all there, all the men and women who made up Wilson Manufacturing, and in a way they were as much Catherine's family as her mother and Nancy were.

"Let's hear it for the boss!" Frank Petrie, one of the old guard who revered her dad, sent up the call from the other side of the room. Not many voices joined him in the cheer.

I wish you were here, Dad, she thought as she walked to the front of the room. There were so many things she wanted to ask him, so many decisions she needed to talk over with him. It had been months since anybody had heard from Tom, and while she continued to worry about him, she hadn't let the company's progress slow down one whit.

Tom Wilson wasn't there to make the decisions; his daughter Catherine was. And although this wasn't the life she had imagined for herself, it was the life God had chosen to give her, and she'd be damned if she gave it—and Wilson Manufacturing—anything less than her best.

She picked up the bright red basket piled high with envelopes. "Come on, everyone," she called out gaily. "Gather 'round. This is what we've all been waiting for."

Of course, playing Santa Claus was always fun. No wonder her dad had always looked forward to the Christmas Eve party. By noon the Christmas bonus envelopes had been given out, the fresh turkey from Sampson Farms in New Jersey raffled off, and the last of the eggnog enjoyed. Everyone joined voices in a rousing rendition of "Jingle

Bells'', then some of the older employees gathered around Catherine to wish her a merry Christmas.

"Have you heard from Tom lately?" asked Wally Arnsparger, from the shipping department. "I thought of him the minute I heard about what's going on in the Ardennes."

Catherine swallowed hard. The vicious battle in the Ardennes forest near the German border had been uppermost in her mind for days. "I'm sure he's fine, but the mails have been a little slow lately." She had to struggle to maintain the composure she was known for. Ten days ago when Glenn Miller's death had been announced, she'd openly wept. She couldn't do anything so foolish again.

Wally nodded. "Heavy casualties," he said, ignoring the crowd of well-wishers waiting their turn to greet the boss. "Frank O'Brien thought he saw his son's name on the KIA list and started bawling over his morning coffee." He shook his head sadly. "Turns out Dennis wasn't on, but his nephew Georgie was." He pumped her hand heartily, then said goodbye.

"Did you know George?" Eddie whispered as Wally disappeared through the cafeteria doors.

"Not well." Catherine conjured up the image of a tall lanky boy with dark hair and eyes. It disappeared as quickly as it had come. "I think he went to school with Mac Weaver."

"That reporter who joined up?"

"That's the one." Mac had come home a few weeks after Douglas died, only to enlist in the army. He was somewhere in the Pacific now, doing something very hush-hush.

"Lucky dog," mumbled Eddie.

"Fool," said Catherine. "The draft had passed him by. He could have gotten his quota of excitement covering the war as a reporter."

"That's not why a man signs up, Cathy."

"I know why a man signs up." They turned to see Bill Collins from accounting. "The whole point is to kill the enemy before he kills you."

Catherine excused herself and hurried down the hallway to her office. Eddie caught up to her at the doorway.

"You're crying," he said.

"Say one word about it and I'll fire you."

"You know your dad's fine," he said with an admirable display of bravado. He took her hand. "They wouldn't put a guy his age in the front line."

She laughed despite her fear. "You're a great comfort, Martin. You should try volunteering at the hospital."

"You'll hear from him soon."

"You're right," said Catherine squeezing his hand. "Any day now."

She lingered awhile to finish off some correspondence. The factory was deserted. Not even Maury, the cleaning man, was anywhere around. She hurried through the gate, head ducked against the snow, and made it to the subway in record time, glad to leave the empty building behind. The train was filled with last-minute shoppers with their holiday packages peeking out of paper shopping bags, and her spirits lifted as a little girl in the next car sang Christmas carols at the top of her tiny lungs.

The subway steps were slippery with icy snow and she hung on to the railing for dear life as she exited onto Continental Avenue. "Going to be a beaut of a storm," said an old man waiting at the corner to cross the street. "You take care getting home, girlie."

He disappeared into the swirling snow. He was right about the storm; Catherine had to bend low into the wind in order to keep from being lifted off her feet by the vicious gusts. Not only were they going to have a white Christmas, it looked as if they might have a blizzard.

Finally she turned onto Hansen Street and made her way to her house.

"Anybody home?" Catherine hung her cloth coat on the rack in the hallway and draped her snowy scarf over the banister. "Mom? Nancy?" She sat down on the bottom step and yanked off her rubber boots and shoes.

Her voice echoed throughout the empty house, and for a minute she wished she had stayed back at the office and worked on the production schedule for 1945.

"Wonderful," she said aloud as she padded barefoot to the kitchen. "The only other person who likes to work on Christmas Eve is Ebenezer Scrooge."

The kitchen was as quiet as the rest of the house. A covered pot of soup sat on the front burner and a note rested against a plate of freshly baked bread.

Your sister and I have gone off to serve Christmas Eve dinner at the hospital. We'll be home in time for supper. Get some rest!

Love,
Mom

P.S. Remember midnight mass tonight with Edna and Les!

She made quick work of the soup and devoured two slices of bread as if she were famished. Truth was she had hoped the simple fare would fill the emptiness inside her, but that emptiness couldn't be satisfied with food. She wished her mother and Nancy were home, chattering and laughing and turning the house into a home. A long time ago Catherine had known how to do that sort of thing, but it was a skill she had forgotten. Married women were good at turning on the lamps and drawing the drapes and doing whatever magical things it was they did to make four walls into a haven.

Young girls were good at that, too. Girls like Nancy who believed in love and happily-ever-after and that good things happened to good people, no matter how hard the world tried to tell them otherwise.

But Catherine was no longer a girl, and fate had seen to it that she hadn't become a wife.

"I never should have had that eggnog," she muttered as she finished washing her lunch dishes and putting them away. Alcohol went straight to her head, and that spike of rum had obviously been enough to release a flood of melancholy emotions better left hidden.

She tidied up the kitchen and wandered into the living room. The heavily carved mahogany furniture glistened with lemon oil, and the scent mingled with that of cinnamon and bayberry. The tree, a beautiful pine, occupied a place of honor near the picture window, waiting for evening when the Wilson women would transform it into a thing of beauty. In the old days they would invite everyone on the block—from the Weavers to the Lewises to the Fiores—to join them as they strung popcorn garlands and sang carols and draped tinsel on the welcoming branches.

Thanks to the war, of course, everything was different now. It was hard to celebrate Christmas with the same excitement, what with Douglas gone and her dad somewhere far away. Last year Johnny Danza had written to her, telling Catherine of the USO show and a first-run movie they'd watched by the light of a December moon.

She looked out the dining-room window and shivered. The sky was the color of heavy cream and the falling snow had already obliterated her footprints from the path to the front door. The postman had already delivered a batch of Christmas cards and, given the weather, it was unlikely he'd be back to make a second delivery. "A white Christmas," she whispered, her breath fogging the glass. How she wished there was something to celebrate, some sign that the war would end and those she loved would come home safe and sound.

The grandfather clock in the foyer announced the hour. Three o'clock. Her mother and Nancy wouldn't be home for hours. An endless afternoon stretched out before her, as bleak as the weather.

"YOU OKAY, PAL?" The cabbie peered at his passenger through the rearview mirror. "You don't look so good." The man's face was as white as the snow blanketing the city streets.

"I'm fine," the soldier mumbled, his voice muffled by his upturned collar.

The cabbie hung a left at the corner of Queens Boulevard and Seventy-first Avenue. "Now what was that address you wanted?"

"Hansen," the soldier managed. "Seventy-fifteen. One of those Tudor jobs."

The cabbie laughed and clamped his teeth more tightly around his cigar. "They're all Tudor jobs in that neck of the woods, kid. You gotta have some dough to live there." He took another look at the soldier. "When was the last time you had a good meal?"

The soldier turned green around the gills. "Just drive, would you?"

"Hangover is it?" The cabbie eased off the gas. "Don't worry, old pal. I'll get you home in time to trim the Christmas tree...."

CATHERINE FROWNED and buried her face more deeply into the sofa pillow. Who on earth was making that racket? Didn't they know people were trying to sleep?

She squeezed her eyes tight and tried to conjure up the dream once again. It was Christmas Day and President Roosevelt came on the radio and announced that the war was over. The sun was shining, the birds were singing, the doorbell was ringing—

Wait a minute.

She opened one eye and listened closely. "Must have been my imagination," she said, then pulled the afghan up over her shoulders. But then there was the noise again, only it wasn't a doorbell ringing. No, it was more like a faint tapping.

She threw back the afghan and sat up, yawning. Maybe the mailman had made it back through the snow, after all, with one last batch of Christmas cards. And maybe this batch would bring the long-awaited letter from her father—and one from Johnny. She hurried out into the hall, praying to see a welcome stack of cards and letters pooled on the floor beneath the mail slot.

Not so much as a postcard. She turned to hurry back to the sofa and the cozy comfort of the afghan when she heard it again, louder this time, a tap-tap-tap at the door. If Danny Tesch from down the block was throwing snowballs again, she'd take him by the ear and march him back to his mother so fast, his ten-year-old head would spin! One broken window per winter was more than enough.

"Danny," she said, swinging the door open wide, "you stop that this minute."

But it wasn't Danny Tesch.

It was Private Johnny Danza.

And he was unconscious on her welcome mat.

Chapter Six

"Oh, my God! Johnny!" She bent down, unmindful of the chill wind whipping through her pink chenille bathrobe. His skin was as white as the falling snow, his jet black hair an angry slash across his forehead. She touched his cheek. "Johnny? Please say something."

Dear God, what was wrong? She moved her fingers down to the base of his throat, exposed by the ill-fitting army-issue overcoat. A pulse, shallow but steady, beat beneath her fingertips. She shook him by the shoulders. "We have to get you inside, Johnny. Wake up, please!"

He moaned softly and his eyelids fluttered then opened. He started to say something, but she pressed the tip of her index finger against his lips. "Save your strength. You'll catch your death out here in the snow."

Struggling to keep her balance on the icy top step, she managed to get her arms around him and slowly, carefully, she pulled him to a sitting position. His head rolled back against her shoulder.

"You have to help me, Johnny. I can't do this without you."

He was barely conscious. His lean body was a dead weight as she tried to maneuver him into the house. Her bare feet slipped on the top step, and it took every ounce of strength at her command to keep from tumbling backward, taking Johnny with her. God must have been watching over them both because somehow she regained her footing and half-dragged, half-carried him into the foyer where she laid him down on the braided rug.

"Cathy..."

She knelt next to him in a puddle of melted snow and brought her ear close to his mouth.

"Sorry..."

"You don't have anything to be sorry about," she said vehemently. "I'm going to take care of you."

But how?

She loosened his tie and unfastened the top button of his shirt. How thin he was; those proud angular cheekbones stood out in stark relief in his strong-boned face. He was shivering uncontrollably, so she kept his coat on and covered him with the afghan she'd cuddled under during her nap. She ran to turn up the thermostat, coal shortage be damned. She didn't care if they froze the rest of the winter; all that mattered was Johnny.

A shuddering cough racked his body, and it was her turn to tremble at the labored, erratic sound of his breathing. She raced upstairs and yanked the blankets from both her bed and Nancy's, then hurried back down to the foyer and bundled him up with a few more layers of warmth. Unfortunately it wasn't enough. His brow was slick with sweat but the shivering increased, and she knew that whatever was wrong with him couldn't be cured with an extra blanket and a cup of cocoa.

She rushed to the telephone in the kitchen. Her fingers fumbled with the dial and for a moment Dr. Bernstein's number played hide-and-seek with her memory. She held her breath as it started to ring. "Please be there," she whispered. "Please...please..."

He was. "I'm closing up shop in ten minutes," he said, after she explained the problem. "Keep him warm and I'll be there as quick as I can."

A half hour later she ushered the doctor into the foyer. "Oh, thank God! I was terrified the storm would—"

"Storms don't stop me, Cathy Wilson. You should know better." Dr. Sy Bernstein had delivered both Catherine and Nancy and over the years seen them through measles and chicken pox and assorted cuts and bumps. Seeing him standing there looking competent and trustworthy, Catherine felt better already. Dr. Bernstein handed her his coat and hat. "Toss them anywhere," he said, bending down over the unconscious Johnny Danza. "First thing we need to do is get this young man comfortable."

She draped his coat over the banister and balanced his hat on the first step.

"Take his feet," ordered Dr. Bernstein. "I'm going to grab him under the arms. I'll bear most of his weight, Catherine, but I'll need your help."

"Anything," she said. "I'll do anything." Johnny's boots were huge and heavy, deeply scuffed around the toes and heels, and she found it difficult to get a good grip on his ankles. "Okay, Dr. B. Whenever you're ready."

"On the count of three. One...two...three. That's it...that's it...." They maneuvered their human burden through the foyer and into the living room.

"The sofa by the window," said Catherine, wincing as a pine needle stabbed the underside of her bare foot. "That's closest to the radiator."

Johnny moaned as they lowered him to the cushions, and Catherine felt as if a fist had grabbed her heart and was slowly squeezing it.

The doctor leaned over Johnny and began to undo the buttons on his overcoat.

"Don't just stand there, Catherine," Dr. Bernstein barked. "Let's get this boy undressed."

Her cheeks flamed despite the chill. Dr. Bernstein noticed.

"You're a sensible young woman, Catherine. Don't go turning coy on me. I need your help." He gestured at Johnny. "He needs your help."

She took a deep breath then knelt next to the sofa. Her fingers fumbled at the buttons of his army-issue shirt as if she was wearing mittens. The doctor was unfastening the soldier's trousers and she kept her gaze firmly fastened to the task before her. "Danza John," read his dogtags. "O positive." Her vision blurred as she tried to make out his birthdate and religion.

"Get a grip on yourself," said Dr. Bernstein, his voice gruff but kind. "You'll have plenty of time to cry later on."

He was right. She knew he was right but she couldn't help the tears. This couldn't be happening. You simply didn't fall asleep on your living-room sofa one minute and awake to find an unconscious soldier on your welcome mat the next. Johnny Danza was somewhere in Europe with her father, fighting the war.

She stripped off his shirt and grasped the hem of his undershirt. Her fingers brushed against his flat abdomen and she watched, mesmerized, as the taut muscles reacted to her touch.

"I'll lift him," said the doctor, gripping Johnny by the shoulders. "You prop him up with pillows."

She nodded, smoothing the white undershirt over his stomach once again. He moaned again as the doctor repositioned him on the couch, and Catherine struggled to contain her tears. She wasn't imagining this. Johnny wasn't somewhere in Europe with her father; he was right here in Forest Hills. Dr. Bernstein cradled the man in his brawny arms while Catherine arranged those foolish, frilly chintz pillows behind his back for support.

"Get my bag from the hallway," the doctor ordered.

Catherine was back in an instant with the heavy black leather satchel.

"Take off his undershirt."

She did as he requested. Then both he and Catherine gasped at the sight of Johnny's bare chest. She felt her knees buckle beneath her, but Dr. Bernstein steadied her and she took a deep breath to calm herself.

"Shrapnel wounds. I haven't seen anything like this since the last war. And look at that arm. Nasty infection setting in. Darn good thing the boy made it here or he wouldn't've lasted the night in that storm."

This is what it's all about, she thought, staring at the ugly wounds zigzagging across his upper torso. *This is what's happening over there—to all of them. Dear God, forgive me...I never knew...I never imagined...* She'd been as foolish as her little sister, thinking of USO tours and war bonds, knitting scarves for brave young men to take into battle. How wrong she had been. How wrong they all had been.

She pushed an image of Douglas, torn and dying, from her mind.

Douglas was beyond her help now.

And—God help him—her father might be, as well.

But Johnny Danza was here right now and this was her chance to do for him what she couldn't do for Douglas. She took a deep breath. "What can I do to help?" she asked Dr. Bernstein.

The doctor eyed her for an instant. "I'm going to depend upon you, Catherine."

She nodded, swallowing hard. "I understand."

"First thing, I need more light in here." He glanced around the darkened living room. "Turn on the lamps and raise the shades. You could develop photographs in this place."

Catherine quickly did as he asked. The lamps cast a yellow glow, but raising the shades had little effect, for it was already dark outside.

"Turn the heat up higher and don't worry about restrictions. I'll make certain you good people don't freeze this winter. Light a fire in the grate, then bring me all the clean towels you have."

The doctor rolled up his sleeves and reached into his bag. Johnny moaned again with pain and the sound acted on Catherine like a shot of pure adrenaline. She dashed into the hallway and raised the thermostat, then hurried out into the backyard, still in her bathrobe, to grab an armload of firewood. The wood was wet with snow and she thanked the good Lord her mother had thought to place a basket of dry kindling near the fireplace. Without it she never would have managed the roaring fire that soon warmed the living room.

Dr. Bernstein was bent low over Johnny's body. "Towels!" he snapped. "On the double."

She was back downstairs with a stack in seconds. Dr. Bernstein motioned for her to drape a towel over Johnny's bared midsection.

"Look at this." The doctor placed bloodstained metal fragments on the white bath towel. "Set up an infection throughout his system. Damn war." Sweat, which had beaded on Dr. Bernstein's forehead, began to trickle down until drops were balanced on the edge of his eyelashes. "He wasn't hurt badly enough to die, but he's not well enough to go back into battle, so what do they do? They give him a thirty-day furlough and the damn fool finds his way back home. What the hell was he thinking of, anyway?"

Catherine trembled as Dr. Bernstein probed Johnny's flesh with a fierce-looking pair of tweezers. "Should I call for an ambulance?"

"Look out the window, girl. Patton's tanks couldn't make it through that snow."

"What are you going to do?" Her voice rose an octave. "How will you take care of him?"

"I won't," said the good doctor, casting a sharp-eyed glance in her direction. "You will."

"But you said he's in terrible shape."

"He is, but he won't be for long."

She almost swooned as he swabbed the angry network of wounds with an alcohol-soaked towel. "I'm not a nurse."

"You will be by the time this boy is on his feet again."

"Is . . . is he going to die?"

Dr. Bernstein chuckled. "No," he said. "Absolutely not. The kid's strong as an ox. Get that fever of his down and we're halfway home." The medicine would make short work of the fever. Johnny was also exhausted and underweight. With lots of sleep and good home-cooked food, he'd be on the mend before they knew it.

She listened carefully as he told her what she would have to do, then wrote down every last detail on a piece of pale blue stationery.

"Do you have all that, Catherine?"

"I think so, Dr. B." She read back the instructions. "Bathe him. Dress his wounds every two hours. Medicine every four. Keep him warm, dry, well fed, and let Mother Nature do the rest."

He patted her on the shoulder. "You're a good girl, Cathy. Always have been. Dot and Tom should be very proud of you."

"I'll tell them. I've been feeling unappreciated lately."

He narrowed his eyes and took a closer look at her. "Have you been getting enough sleep?"

"Probably not. The factory keeps me hopping."

"I hope you've been getting out and seeing your friends."

"Not as often as I'd like. I did get out to see *National Velvet* at the Elmwood last week."

"This blasted war won't last forever, Cathy. Before long your dad will be home again and you can go back to being a happy young woman."

She led him into the foyer and helped him into his coat. "I'm doing just fine," she said. "I enjoy the challenge."

"Home and children," he said, nodding sagely. "That's the best challenge of all."

She said nothing.

"Damn insensitive of me, that last remark, what with Douglas and all. I'm sorry, Catherine."

"There's nothing to be sorry for, Dr. B. I've made my peace with it."

"You have a merry Christmas," said Dr. Bernstein.

"And you have a happy Hanukkah." She kissed his weathered cheek and opened the front door. "Get home safely."

A blast of wind raced into the foyer, and Dr. Bernstein turned up the collar of his coat. "It's going to be a hard winter," he said as he headed down the snowy steps. "A very hard winter."

Catherine stood in the doorway and watched until the man disappeared down the street, obliterated by the swirling snow. Another blast of wind raced up under her bathrobe and she ducked inside and closed the door behind her. All she needed was to come down with a case of the grippe. Who would take care of Johnny?

Johnny! Energy flowed into her limbs and she raced into the living room. He was sleeping peacefully on the sofa, his lanky frame an incongruous sight against the feminine-looking cushions. She tucked the granny afghan more tightly under his chin. "Sleep," she whispered, looking down at the man in her care. "I'll take good care of you. I promise."

She took the stairs two at a time and raced to her bedroom to change into dungarees and one of her dad's old shirts. The dungarees were long so she rolled them up to just above her ankles and folded the sleeves of the shirt to her elbows. She slipped her feet into a pair of comfortable old slippers, gave her hair a lick and a promise, then was back downstairs before Johnny had a chance to so much as change position.

Grabbing the piece of blue notepaper from the mantel, she scanned the list of nursing duties. Bathe him. Her breath caught. *Bathe him?* Dr. Bernstein's words came back to haunt her: "We want to break that fever. Give him a sponge bath, then rub him down with rubbing alcohol before you bundle him back up."

Her mother and Nancy wouldn't be home for hours. The notion of bathing a man was shocking, but Johnny couldn't wait for her mother to come home and tend to his needs.

Catherine placed her palm against his forehead. Dr. Bernstein was right—he was burning up.

This was no time for maidenly virtue. Mustering her resolve, she went into the kitchen and filled a soup kettle with warm water, then grabbed a bar of Ivory and the clean towels Dr. Bernstein hadn't used.

She carried everything back into the front room where Johnny slept and placed the paraphernalia on the floor next to the sofa.

"Johnny." She laid her hand against his cheek. "I'm going to take care of you, okay?"

His breathing was labored. His lips looked dry, cracked. She went into the kitchen and filled a jelly glass with cool water. Back in the living room she knelt by his side and held the glass to his mouth. "Come on, Johnny. Take a sip." She dipped her fingers in the water and ran them across his lips. He swallowed reflexively, his tongue touching the moisture on Catherine's fingers then darting away. Her breath caught for an instant, then escaped in a long shaky sigh.

His lids fluttered open. She'd forgotten how blue his eyes were. Even glazed with fever, they were as deep and beautiful as lapis. Hands trembling, she pulled down the covers and draped them over the back of the wing chair near the fireplace. His chest was bare, save for the light layer of bandages Dr. Bernstein had placed across the shrapnel wounds, and she was horrified to discover that only a pair of army-issue boxer shorts covered him below the waist. Even his feet, long and narrow and pale, were bare. Somehow the sight of his bare feet seemed more intimate, more disturbing, than his bare chest and legs.

The Johnny Danza she had met that long-ago night at the Stage Door Canteen had been brash and cocky and funny. The kind of guy you imagined would breeze through life with a smile and a wisecrack for everyone. Through his letters she had slowly come to know a different Johnny Danza, one who was sometimes vulnerable, sometimes angry, sometimes a better friend than she thought she deserved.

But eighteen months of letters hadn't prepared her for the sight of him, helpless and sick, on her mother's sofa. She felt as if she was invading his privacy and she was sorry about that, but it was unavoidable.

She tested the wash water with her elbow, then soaked a clean face towel and lathered it up with soap. "I'm going to give you a sponge bath," she murmured as she brought the cloth to his chest. "This will make you feel so much better...."

He winced as the fabric touched his skin but—thank God!—he didn't shiver. Working swiftly, she moved the towel across his shoulders, over the unbandaged portions of his chest, down to his rib cage and—

No! She bypassed the narrow portion of flat belly exposed above the waistband of his shorts and drew the soapy towel over his lower thighs and legs. Despite the fact that he was skinnier than when she saw him last, his legs were still strong and well muscled, heavily furred with crisp curling black hair. They were also covered with goose bumps, so she quickly finished and rubbed him dry with a large towel she'd left near the fireplace, then massaged rubbing alcohol on his burning flesh. The important thing now was to keep him warm.

A low sound of contentment broke the silence, and Catherine smiled as she covered him again with the afghan and quilt. The worry lines between his thick dark brows had eased, and she could almost swear that color was coming back into his face.

She picked up the makeshift washbasin, then started for the kitchen to empty it in the sink.

"Don't go."

She stopped in the doorway and tilted her head. No. It must have been her imagination. Once again she headed for the kitchen.

"Cathy."

She put the washbasin down and was beside the sofa in an instant. His eyes were closed, his lashes casting shadows on his cheeks. She touched his hand. "I'm here."

A smile, shaky but very real, flickered across his face as his fingers linked with hers. "Stay with me."

Tears blurred her vision. "Don't worry, Johnny," she said, her voice soft. "I'm not going anywhere."

The grandfather clock tolled seven, then eight, and still Catherine sat on the floor next to Johnny. He slept as if drugged, awakening only to hold her hand more tightly and reassure himself of her presence. Her back ached, the fire needed tending, and she knew she should give her mother a call at the hospital and tell her of their unexpected visitor, but she couldn't bring herself to leave his side.

With her fingers linked with his, she felt connected to another human being for the first time in so very long. She willed her strength and warmth to become his. She wanted somehow to communicate how important he was—and how she would do anything in her power to make him well again.

Outside the winds howled and rattled the windows in their casings. From her spot on the living-room floor she could barely make out the Weavers' house beyond the window, for the falling snow obscured everything beyond the foot of their front path.

But inside, the radiators glowed with blessed heat and the lamps blazed merrily and, as she held Johnny's hand and prayed, Catherine felt her icy heart slowly begin to thaw.

"THANK HEAVEN for the subways!" said Dot as she adjusted her scarf and smiled at her daughter. "We'd be stranded at the hospital all night."

"If it wasn't Christmas Eve you wouldn't have been able to drag me out. I was having a swell time at the party."

"Now, none of that. You know we couldn't leave your sister home alone tonight."

"She'd never notice," said Nancy, grabbing for the railing as they climbed the slippery cement steps to street level. "She's probably still at the factory."

Dot glanced at her younger daughter. "Are you two having difficulties?"

"Things are fine, Mom, but you have to admit she works longer hours than President Roosevelt."

"Your sister takes her responsibilities seriously. She's determined to make Daddy proud."

Nancy looked down at her feet in their battered rubber galoshes. As if Catherine needed to do anything special to make their father proud. All Catherine had to do was smile and all was right with Tom Wilson's world. And now she was running Wilson Manufacturing single-handedly—and turning a profit to boot! Nancy had been working there since her return home from her Long Island adventure, and half the employees still didn't know her name. She bet she could tap-dance on top of the tool-and-die machine and not one person would take notice.

The street was deserted and it took a second for them to gain their bearings. It was difficult to tell earth from sky; everything, everywhere was a uniform shade of white.

"Well, one good thing," said Nancy as they made their way down Hansen Street through knee-deep snowdrifts. "At least we got a white Christmas."

Dot looked at her and laughed despite the cold. "You're right, honey. A white Christmas! We should be happy we're healthy and together to enjoy it."

Of course they weren't all together. For months they'd waited in vain for a letter from Tom. This was their second Christmas without him and the old saw, Absence makes the heart grow fonder, was truer than Nancy had ever imagined. How she missed the way things used to be, with the whole family gathered around the fireplace, singing carols and sipping eggnog. Last year she had wanted to run as far and fast from Hansen Street as her legs would carry her. This year she was glad to be home.

James F. Byrnes, the director of War Mobilization and Reconversion, had placed a ban on horse racing, effective January third of the new year. Severe meat shortages were predicted, and citizens were being asked to save their Christmas wrappings for salvage because "paper is too precious." Across the ocean, the Maginot Line was cut as the Twenty-sixth and Thirty-fifth Infantries united and the Seventh Army was only four miles from the Reich. *Peace on earth, good will toward men . . .* Nancy thought.

Her mother looked up at the snow-laden sky and frowned. "I'm afraid we might not make midnight mass, honey, if it keeps up like this."

Nancy peeked at her graduation watch snuggled under her mittens. "It's not even eight o'clock yet, Mom. It might slow down."

"Strange," said Dot as they approached their house. "I'm surprised Cathy doesn't have the blackout shades drawn."

"I know what's even stranger," Nancy offered. "The only light on is in the living room." Usually Catherine was holed up in Tom's den, working on budgets or forecasts or whatever other boring things were necessary for running a business.

"Will you look at these front steps," her mother exclaimed as they struggled their way up to the front door. "We'd better get these shoveled before somebody breaks a leg."

"I'll do it after supper. It'll be fun." That was most likely the biggest fib Nancy had told in her entire life and it made her mother smile. Catherine's time was considered to be more important than Nancy's, what with the factory and all, and no one expected her to go outside and shovel snow like the rest of the world. And Nancy certainly couldn't imagine her mother doing it when a perfectly healthy girl of eighteen and a half lived under the same roof. Besides, Aunt Edna and Uncle Les were coming over before mass, and the last thing she wanted was for either one of them to slip and get hurt.

The two women stomped into the hallway in a swirl of icy air and snow. Nancy leaned against the wall and struggled with her galoshes while her mother simply balanced first on one foot and then the other and neatly removed her ankle-length fur-trimmed boots. If Nancy had tried that, she would have fallen on her head. There truly was no justice in the world.

Nancy sniffed the air. "I don't smell dinner cooking." She couldn't keep the note of satisfaction from her voice. "I'll bet she forgot."

Her mother lined their boots in a neat row next to Catherine's on the straw mat by the doorway. "Cathy's been working very hard lately." She aimed a sharp look at Nancy who looked away. "She probably fell asleep on the sofa."

Dot turned and headed into the living room, no doubt to tuck a down pillow under Sleeping Beauty's head. Nancy hated feeling jealous and ugly like that, but there were times she simply couldn't help it. Wasn't she the one who'd spent her whole day off helping their mother at the hospital? Everyone forgot that she had loved ones overseas, too. Tom Wilson was her father, as well as Cathy's. She loved Mac Weaver as much as anybody on the block and prayed for his safe return when the war was over. And Gerry Sturdevant—well, what could she expect? No one believed you could fall in love through the mail, especially not if you were only eighteen and had never met the boy in question.

She started up the stairs to change into a nice cozy robe and slippers when her mother's voice stopped her.

"Cathy! What on earth...?"

Nancy cocked an ear in the direction of the living room. She heard her mother's voice, low and animated, and Cathy's sleepy mumble. Curiosity got the better of her and she headed downstairs to the living room where she got the surprise of her life.

Her sister Cathy, the paragon of virtue, was curled up on the floor, holding the hand of a sleeping—and possibly *naked*—man. Who said there wasn't a Santa Claus? This was the most exciting thing to happen around the Wilson house in a very long time.

"Well, big sister," she said, unable to keep the giggle from her voice, "who's your friend?"

The man, whose face was hidden by a large down pillow, roused for a moment and Catherine glared in her direction. "You wake him up, Nancy Wilson, and I'll tar the hell out of you."

"Catherine!" Their mother sounded scandalized. "Your language!"

"I mean it, Mother. If that twerp wakes Johnny up, I'll—"

"Johnny?" Nancy stepped closer to the sleeping man. "That's not Johnny Danza, is it?"

"Yes, it is." She had never heard Catherine sound like that, all fierce and fiery. It made Nancy feel young and terribly backward and she didn't quite know why.

"But how...?" She stared down at the man stretched out on the sofa. "I thought he was overseas. I thought—"

"We all thought the same things, honey." Dot put an arm around her younger daughter's shoulders. "Cathy doesn't have any answers yet." Dot quickly told Nancy how the ailing soldier had popped up on the doorstep, barely conscious and burning with fever, and how Cathy had managed to drag him inside and call Dr. Bernstein.

That still didn't explain the soft expression on Cathy's face or the way her hand was entwined with his in such a possessive manner, but Nancy knew better than to ask. There was one other question, however, that she simply couldn't put aside.

"Daddy," she said, meeting her mother's eyes. "Is he on his way home too?"

She regretted the words as soon as they left her mouth, for the stricken look in her mother's eyes was something she wouldn't soon forget.

"I don't know, honey." Her mother's hand trembled as she stroked Nancy's hair off her forehead. "We won't know until Johnny is well enough to tell us."

Cathy scrambled to her knees and placed her ear against the soldier's lips. "He's hungry," she said, smiling up at them as if FDR had just announced that the war was over. She met Nancy's eyes. "Would you sit with him while I make some scrambled eggs?"

Nancy felt cold all over. She had just spent an entire day doing volunteer work at the hospital, but nothing she had seen there came close to the reality of Johnny Danza there in the living room. "I . . . I guess so." The men and boys in the hospital were strangers. She'd never seen them drink beer or laugh at Bob Hope's jokes or dance to "Boogie Woogie Bugle Boy." They were patients in a hospital, meek and mild and doing their best to get well so they could go back and serve their country.

Johnny was different. She had seen him do all of those things. She had even danced with him once herself. She could still remember the way the black taffeta skirt had swirled about her knees and thighs as he swung her about. Her sister, she knew, had sent him letters and scarves, and not once had it ever occurred to Nancy that anything could possibly happen to him.

"Come on," Cathy said as she rose to her feet. "I don't want to leave him alone even for a minute."

Nancy took her sister's place on the floor beside Johnny. He shifted position slightly and a low moan issued from deep in his throat. "What does that mean? Is he in pain? Should I do something?"

"I'll bring him his medicine with dinner," Cathy said, straightening out the tails of the big white shirt she was wearing. "Just sit with him. Hold his hand. That's all."

It was clear from Cathy's tone of voice that she didn't think Nancy was up to the task. Truth to tell, Nancy wasn't entirely sure she was, either. Her mother and Catherine left the room, whispering together as if they had secrets too important for a girl like Nancy to hear.

On the couch Johnny grew fitful. She tried to hold his hand the way her sister had, but he pulled away. "Cathy..." His voice was weak but insistent. "Cathy..."

She patted his hand. She wasn't even a good substitute. "Cathy'll be back in a minute, Johnny. I promise."

He fell back asleep. She watched his chest rise and fall beneath the blankets and a sadness so deep it took her breath away rose inside her chest. "Welcome home, Johnny," she whispered.

CATHERINE WORKED as if possessed. Her mother had scarcely had time to fill the teakettle with water from the tap before Catherine had the eggs cracked and the skillet heating atop the stove. "Toast!" She lit the oven, then pulled a cookie tin from the cabinet beneath the sink. "Do we have any bread?"

Her mother's low chuckle floated across the kitchen. "In the bread box, honey."

Catherine sliced two thick slabs of homemade bread and set them in the oven to brown. Then as she cooked the eggs her mother set up a tray complete with a pot of warm cocoa, clean linen and silverware.

"Now comes the hard part," said Dot, leading the way into the living room with the piping hot supper. "Getting him to eat."

"That won't be hard at all," said Catherine, shooing her little sister away from the ailing soldier's side. "I'm sure he'll do whatever I say."

"Sick men are as stubborn as little babies," said her mother. "Especially men as under the weather as Johnny. You have your work cut out for you."

"Oh, don't worry," said Catherine confidently. "You'll see."

A few minutes later she was ready to throw in the towel and admit defeat. Not only would Johnny not take a single morsel of food from her, he persisted in dozing off with his head against her shoulder. Nancy was outside shoveling snow off the steps. The scrape of metal against brick sounded loud against the Christmas Eve silence. Thank God, because her sister's teasing would have driven her insane.

"I give up," Catherine said at last. "This is harder than feeding a two-month-old child!"

Dot laughed and placed a shiny red ornament on the tree. "Why don't you take over Christmas-tree duty and let an old expert have a try?"

"I know when I'm licked." Catherine rose to her feet and exchanged a plate of scrambled eggs for a garland of popcorn. "He must eat something, Mother. It's very important."

DOT DID HER BEST to hide her smile as she took her daughter's spot on the floor next to Johnny. How many nights had she spent nursing a sick child, trying to tempt a finicky eater into taking some nourishment? How quickly children forget the days when they were as helpless as this young soldier.

Of course, she voiced none of this aloud. Her darling and serious older daughter was standing by the Christmas tree watching her as if she had never so much as warmed a baby's bottle in her life. Gently Dot put her arm behind Johnny's shoulders and cradled him in a sitting position. His eyes opened and he gave her a dazed glassy stare that she remembered well from the girls' bouts with fever. A rush of maternal emotion flooded through her, and she had to blink rapidly to clear her vision.

Sentimental old fool, she thought as she coaxed him to open his mouth. *Just because it's been ages since you've had someone you can really mother...*

"I'll be darned," muttered Catherine as she arranged the popcorn garland along the boughs of the tree. "He's eating."

"Of course he is, honey." Dot swallowed around a huge and painful lump in her throat. "He knows I won't budge until he's swallowed every single bite."

It was a long and tedious process, getting the meal into Johnny, but Dorothy persevered. When he fell asleep again, it was on a full stomach. Nancy came in after shoveling the walk, grumbling loudly that her parents could at least have had the foresight to make certain they had a son, as well as two daughters. Both Catherine and Dot laughed, and to Dot's amazement, Nancy did, too. There were times she felt as if she was living in an armed camp, with the two sisters on opposite sides, but for once there was nothing barbed in Nancy's comment and nothing angry in Catherine's laughter.

Nancy disappeared into the kitchen, then returned a few minutes later with three mugs of hot cocoa. "Wonderful," said Dot, smiling up at her younger child. "I've been envying Johnny his supper."

Catherine finished placing the popcorn garland on the tree, then brushed her hands against the legs of her dungarees. The tree looked wonderful with the glass and wooden ornaments and popcorn garland; with the lights on, you'd scarcely notice the missing tinsel. "Why don't I go into the kitchen and rustle something up for us?"

"I don't mind doing it," said Nancy. "How about tomato soup?"

"Sounds wonderful," said Dot, her heart soaring at these signs of amity between her children. She looked at Catherine and mentally crossed her fingers for luck.

"I could make some egg-salad sandwiches to go with it," Catherine volunteered after a moment. She hesitated. "That is, if you don't mind company in the kitchen, Nance."

"Just don't tell me how to cook, okay?"

Catherine laughed and ruffled Nancy's red bangs. "That's a promise."

"Well, well, Johnny Danza," Dot said as the two girls left the room. "You've brought me quite a wonderful Christmas present tonight."

She couldn't remember the last time such a feeling of harmony had existed in the Wilson household—and it had taken the arrival of this young man to make it happen. Her eyes misted once again and this time she did nothing to stop the flow of tears. There was nothing wrong with crying, after all. These were tears of joy, not sorrow, joy that Johnny had sought them out, that Catherine had opened their door and her heart to the desperately ill young soldier.

The war made you feel so powerless. Reports about cities with names that lay strange upon your tongue were made by voices on the radio that had become as familiar as that of your local butcher. It took something like this, the simple act of caring for another human being, to remind you that there was still goodness in a world gone mad.

"Where's my Tom?" she whispered to the sleeping soldier. "Is he all right?" She was thankful for Johnny's safety, but she longed to know that the man she loved was alive and well somewhere across the ocean.

"Here we are," said Nancy as she entered the room with a tray of soup and sandwiches. "It isn't fancy but it tastes swell."

Catherine, hands clutching silverware and napkins, brought up the rear. She looked happier than Dot had seen her since Douglas went into the service. "I have to hand it to my baby sister," Catherine said. "She heats up a mean bowl of Campbell's soup." She set the items on the end table near Dot.

"It's Christmas Eve," said Nancy, putting the tray down on top of the coffee table. "No wisecracks allowed." She glanced at Catherine, who was throwing a few more logs on the fire. "At least *I* know how to cook."

Catherine sat down on the floor near the sofa. The look she gave Johnny made Dot's chest feel tight with remembered emotion.

"I may not be Fanny Farmer," said her older daughter, "but I know my way around the kitchen."

They kept up a stream of easygoing banter during supper, broken only when Catherine jumped up to get a damp cloth to mop Johnny's brow. Dot watched as she pressed her lips to the soldier's forehead. "His fever's broken," she said, a wide smile on her lovely face. "Dr. Bernstein said that would be a good sign."

Oh, honey, thought Dot as Catherine sat back down and reached for her soup, *do you know what's happening to you?* It was the oldest story in the world. Was there a woman alive whose heart didn't beat faster at the sight of a helpless man? All those deeply female instincts Catherine had had to bank when Douglas died were coming to life again as she tended to the wounded soldier. An old story but a good one; Dot only wished she could play God and ensure a happy ending.

The clock struck ten. Dot rose and moved to peer out the front window at the snow-blanketed street. St. Mary's Church was only eight blocks away, but considering the storm it might as well have been eight miles. She looked forward to midnight mass all year long. There was something ineffably beautiful about the ritual: candles twinkling on the altar amidst masses of poinsettias and holly; the priest's deep voice intoning those ancient and wondrous Latin phrases of hope and joy and salvation; the choirboys, in their white robes with bright red bows tied at the neck, whose voices seemed to bring the angels right down here to earth.

She leaned her cheek against the cool pane and let her mind drift back to Christmas two years ago. Tom had made the decision to enter the service, pulling every string there was to pull in order to have the rules bent just enough to allow him to serve. They had fought bitterly for weeks about his decision. Her heart had ached, because the man she loved, the father of her children, could care so little about them that he would put his life in danger.

Tom, however, had other ideas about how best to care for his family. How like a man to see the bigger picture, to focus in on Hitler and Hirohito and Mussolini, and completely overlook the day-to-day needs of the wife and daughters who loved him so.

That last Christmas Eve together they had walked to St. Mary's without speaking. The girls had walked ahead of them with Edna and Les Weaver, laughing and singing carols. Tom and Dot had maintained a silence as brittle as the icicles hanging from the eaves on the buildings they passed, a silence they'd maintained for the previous two days. But with the first soaring notes of "O! Holy Night," Tom's hand had found hers and they'd looked at each other. "I love you," he'd mouthed silently, as those glorious voices filled the church. She'd squeezed his hand tightly and made her peace with his decision.

"Mom."

She turned at the sound of Cathy's voice to see both of her girls looking at her with concern. "Just daydreaming," she said with an embarrassed laugh. "I guess I'm getting old..."

Cathy pointed to the pile of clothing stacked on the wing chair. "His uniform and things. Do I wash them myself or take them to the Chinese laundry? Maybe the dry cleaner on Continental?"

"Depends." She held out her hands. "Let me see them."

Cathy scooped up the stack of drab clothing. "Oh, darn!" She bent down to retrieve his wrinkled shirt. "What on earth is this?" She reached into the breast pocket and withdrew a thin white envelope with no address, then a thick pale blue envelope with a name scrawled across the front. "Oh, my God." Hand trembling she pressed the letter into Dot's hand. "It's for you, Mom." A pause, then, "It's from Daddy."

Dot didn't know whether to laugh or cry. The letter seemed to have a life of its own; it fairly burned the skin of her palm. Catherine put her hand on Nancy's shoulder. "Why don't we take these dishes into the kitchen and straighten up?" she suggested to her younger sister. Nancy's eyes were wide with fright, but she got to her feet and dutifully did Catherine's bidding.

Dot ripped open the envelope and unfolded the thin sheets of letter paper. Her eyes misted over at the sight of his beloved handwriting. She didn't know what to expect, but a refrain sounded over and over inside her head: *Please ... please ... please ...*

Chapter Seven

Catherine placed the soup plates in the sink and rubbed a sponge across a bar of brown soap. "Bring me the cups, Nance," she said, keeping her voice level and unconcerned. "May as well wash everything while the water is nice and hot."

Nancy stared at her from the doorway. "How can you even think about washing dishes at a time like this?"

Catherine glanced over her shoulder at her sister. "Is that a rhetorical question?"

"Yes—I mean, no! Darn it, Cathy, don't you ever care that we finally have a letter from Daddy after all these months?"

"Correction." Catherine plucked the cocoa cups from the tray her sister was holding and placed them in the sink with the rest of the dirty dishes. "Mom has a letter from her husband."

"I don't see the difference."

"Believe me, there is one." Catherine started to say that Nancy was too young to understand but caught herself. "Think about your pen pal, Nance."

Nancy slumped into a kitchen chair.

"Think about Gerry and how you feel when his letters arrive. Would you like Mom and me peering over your shoulder when you first read them?"

Nancy plucked at the fringed edge of a Christmas-red place mat. "No, but that has nothing to do with Mom and Daddy." She paused a moment. "Does it?"

Catherine wiped her hands on her apron and sat down opposite her sister. "First they're husband and wife, Nance, *then* they're parents. If they forget about that first truth, nothing else they do will matter very much, will it?"

Nancy's cheeks flamed and Catherine longed to comfort her but knew she didn't dare. Nancy's moods were as changeable as the weather; her internal barometer measured highs and lows that made it impossible to guess her reaction to anything.

"I'm scared," Nancy whispered, still staring down at the place mat. "I'm scared something terrible has happened to Daddy."

"If something terrible had happened, wouldn't we know about it by now?"

The expression in Nancy's eyes was easy to read, and it was Catherine's turn to look away. The news of Douglas's death had come with terrifying swiftness. She would never forget the horror of receiving a letter from him the day after the funeral.

"Daddy's not at summer camp, Nance," she said after she collected her emotions. "He's fighting a war. You can't expect him to write every day—or for the letters to get through with no problem."

Nancy pushed her chair away from the table. "I can't stand it another second. I have to know what's in that letter."

Catherine sighed and admitted defeat. "So do I."

Nancy tilted her head in the direction of the living room. "She's not crying. Is that a good sign?"

"I don't know." The Wilson women cried when they were happy and they cried when they were sad. They also *didn't* cry for the same reasons.

Slowly they headed toward the living room. Catherine's heart beat so loudly she was sure her mother could hear it from a room away.

"I know you're out there, girls!" Dot's voice sailed down the hallway.

They ran into the living room and found their mother clutching the letter to her bosom. "He's all right." Dot's words mingled with her daughters' cries of joy. "Your father is going to be fine and we have Johnny to thank for that."

Both girls looked at the soldier asleep on the coach.

"Was Daddy injured?" Nancy cut through to the heart of the matter.

"Your father's hale and hearty," said Dot, eyes glistening. "They were out on patrol and walked straight into an enemy ambush." Her voice trembled, but she cleared her throat and continued. "Five men were killed. It would have been six if Johnny hadn't thrown your father into a ditch and shielded him with his own body."

"You're a hero," Catherine whispered, crouching down near Johnny and adjusting the quilt. "How can we ever repay you?"

Her mother, of course, knew exactly how. "'Our house is his for as long as he wants,'" Dot declared, reading from Tom's letter. "'There's no guarantee the army will welcome him back once he's well. He seems gruff and hotheaded but he's a good Joe. He had no family. Now he does.'"

"You bet he does!" Nancy wiped her eyes with the sleeve of her pink cardigan.

"You don't have to worry about a thing." Catherine brushed a lock of dark hair off his brow. "We'll take good care of you."

Dot read selected portions of Tom's letter while Nancy threw more wood on the fire and Catherine sat on the floor next to Johnny and listened to her father's graphic description of battle—and of death.

"'Johnny will be going home on medical furlough any time now. I am passing this letter on to him through a medic. I hope it reaches him—and you. You were right, Doro. I had no business leaving you and the girls. War is a young man's game and I don't feel young anymore. I feel tired and I want to come home....'" Dot's voice cracked but then she continued, "'Take good care of Johnny. He's one of us. Tell Nancy I'm proud of her independence and determination. Tell Cathy that her hard work has made her old man prouder than he can say. And most of all tell them both that I love them....'" Dot refolded the letter and put it back in the envelope.

The only sounds in the room were the crackle of wood in the fireplace and the soft sounds of Johnny's breathing as he slept. Tom's letter had brought the war into the living room the way no newspaper article or radio broadcast ever had. They could almost smell the gunpowder and feel the bitter winds of a European winter.

But there in the house on Hansen Street it was Christmas Eve, and for the first time in years Catherine felt like celebrating. "Look," she said, pointing to the living-room window. "The Weavers are on their way over."

Dot leapt to her feet and smoothed her hair with the palms of her hands. "Will you look at the time! It's after eleven. They must be on their way to midnight mass!" She untied her apron and hurried toward the stairs. "You answer the door, Cathy! I have to powder my nose."

Catherine met her sister's eyes. "It's been a long time since Mom's been that happy."

Nancy, whose eyes were suspiciously wet, nodded. "A very long time."

Catherine flew to the front door and opened it wide. "Merry Christmas!" She hugged Edna and Les. "We've received the most wonderful present! We—"

"So have we, sweetheart," said Edna, hugging Catherine in return. "Our Mac is home for the holidays!"

Catherine looked up in time to see Mac Weaver, resplendent in his navy uniform, march up the snowy path. "Mac!" She flew down the steps and hurled herself at the handsome man. "I can't believe you're here!"

"Merry Christmas, princess!" He swept her up into his arms and spun her around.

"What are you doing here?"

"They sent me back to speak at a fund-raiser in D.C. You think I could resist coming home for Christmas?"

She threw her head back and laughed. "I'm so glad to see you."

He put her down and draped an arm around her shoulder. "We'd better get in before you catch cold, princess." He bent down and playfully scrutinized her face. "Am I crazy or have you gotten prettier since I last saw you?"

"You're crazy," she said, laughing as they entered the house. How wonderful it was to see Mac again! He was Douglas's big brother and had always felt like a big brother to her, too.

She took his scarf and overcoat and draped them over the banister.

"What's going on in the living room?" he asked, inclining his head in that direction. "Sounds like a revival meeting."

"We have company." Quickly she explained about Johnny and Tom and the shock of finding the young man unconscious on the welcome mat just a few hours ago.

"That's one hell of a story."

"Don't go turning into a reporter on me, Mac Weaver. It's—"

"Mac!" Nancy's squeal split the air and the teenager catapulted herself into Mac's arms. Dot wasn't far behind. Edna and Les stood in the archway to the living room, beaming proudly, while Dot's smile could have lit up Times Square before the dimout.

The grandfather clock tolled the half hour.

"Thirty minutes to get to church for mass," said Les. "We better hit the road."

"Do you think we can get there through the snow?" Dot asked.

"Christmas isn't Christmas without midnight mass," Edna said. "Father O'Herlihy has had kids out shoveling the sidewalks."

"Goodness knows we have a lot to be thankful for," said Dot, glancing at her daughters. "What do you say?"

"I love the snow," said Nancy. "I'm game."

"I think you're all forgetting someone." Catherine gestured toward the living room. "Johnny."

"I'd better pass this time, Edna," Dot said. "I'll stay home with Cathy."

"No!" They all turned and looked at Catherine, whose cheeks reddened. "I mean, why should you and Nance miss out? I don't mind staying home with Johnny." She could attend mass the following morning.

"Don't have time to stand there debating the issue, ladies." Les Weaver winked at his son. "Father O'Herlihy doesn't wait mass for anyone."

Catherine waved goodbye from the top step, then went back into the house. It seemed as if laughter still echoed in the hallway. It had been a long time since the old house had been so filled with holiday spirit. The Weavers—including Mac—would be over for dinner the next afternoon. How wonderful it would be to celebrate the Christmas season with the people she loved most in the world!

Her blood fairly bubbled through her veins with excitement. Johnny Danza, a hero. In an act of stunning courage he had risked his own life to save her father. She'd never imagined she would ever know a hero—or that the hero would be someone as unlikely as the wisecracking Johnny. She stood in the archway to the living room and looked over at him. A fire still crackled cheerfully in the grate, casting an orange glow over the room. Shadows danced against the walls, throwing strange patterns of light and dark across Johnny's face.

Dr. Bernstein had said the medicine would make Johnny sleep deeply, and he was right. He had slept right through the excitement when they found her father's letter in his jacket pocket, and he hadn't so much as batted an eye when the Weavers arrived. She supposed she should be thankful that he was getting his rest; sleep, after all, was the body's best healer. But still...

"Wake up, Johnny," she said softly, leaning her head against the archway. "There's so much I want to say to you."

"I'm listening."

She took a step into the room. "Johnny?" She hadn't seen him so much as move his lips. "Are you awake?"

"Mmm."

What she wanted to do was run to his side, take his hands in hers and pour out her gratitude for all he'd done for her father. What she did was stand in the doorway, feeling as awkward and foolish as she had at her first high-school dance. *This is ridiculous, Catherine. You've bathed this man, for heaven's sake. Certainly you can talk to him.* She took two more steps into the room. *If you're awake, Johnny, I wish you'd open your eyes.*

"You don't have to tiptoe...." His voice was foggy but his words were clear. "I said I'm awake."

She jumped, startled. Was he a mind reader, as well? "If you're awake, why don't you open your eyes?" Ten more steps and she was at his side.

He opened one eye and looked up at her. "You always so bossy?"

"Yes. I take after my father."

His laugh was sleepy, his smile a bit goofy. "Sit down. You look ten feet tall."

"I am ten feet tall." She pulled a chair close to the sofa and sat down. "I'm surprised you're awake."

"So'm I." He swallowed with obvious difficulty, then ran his tongue across parched lips. "Those pills could knock out a horse."

She placed her hand against his forehead. "They're also doing a pretty good job of knocking out your fever."

He glanced around the room. "Y'know, I don't really know how I got here. Last thing I remember, I was in a cab with a guy who smoked cigars."

She laughed and smoothed the quilt that covered him. "You're heavier than you look, Private Danza."

"You carried me into the house?"

"Let's say I managed." She told about finding him on her doorstep and getting him in from the storm. "You did give me a little help."

"I don't remember a damn—excuse me—darn thing."

"I'm not surprised. You were running a high fever. When Dr. Bernstein got here you were hallucinating."

He grinned that cocky grin she remembered from the night at the Stage Door Canteen. "I owe you one, Cathy."

"I'd say we were even."

Color stained his cheeks. "You, uh . . . you know about it?"

"Yes, I know about it. We gathered up your clothes to clean them and found the letter from Daddy."

He looked away. "The old man exaggerates."

"I don't think so." He looked so embarrassed that her heart went out to him. "Not many men would do what you did, Johnny."

He shrugged. "You asked me to take care of him."

Please take care of him, Johnny. . . . She took his hand and held it. There were no words for the emotions churning inside her chest. The grandfather clock tolled midnight, and from the church eight blocks away came the sound of bells.

"Merry Christmas," she said, pressing a kiss to his forehead.

He held her hand more tightly. "Merry Christmas."

"I'm glad you're here with us."

He nodded. How simple—how amazing!—it was to sit there by the fire and hold his hand, to feel hopeful when for so long she had felt nothing but despair.

"Cathy?"

She looked at him, eyes misty. She was awash in Yuletide cheer. It wouldn't surprise her if Santa Claus himself came bounding down the chimney. "Yes, Johnny?"

"Am I naked?"

MAYBE SHE HADN'T heard him, he thought. He'd try again.

"I said, am I naked?"

He wouldn't have figured her for the type to blush as red as the Christmas stockings dangling from the mantelpiece.

She released his hand and stood up. "Wh-why would you ask such a thing?"

"Something itches. I figure I'm either naked or I have sand in my shorts."

"Good grief!" She stared at him as if he was wearing his shorts on his head. "You're not naked. You're wearing your...your underwear. The blanket's what's making you itchy."

"Where are my clothes?"

"I told you—we're cleaning them. Your uniform was a mess, all covered with soot and snow and God knows what else."

"Who took my clothes off me?"

"Dr. Bernstein."

"Were you here, too?"

Her face flamed even more. "He needed help with the bandages."

He thought for a second. "You gave me a bath, didn't you?"

Some of her embarrassment turned to anger, and she turned the anger on him. "Why are you asking me so many questions? You're supposed to be sick."

"Don't I have a right to know who's been doing what while I was out cold?"

"You weren't out cold. You were actually pretty cooperative."

This time it was his face that reddened.

Her blue eyes narrowed as she looked at him. A smile flickered at the corners of her mouth but refused to commit itself. "Now let me ask you a question—why did you ask me if you were naked when you could have looked for yourself?"

"I figured it would be rude to lift up the blankets and see what was going on."

"What's rude is all this conversation about your underwear or the lack thereof."

"'Thereof'?" He played with the word, examining it from all angles. "I never met anybody who used a work like 'thereof.'"

"Stick with me, Private." Her smile flickered again, then decided to stick around. "I have a whole list of words I can teach you. You'll be a walking dictionary by the time you head back overseas."

"No guarantee I'll be going back. By the time I'm on my feet again, I might have enough time for them to muster me out. Cheaper than keeping me on Uncle Sam's payroll."

"Well, don't you worry." She was all crisp and businesslike again, the cool blond princess he remembered from that night at the Stage Door Canteen. "We'll see to it that you have nothing to worry about."

"I don't need anybody taking care of things for me. I've done all right by myself."

"Spoken by a man who's flat on his back and weak as a kitten."

"The hell I am." He couldn't argue the flat-on-his-back part, but he'd never been called weak in his life.

Her laughter was sweeter than the church bells that had tolled the arrival of Christmas. "I can see you're going to be a difficult patient. Dr. Bernstein said it will be at least two weeks before you're on your feet again."

"If you think I'm going to lie here for two weeks causing trouble for your family, you're—"

"Oh, will you please stop pretending you're in a John Wayne movie? You're skinny, you're feverish, and you're not going any place until I say you can."

"I'm not going to sponge off your family."

"You're not sponging, Johnny. It would be an honor."

She looked sincere. Hard to believe, but she did. "I'll pay my own way."

She waved a hand in the air. "We'll talk about it."

He tried to lift his head off the pillow, but a wave of dizziness swept over him.

"See?" Her voice was triumphant, almost happy. "You're not well, Johnny."

The room was spinning and he closed his eyes. "Maybe you're right." He also felt hot and cold at the same time, and the shrapnel wounds on his chest were screaming for attention.

"Johnny?" She bent down next to him, and he smelled vanilla and cinnamon. She touched his forehead, his cheek and the base of his throat. "Don't worry. Dr. Bernstein said it would be like this. You're due for your medicine and another alcohol rub."

The thought of alcohol on his chest made him wince. "Just the medicine."

"The alcohol will help bring down your fever."

"That's okay. I don't mind the fever."

"Forget it, Private Danza. I'm the one in charge around here."

Knowing she had given him a rubdown when he was out cold was bad enough. But he couldn't be expected to lie there, almost naked, and let her trail her hands all over him. He knew he was sick, but *that* sick he wasn't.

"What about the medicine?" The stuff knocked him out cold. It was the only way he'd make it through the rubdown.

"Do you want that first?"

"Yes."

She disappeared down the hallway. If he wasn't so damned tired and sick, he'd find his clothes and get the heck out of there. Even though she'd been engaged once, he couldn't expect her to understand the effect her hands on his body would have. Just thinking about having her so close to him was enough to send his blood rushing to points south.

It had been a long time since he'd been close to a girl, especially a girl like Catherine Wilson, a girl whose hair sparkled like the ornaments on the tree. There was no telling what would happen when she started rubbing him down. If there was one thing a man learned, it was that his body sometimes had a mind of its own. They could be wheeling you into the operating room, and if a pretty girl walked by, you just couldn't help doing a double take.

Especially if the girl in question had been on your mind for longer than you cared to admit.

Who'd have thought it? Johnny Danza mooning over a girl he'd met only once. The last time that had happened he'd ended up getting married, and he saw where that had landed him. He wasn't much good as a husband—at least, Angie sure hadn't thought so. She'd run off with a guy she worked with not long after Pearl Harbor. Being an army wife didn't hold much allure for her; looking back over the past few years, he couldn't say he blamed her.

What kind of life was it for a beautiful young girl— spending her days at work and her nights waiting for her man to come home. Week after week, month after month, year after year. That was more than a man could ask of any woman.

Catherine bustled back into the room carrying a tray loaded with towels, rubbing alcohol and all manner of things. She shook two tablets from a brown pharmacy bottle into the palm of her hand and held out a glass of water. "Sit up and take these," she ordered, tougher than his drill instructor at boot camp.

The quicker he took them, the quicker he'd be asleep. At least then he wouldn't have to be witness to his own humiliation. He popped them into his mouth and washed them down with a gulp of water.

She knelt on the floor next to him. "Let me see that bandage." She reached for the blanket and folded it down, exposing his chest. With gentle hands she lifted the dressing. "Just as I thought. You need more salve."

He yawned loudly. "Maybe you could wait until tomorrow. I could use some sleep."

"Once the pills start working, you'll fall asleep no matter what I'm doing."

Sorry. He wasn't buying any of it. No red-blooded American male could fall asleep with someone like her sitting right next to him, no matter how sick he was. She lifted the bandage away then discarded it. The air was cold against his chest and despite himself, he shivered.

"I'll work quickly. Just let me squeeze some salve onto my hand...." He watched, mesmerized, as a ribbon of beige cream curled into the palm of her hand. "This might hurt, Johnny. I'll use as light a touch as I can."

His breath caught sharply as her palm found his chest.

"I'm sorry. I don't mean to hurt you."

He nodded. He didn't trust his voice. Pain was secondary to his acute awareness of the touch of her fingers against his skin. The shrapnel wounds were red and angry-looking, but she didn't flinch or look away. The last nurse who'd changed his bandage—could it really be less than seventy-two hours ago?—had turned white when she saw the network of ugly gashes.

Not Catherine. She talked to him about Christmas, about midnight mass with Father O'Herlihy, about how much her father had loved to put on his best bib and tucker and parade to church with his whole family.

"But only twice a year, mind you," she said, laughing, as she placed a fresh bandage over his chest. "Midnight mass and Easter Sunday. That's it."

He yawned again, this time for real. "I made you miss the services, didn't I?"

"Don't worry about it," she said, reaching for the bottle of alcohol. "There's always next year."

He'd been worried that his body would do something to embarrass him. He never figured that what it would do was fall asleep. He stifled a third yawn and eyed the bottle. "Isn't that stuff going to sting?"

"Don't worry. I won't let any of it get near your bandage."

He braced himself for the cold harsh feel of it against his skin, but it didn't come. His lids lowered and instead of an icy shock, he felt soothed...cared for...as if he were floating in midair with only cotton candy clouds beneath him for support....

"Can you turn over?"

"Mmmph..."

He did his best, but it was like moving through a vat of thick honey. He felt distant from it all, as if his arms and legs belonged to somebody else. Somebody clumsy and slow. Ah...there it was again. Those hands sliding across the muscles of his back, trailing down his spine, spanning his rib cage.... She was talking to him, but she was so far away he couldn't make out her words.

But then words didn't really matter. All that mattered was the way she touched him. He couldn't remember the last time he'd been touched like that—with kindness or compassion or friendship. This couldn't be happening. Not three weeks ago he'd been crouched in a foxhole, praying he'd have a chance to shoot before an enemy bullet found him.

It wasn't supposed to be like this, with him lying there on her couch, sick as a dog, the most pathetic war hero you could possible imagine.

"Sorry..." he mumbled as the medicine kicked in. "Sorry..."

He fell asleep.

THE GLORIOUS VOICES of the St. Mary's choir rose toward heaven, carried upon the beautiful notes of "Ave Maria." Dot clutched her missal as her heart soared right along with them.

Tom was alive! She was sure her smile could light up the entire church. Tucked inside her prayer book was that precious letter from her husband. Not that she needed to look at it again—she had every single precious word memorized. She squeezed Nancy's hand and her daughter looked over at her, a grin on her sweet face.

What a wonderful Christmas! Although she wished with all her heart that her husband could be with them tonight, it was enough to know he was safe and sound somewhere across the ocean. How little it took to change the way you looked at the world. That morning she had awakened with the same heavy sense of dread that had dogged her these past few months. Each day without word from Tom had seemed a lifetime. She'd wondered how she would manage to keep up a happy front during the holiday.

But now her prayers had been answered!

Her husband was safe and sound. Nancy was home to stay. And Catherine...

Catherine was coming to life right before her mother's delighted eyes. There was no mistaking the way she'd thrown herself heart and soul into caring for Johnny. That stone wall she'd built around herself after Douglas died was crumbling at last, and Dot offered a prayer of thanks—and another one that Johnny would stay around long enough for one more miracle.

December 25, 1944

Merry Christmas, Gerry!
I have the best news in the whole world. Daddy is fine! Mom had a letter from him tonight. Remember I told you about Johnny Danza, the kid from Brooklyn who's become my

dad's friend? Well, Johnny saved Dad's life and got himself injured in the bargain. They sent Johnny home to recuperate and he carried a letter from Daddy, since the mails hadn't been going in and out of their position.

An uncensored letter! Can you imagine a letter without holes cut into it and words missing and a hundred other people poking their noses into really personal things?

You should have seen Mom's face when she read it. Her eyes were all wet with tears and a smile lit up her face.

And as if that isn't wonderful enough, there's even more. When we came into the house tonight after mass, Johnny was sound asleep on the living-room sofa right where we'd left him. And curled up on the floor next to him was Cathy. Her head was resting on his shoulder, and she looked so young. I know she's only twenty-two, but losing Douglas the way she did made her grow up quicker than she should have.

Mom and I just stood there in the doorway. All we did was look at Cathy and Johnny and I think I'm pretty safe saying that Mom and I were making the same wish.

I miss you so much, Gerry. The locket you gave me for my birthday never comes off. I keep all your letters tied up together with ribbon and tucked away in my sweater drawer. Everyone says the war is winding down, that Hitler can't run forever, that the Japanese are running out of steam, that the day is going to come when everything is back to the way it's supposed to be.

Only thing is, I don't know if anybody remembers exactly how that is.

I love you very much, Gerry.

Nancy

Chapter Eight

Sometimes a guy just got lucky.

You could go your whole life looking for the reasons some men got all the breaks while others came up empty and never come close to understanding why God made the choices He did.

When Johnny woke up a little after dawn on Christmas morning, it took him a full minute to realize he wasn't dead and gone to heaven. In all of his twenty years he'd never known a moment as completely happy as the moment he opened his eyes and saw Catherine Wilson asleep in the armchair beside him. A bright blue blanket covered her from ankle to chin. Only the cuff of her yellow pajamas peeked out at the bottom—along with her delicate feet.

He felt funny watching her sleep. Sleep was a private thing, and he knew she probably wouldn't like knowing he was looking at her, but he couldn't help it. It had been a long time since he'd seen anything as beautiful as the sight of her long honey-colored hair drifting across her shoulders. He couldn't have turned away from that sight if General Eisenhower himself had issued the command.

Especially since for the past year and a half he'd carried around another, more painful, image of the girl now asleep in the chair . . .

"A DOZEN ROSES?" The cab driver whistled low and long. "Who's the lucky gal?"

Johnny Danza laughed as he climbed into the taxi and gave the Wilsons' address. "Would you believe 'lucky gals'? I'm having breakfast today with three beautiful ladies."

The cab driver shook his head and headed toward the Queensboro Bridge. "You soldiers got all the luck. Dames are suckers for guys in uniform."

Johnny wasn't about to deny it. For the first time in his life he had stature, a place in the world, and he had the army to thank for it. With that uniform on, it didn't matter that he was a nobody with no home or family to call his own. That uniform made him special. Important. Someone worth knowing.

He leaned his head back against the seat and closed his eyes. Last night, after leaving the Wilsons, he and the guys had hit all the night spots New York City had to offer. The Folies Bergères had been a real eye-opener. Not only were the costumes even skimpier than he'd figured, but after the show was over the dancing girls had applauded all the soldiers in the audience for going out there and defending their country. Drinks were on the house everywhere they went and it wasn't hard to figure some of the girls wouldn't have minded spending the night with a soldier on his way to war.

But wouldn't you know it? Damned if he could get Catherine Wilson off his mind. He'd be talking to some glamorous redhead with a dress cut down to there and his thoughts would wander back to the way Catherine had felt in his arms as they danced. A whole night to raise hell, with everyone's blessing, and he spent most of it mooning over another man's girl.

Big man, Danza, he thought as the taxi jounced its way across the bridge. Like she'd give him a tumble even if she didn't belong to somebody else. Catherine wasn't like anybody he'd ever known. You didn't meet girls like that where he came from. Orphanages were places where you grew tough and lonely, where you learned how to make your way in the world without extras like affection and warmth and trust.

She'd cut her teeth on all of those. You could see it in the way she moved, all confidence and grace, and in the way she met your eyes when you talked as if what you said really mattered.

So who could blame him for wanting to spend a few more hours believing in miracles? Besides, if he was being really honest with himself, it was more than Catherine that drew him to the Wilsons' home for breakfast. Although he couldn't put words to the emotions churning in his heart, he understood that he needed to belong somewhere, even for an hour, before he headed overseas to the unknown. He wanted Mrs. Wilson fussing over him with French toast and fried eggs; he wanted Nancy to make him laugh with her *Photoplay* gossip. For months he'd listened to Tom's stories about his wonderful family, and the moment he'd met them, he knew they were all true.

Tom Wilson was one hell of a lucky man.

"Mind if I let you off here?" asked the cabbie as he stopped at the corner of Hansen Street. "I'm trying to keep my tank full for as long as I can." Gasoline was getting harder and harder to come by for civilians, even those who needed it to make a living.

Johnny paid him and added a healthy tip. Might as well spread it around where he could. He didn't have anybody to save it for and he doubted there'd be much use for American dollars where he was going.

"Enjoy yourself, soldier!" The cabbie pocketed the money as Johnny climbed out of the back seat and closed the door behind him.

Hansen Street was a broad, tree-lined avenue with maples and oaks towering over the roofs of the houses, dappling the morning sunlight with a green and golden glow. An old couple in their Sunday best strolled past and Johnny tipped his cap. The old guy saluted while his wife smiled at Johnny and wished him well. Up ahead of him a kid on a rusty Schwinn tossed rolled-up newspapers toward the front doors. He'd already seen the headlines. The Fifth Army was moving toward Rome. Any day now the Allies would converge on the Eternal City. For a change, however, the war didn't matter. All he could think about was the blue of Catherine's eyes.

70-33 Hansen Street. 70-27. 70-21.

There it was. 70-15.

He squared his shoulders and smoothed the crisp green florist's paper that hugged the roses. He mounted the stairs, pressed the doorbell and heard Westminster chimes sound inside the house. Smoothing his hair, he cleared his throat and swallowed his nerves.

Nothing.

He rang the bell again.

"You lookin' for the Wilsons?"

He turned in the direction of the voice and saw a man of medium build looking up at him from the foot of the steps.

"Yeah. I'm invited for breakfast."

"Won't be having any breakfasts at the Wilsons' today, soldier. Not after what happened."

He was down the steps in a flash. "What do you mean, 'after what happened'?"

"You don't know about Douglas?"

Johnny shrugged. "I don't even know who Douglas is." As far as he knew, Tom didn't have any sons.

"Cathy's beau. Got himself killed in the Aleutians a week ago. The Weavers just got word last night. Tom and the family have been across the street since midnight." The man motioned toward the only house where the porch lights still blazed. "Guess the best way to get through it is together."

"Thanks," Johnny mumbled, looking at the garish red roses tucked under his arm. "Thanks for telling me."

The man moved off down the street. Johnny looked across at the Weavers' house. The curtains were open wide and he saw figures moving back and forth in front of the big window. He started toward the house, then stopped. What right did he have to knock on the door and say he was sorry? He sat down on the bottom step. He was a stranger to all of them except Tom. His condolences wouldn't matter a damn. They sure wouldn't bring Cathy's boyfriend back.

Nothing could do that.

At least she wasn't alone. It would be rough, but she had her family and her friends to hold her hand and ease her through the worst of it. Her heart was broken but it would mend one day. God wouldn't let a girl like Cathy shrivel into an old maid. There'd be another guy, one just like Douglas, from a happy family who would love her the way she was meant to be loved. She'd never forget Weaver but she'd go on.

That's the way life was.

He stood up. There were only a few hours left until he and Tom were due to report at the pier. He'd grab himself some breakfast at a diner then come back around noon to try to catch up with Tom. He turned to go and as he did his eye caught the flash of something at an upstairs window.

Catherine stood there, arms folded across her chest, gazing off across the street. A world of sorrow was in her eyes. *I understand,* he thought. He knew all about loneliness.

He ducked behind a maple. The last thing she needed was to see him hanging around with those stupid roses in his arms. He watched as she pressed her forehead against the windowpane and looked as if her heart was breaking.

It occurred to him that in his entire life no one had ever cried for him and it was unlikely that anyone ever would. Even in death, Douglas Weaver was luckier than Johnny would ever be.

THE MEMORY OF THAT MORNING was as fresh now eighteen months later as it had ever been. The look of sorrow on Catherine's lovely face had never left him. In his darkest moments he thought about how it would feel to have some-one who cared, someone who would stand by him through the good and the bad, and each time the face he saw was hers.

Which was why he had no business seeing her face first thing Christmas morning.

This was dangerous. Probably more dangerous in some ways than squatting in a foxhole fighting the Nazis. He knew about guns and rifles and bombs. He didn't know a damn thing about families and Christmas and girls with hair like molten honey. The blankets were wound tightly around his body and he struggled to kick his way free. If he had half a brain he'd find his clothes and get out before the rest of them woke up. With a little luck he'd find himself a cab and head for the nearest hospital where he could heal his body among strangers, the same way he had done most things in his life.

She was still asleep, her breathing soft and sweet in the quiet room. Gingerly he sat up, shivering in the cold morning air. The wounds on his chest burned and it took all of his strength to sit up straight, what with the way the room was spinning.

So how could it hurt, staying there one more day? By tomorrow he'd be back on his feet and he could find himself a place to finish getting well. Besides, this was Christmas, and for once in his life he was going to spend Christmas with a real family—even if that family didn't belong to him.

CATHERINE AWOKE with a start a little after seven. For a few seconds she couldn't place her surroundings or remember why she was sleeping curled up on the armchair in the living room. The tree loomed in the half-light filtering through the draperies, and the gaily wrapped packages stacked beneath the boughs reminded her it was Christmas morning.

The events of the previous day rushed back at her. The knock at the door... Johnny sprawled across the welcome mat... the miraculous letter from her father. She would almost believe it had been a dream if it wasn't for the fact that Johnny was sound asleep on the sofa a few feet away from where she sat. She smiled at the way his covers were tangled around his legs and torso. She padded over to where he lay and smoothed the blanket and quilt back into order. His breathing was even; that labored sound of the night before was gone, and his forehead was cool to the touch.

"You're going to be just fine," she whispered. He was young and strong and she was determined enough for both of them.

EIGHT O'CLOCK MASS was crowded with familiar faces—the Dustins, the O'Learys, Rose and Agnes Schellenbarger from the newspaper store at the corner. Everyone offered a smile and a holiday greeting.

Rose cocked her head to one side and looked closely at Catherine. "Is there a reason for that smile on your face, or is it just the holiday spirit? I do hope it means you've heard from your dear father."

Catherine felt her smile widen. "Not only have we heard from him, but his letter was delivered by special messenger." She told them the story about finding Johnny on her doorstep and finished with a rousing version of his heroism.

The two sisters crossed themselves. "Saints be praised," said Agnes. "It's good to hear some happy news."

Before Catherine had a chance to think, she found herself inviting the elderly women to the house for eggnog later on. And as if that wasn't enough, she invited Father O'Herlihy, the Dustin family, the O'Learys, and everyone within earshot.

What was the point of having wonderful news if there was no one to share it with? It had been years since the house had been filled with friends and family, singing carols and sipping eggnog and arguing over the turkey roasting in the oven. That was exactly what they needed: a real old-fashioned celebration.

She flew home, scarcely noticing the cold winds and the snowy streets. A lovely rich bread pudding—just the thing to tempt Johnny's appetite and fill out the hollows in his cheeks. Of course her mother was probably already up and, if she knew her, scrambling some eggs for their unexpected guest.

As she turned onto Hansen Street, clear winter sunlight sparkled against the crusty snow, crisply outlining walkways and steps and the bare branches of oak trees spreading their limbs toward the sky. Why hadn't she noticed lately how beautiful this street was? She felt as if she'd been walking through fog, and now that fog had lifted and she was able to see—really see—for the first time.

The storm had passed during the night and the sky was a clear deep blue frosted with wisps of pink-tinged clouds. Peals of laughter rang out from down the block as the Bellamys' four grandchildren piled onto their new bright red sled and skimmed down the quiet street.

She waited, expecting that old familiar ache to clutch at her heart, and when it didn't, her own laughter rang out into the morning air.

"Hey, Cathy!" The oldest Bellamy grandchild waved a mittened hand. "Merry Christmas!"

"Merry Christmas, Frankie!" She smiled at the kids as they skidded to a stop at her feet. "Looks like Santa was good to you."

"You bet!" The boy yelped as his younger brother pelted him with a snowball. "Want us to give you a ride?"

"Maybe this afternoon," she said, wrapping her scarf more tightly about her throat. "My mom's making breakfast. I'd better get inside." She escaped just as the Bellamy grandchildren launched the first full-fledged snowball attack of the season.

Even their front door looked wonderful and she gave the brass lion's head door knocker a playful tweak on the nose as she entered the house. Christmas carols sounded from the radio in the living room, and she slipped out of her coat and was about to yank off her boots when she heard a commotion upstairs. Quickly she tugged off her overshoes, then dashed barefoot up the wide wooden steps.

To her surprise, Eddie Martin greeted her in the upstairs hallway.

"Breakfast! I clean forgot you were coming over." She patted his arm. "I promised you French toast, didn't I? Well, let's go downstairs and—" She stopped, taking a closer look at the man in front of her. He didn't look happy. "What gives?"

"Mr. High and Mighty, that's what."

"Johnny?"

"That's the one." Eddie made a sour face. "Just tried to give the guy a hand..." His voice drifted away and she noted two scarlet patches blazing on his cheeks.

"Where is he?"

Eddie tilted his head toward the bathroom door. "In there. Les Weaver's helping him."

"Uncle Les?" She frowned. "They weren't coming over until this afternoon. You're a strong guy. Why didn't you—"

"Don't you listen, Wilson?" His tone was harsh, unlike him. "He told me to get out."

"I don't understand." The last time she saw Johnny, he'd been sound asleep on the sofa, weak and sick and docile as a kitten.

"Yeah, well, neither do I." Eddie gave her a curious look. "What's he doing here, anyway?"

She told him.

"When's he leaving?"

"I don't know."

"Why don't you call the hospital? Maybe there's room for him."

"He doesn't need a hospital, Eddie. He just needs some old-fashioned TLC."

"That's why God made hospitals."

"Good Lord, Eddie! What's with you? The man is injured. He's a war hero, for heaven's sake. Can't you show some compassion?"

"I don't like him."

"That's obvious."

"Yeah, well, I'm funny that way. I usually don't like people who don't like me."

"Johnny doesn't know you well enough to like or dislike you."

"Wrong again, Wilson. He knows I'm not in the army. That seems to be enough."

She forced a laugh. "Now come on, Eddie. I doubt he asked to see your dog tags."

"He didn't have to. I'm healthy, over twenty-one, and dressed in civvies. Call it a lucky guess."

They heard water running in the hall bathroom and the sound of male voices talking sports. She sat down on the top step and motioned for Eddie to sit next to her. "Want to tell me about it?"

He sank onto the step. "Not much to tell. Your mom was making breakfast. She took me into the living room and introduced me to Danza. We were having a pretty good talk about the Dodgers, about your dad, then Weaver showed up and the conversation turned to the war—and that's all she wrote. I was done for."

She felt as if she were skating on thin ice. She liked Eddie very much, but there was something about Johnny that had stolen a piece of her heart. Gently she placed a hand on Eddie's wrist. "He's not well," she said, her voice soft. "Dr. Bernstein has him on medication."

Eddie shook his head. "That's not the problem." He met her eyes. "We both know what it is." His sigh filled the hallway. "And he's not the only one, Cathy. I could tell you some stories..."

She listened as he told her of the growing resentment against young men who were not in the armed forces. Fistfights, shouting matches, canceled dates and ruined parties—and that didn't include the simmering angers hidden in people too well-bred to acknowledge them.

"I don't feel that way, Eddie." She clasped his hand in friendship. "I know how hard you're trying to make the grade."

The bathroom door opened.

"Clear the way," hollered Les Weaver. "War hero coming through."

Eddie muttered something under his breath and disappeared down the stairs. Cathy stood up and smoothed her red corduroy skirt. She mustered up a smile. "Heading back to the living room?"

Les appeared in the bathroom doorway with Johnny next to him. Johnny's hair was shiny and neatly combed off his face. He had on a pair of blue flannel pajamas and he looked both embarrassed and pleased.

"Bravo," she said, grinning at him. "I'd forgotten how tall you were."

He smiled back at her. "I guess I spent most of yesterday flat on my back, didn't I?"

"Come on," said Les, pretending to stagger beneath Johnny's weight. "Let's get this young man set up, why don't we?"

"The living room's going to be like Grand Central Station in a little while." Catherine thought of the score of neighbors she'd invited over for eggnog. "I can't believe I did something so foolish."

"Hey, look. I don't want to put anybody out. I could always—"

"Be quiet," she said, sounding frighteningly like her mother. "We'll put you in my room."

Both Johnny and Les Weaver stared at her as if she'd danced out on stage at the Folies Bergères in her underwear.

She threw back her head and laughed. "Don't look at me like that, you fools! I'll move into the sewing room."

"Put me in the sewing room," said Johnny, who was starting to look a little ragged around the edges. "I don't want to put anybody out."

"The sewing room is on the first floor," she pointed out. "Every time you need the bathroom, you'd have to climb the stairs."

"I'm not an invalid."

"For the time being you are."

"*I'm* going to be an invalid if we don't put this boy somewhere soon," Les Weaver pointed out. "I'm not as young as I used to be."

"Follow me." Catherine bustled past them and hurried down the hall. "He's going in my room and that's it."

> *Adeste fideles*
> *Laeti triumphantes...*

Johnny lay in Catherine's narrow bed later that afternoon and listened to the sounds of Christmas floating up from the first floor of the Wilson house. Laughter. The tinkle of glasses raised in toasts. Voices raised in song. He heard all of it, let it drift over and around him until it seeped through his pores and into his bones.

You could almost pretend there wasn't a war going on.

He turned on his side and winced as arrows of pain shot through him from the shrapnel wounds on his chest. *Almost, but not quite.* Oh, it was out there, all right. Superfortresses and tanks and bullets. Blood and broken bones. Telegrams home saying, "We regret to inform you..."

> Jingle bells, jingle bells
> Jingle all the way...

When they'd first told him he could go home on furlough to recuperate, he'd been ready to strap himself to the wing of the first plane out. He didn't care if it was heading for Florida or the frozen harbors of northern Maine. He was going home.

And then it had hit him: he had no home. There wasn't anybody back there waiting for him to walk through the front door, drop his duffel bag by the coat closet, then bound into the kitchen in search of a home-cooked meal. All the way across the Atlantic, sitting in the bowels of a transport plane with a group of other scared sick GIs, he'd wondered where he would go when they landed in Delaware. He was in worse shape than he'd been in the hospital outside London. They hadn't cured him; they'd only diverted the symptoms, and those symptoms jumped on him as he rode the train up to New York. Had they managed to discover the secret he was keeping, he'd have been given his honorable discharge on the spot. Uncle Sam didn't have a hell of a lot of use for a soldier with an arm that didn't always do what he wanted it to. "Shrapnel's caused nerve damage to the muscles in your forearm," the sawbones in England had said, shaking his head. "Permanent most likely. Best learn to live with it."

He could live with it, all right, if the damn fever didn't kill him first.

If he'd had half the brain he was born with, he'd have gotten off that train and checked into the nearest hospital.

What he did, however, was stay on that train all the way to Grand Central Station. There was one thing he had to do no matter what: deliver Tom's letter to his family. Once that letter was safely in Mrs. Wilson's hands, then he'd worry about the fact that he was sick as a dog.

O holy night
The stars are brightly shining...

Well, he'd delivered that letter, all right—and delivered himself right into the middle of the Wilson family's Christmas celebration. Johnny Danza, the kid who'd spent his life on the outside looking in, was in the one place he never thought he'd be—Catherine Wilson's bedroom.

Not that he hadn't spent a few sleepless nights imagining what it would be like to have a girl like that to call his own. And he'd sure as hell imagined what he'd do if he ever found himself in her bed. The only trouble was, none of those daydreams had him in her bed while she enjoyed a Christmas party half a house away.

That's what you get, Danza. Even in his fantasies he couldn't quite bridge the gap between who she was and who he would never be. The kind of guy Catherine Wilson would love was blond and blue-eyed. A guy who played tennis instead of stickball and read the *New York Times* rather than the sports pages of the *Daily News*.

A guy exactly like the guy smiling at him from the framed picture on Catherine's frilly dressing table.

"So you're Douglas," he said, with a mock salute. "I've been wondering what all the fuss was about."

Actually it wasn't hard to see. Douglas Weaver was everything Johnny had figured. Young, handsome, as American as apple pie and boogie-woogie music. If the guy hadn't already paid such a high price for his good fortune, Johnny would have hated him. But how could you hate a dead war hero, even if he was the guy who'd once had Catherine's heart?

Silent night
Holy night . . .

He closed his eyes and let the distant sound of singing wash over him. The bed was soft, welcoming; he shifted his body into the curves made over the years by her slender form. The white cotton sheets smelled of soap and fresh air, but still he caught the faint tantalizing fragrance of her perfume. Sweet, but with a hint of spice. He remembered that perfume. She'd been wearing it the night they met.

He was drifting off to sleep when a knock at the door roused him. He cleared his throat. "Come in."

The door opened and Catherine stepped into the room, bearing a tray piled high with covered dishes.

He raised himself on one elbow. "What's all that?"

"Christmas dinner." A smile danced quickly across her face. "You didn't think we'd forget you."

"Looks like a lot of food. I don't know if I'm up to all that yet."

"We'll see about that." She placed the tray on top of her dressing table and didn't give the photo of Douglas so much as a look. "Can you sit up?"

"Sure." He struggled upright and wedged a pillow behind his back.

"Wait a minute." She was at his side in a flash, rearranging the pillow and adding another one from the easy chair in the corner of the room. "That's more like it."

"Thanks." In the middle of all this luxury he felt like a sultan.

She gave him a funny look, more quizzical than anything else, then placed the tray on his lap. "Enjoy." She turned and headed toward the door.

"Hey, wait a minute!"

She paused in the doorway. "Yes?"

"You leaving so soon?"

"Of course," she said. "You don't need me to cut your turkey, do you?"

"I, uh, thought maybe you would sit here and talk to me while I eat."

She folded her arms across her chest and watched him, her gaze level, measuring. "You did, did you?"

He picked up the fork, studied it, then tossed it back down on the tray. "Look, if I did something wrong I'd be glad to apologize, but first you gotta tell me what it is."

Her level gaze deteriorated into a downright glare and she approached the bed. "You had no right to treat Eddie the way you did."

His brows slid together in a frown. "Eddie?"

She towered over the bed. "Eddie Martin. Short, dark hair—" she aimed her fury at him and scored a bull's-eye "*—civilian.*"

He shoved the tray away from him. "Yeah, I remember the guy."

"How dare you treat a friend of mine that way."

"What did I do that was so terrible?"

"You threw him out when he was trying to help you."

"I didn't need his help."

She waved her finger beneath his nose and for an instant he wondered if she was going to pop him one. "You needed Les Weaver's help."

"That was different."

"Oh, really?" She sat down on the edge of the bed. "Would you mind explaining it to me?"

She bristled with outrage. He wouldn't have believed an angry woman could be so beautiful. "I think you were terribly unfair to Eddie. He deserves better."

He shifted position again. "I'm a big guy. I needed someone I could lean on." Les Weaver outweighed Eddie Martin by a good fifty pounds.

She wasn't buying it. "You can do better than that, Danza. From what I heard, you had no problem leaning on Eddie until you found out he was 4-F."

He turned his concentration back to the Christmas dinner in front of him.

"I don't hear you denying it, Johnny."

"What do you want from me?" Once again he tossed down his fork. "I can't change the way I feel."

"Maybe not, but you can change the way you act."

"What's that supposed to mean?"

She let loose an exasperated sigh. "Good grief! I thought I was speaking plainly enough, but if you want me to spell it out for you, I will." She stood up, blue eyes flashing fire. "As long as you're here, you'll treat my friends with respect."

"What's between you and that guy, anyway?"

"You heard me—friendship."

"You go out with him?"

"That's none of your business."

"Maybe it is."

She sat down at the dressing-table chair. "No, we don't 'go out,' as you put it. We're friends."

"That's what I thought. I figured you'd have mentioned it in your letters if you were seeing someone."

A smile quirked the corners of her mouth. "I didn't tell you everything in my letters, Johnny." She gestured toward the tray of food. "Eat your dinner. It's getting cold."

He downed a generous portion of turkey and mashed potatoes. "Great chow." His stomach lurch ominously, and he washed the food down with a gulp of water. "Tell your mom she's a terrific cook."

"I will." She rose to her feet, and he watched, transfixed, as she smoothed her skirt and ran a slender hand around the waistband, tucking in the silky white blouse. "Enjoy your dinner."

This time he didn't ask her to stay. She headed for the door, and just before she closed it, he called out her name.

She hesitated, glancing over her right shoulder at him.

"About Martin," he said, stumbling over the words. "I'll try. I can't promise anything more than that."

She nodded and before he could say another word, the door swung shut behind her, leaving him alone with his dinner and his thoughts.

"WHAT TOOK YOU SO LONG?" Eddie asked as she came down the stairs into the foyer. He was up on a stepladder, fastening some mistletoe to the ceiling light fixture. "Your mom said this was your job."

"Sorry." She held the ladder for him while he clambered back down. "I was talking to Johnny."

"Right," said Eddie. "The war hero."

She threw her hands into the air in disgust. "Wonderful. Now I have two pigheaded idiots to worry about." She pulled her coat from the closet and tossed it across her shoulders. "I'm going for a walk."

"What about dinner? Les is about to carve the rest of the turkey."

She wound a red-and-white knit scarf around her neck and jammed a matching cap on her head. "I've lost my appetite."

"Come on, Cathy. It's Christmas. You're the only one I know here. If you don't stay for dinner, how can I?"

Fumbling around in the deep pockets of her coat, she found her mittens. "By the way, who asked you to stay for dinner?"

Eddie looked affronted. At that moment she didn't particularly care. "Nancy and your mother. If it's a problem—"

"Everything's a problem," she snapped. "Go eat your turkey."

Eddie folded up the ladder. "Tell me what he said about me. I can take it."

"He didn't say anything." Eddie arched a brow in question and she glared at him. "Look, a few days ago he was in a hospital. He's not feeling well. You can't pay any attention to the way he behaves right now."

"Nothing worse than a 4-F, is there?" Eddie's tone was brash and brittle. "I mean, I'm not a Nazi, folks. I'm a full-blooded American citizen—not that that seems to count for much these days if you're not in uniform."

"Aren't you being a little melodramatic?"

The ladder clattered to the floor. "Forget it. Tell your mom thanks, but now I'm the one who's lost my appetite."

"Where are you going?"

He grabbed his coat from the closet. "To get drunk."

She stared after him as he stormed down the icy walk and disappeared down the street. She couldn't very well go out herself now. Her mother had worked hard to make a delicious Christmas dinner within the boundaries of government rationing. Two absences from the dinner table would be unforgivable. She hung up her coat and scarf, and stuffed the hat and mittens back into the pockets.

"Come on over here, princess," said Mac Weaver as she entered the dining room. He patted the empty seat next to him. "I've been saving this for you."

She sat down and helped herself to turkey and all the trimmings, eager to put all else from her mind.

"Where'd Eddie go?" Mac asked, passing the sweet potatoes.

"To get drunk."

Mac considered her words. "What happened?"

She speared herself some brussel sprouts. "You don't want to know."

Mac's legendary nose for news could still sniff out a story. "That tangle with our friend upstairs?"

She nodded, glancing across the table to make certain her mother and Nancy were otherwise occupied. "Afraid so. Eddie didn't imagine the problem. Johnny doesn't want anything to do with him."

"Danza's overreacting, wouldn't you say?"

"He thinks he has a right to feel the way he does."

Mac leaned closer, eyebrows waggling. "Do I detect romance in the air?"

Her breath caught. "Where on earth did you get that idea? I barely know the man."

"You have that look."

"What look?"

"I know you too well, princess. I've seen that look before."

"Don't say that. You don't know what you're talking about."

"Take a gander in the mirror. It's unmistakable."

She rapped him on the hand with the back of her butter knife. "Stop teasing me. This is Christmas. Whatever happened to good will and peace on earth?"

Instead of a snappy rejoinder, his expression softened and he took the butter knife from her and clasped her hand in his. "It's time to move on, kiddo. Doug would've wanted it that way. He was my brother. I know how he'd feel."

She looked down, vision blurry with tears.

"There's somebody out there for you, princess. I can guarantee it." He chucked her under the chin the way he used to when she was a little girl. "He may even be right under your nose."

Laughter bubbled up. "Are you flirting with me, Mac Weaver?"

"You can do better than an old man of twenty-eight."

She blinked away her tears. "They don't come much better than you."

Her mother smiled with pleasure when Catherine told her that Johnny was tucking into his dinner upstairs.

"Poor boy," said Dot. "I wish he could be down here with the rest of us."

Les leaned forward in his seat. "That's one fine young man, Dot. I got him to open up to me when I was helping him out this morning." He shook his head fondly. "That's some story he has to tell. Brought the war home to me, I'll tell you that."

"I know what you mean," said Mac, with a quick look at Catherine. "Writing about it was one thing. Living it is something else again."

Perspective, it seemed, was everything, and Catherine found her perspective shifting as she listened to Mac talk about the war. The real war, that is. Not the Hollywood version where Spencer Tracy and John Wayne and all the other big strong American movie stars single-handedly won battle after battle and never shed a drop of blood, but the one where boys like Douglas Weaver died and men like Johnny Danza made certain others didn't.

Her mother got up to clear the table and impulsively hugged Mac. "We're so lucky to have you back even if it's only for a couple of days. It seems like you never went away."

Catherine saw an odd look pass across Mac's face, but he hugged her mother in return, then offered to help clear the table.

"I won't hear of it!" Dot looked scandalized. "You sit there and relax." Both Nancy and Edna got to their feet to help her mother.

Catherine knew she should do likewise, but something about the look on Mac's face held her back. Les and her Uncle Frank were locked in discussion about the Allies' incursion into the Ardennes forest. She'd heard enough about the Bulge to last her a lifetime. Nobody else was paying her the slightest heed. She touched Mac's wrist. "Can I ask you a question?"

He gave her the cocky big-brother grin she'd known her whole life. "Shoot."

"What's it really like to be back home?"

"Strange question, princess." He leaned back in his chair and lit a cigarette. "How do you think it feels?"

"I saw your face, Mac, when my mother said it felt like nothing had changed."

"Pretty observant. Have you ever thought about reporting?"

She waved away his words. "Really, Mac. How does it feel?"

He took a long drag on his cigarette. "You know what really hit me when I got off the train? The city was a lot smaller than I'd remembered."

"New York City, small? Oh, come on, Mac. Tell me the truth."

"That is the truth. New York's just a collection of small towns. Doesn't seem so impressive once you realize that."

"What about seeing your family? Your friends? It must have been wonderful to sleep in your old room again."

"Nothing fits anymore. *I* don't fit here anymore. Things look older and shabbier—" He stopped and took another drag on his cigarette. "You all look so damn untouched by it all. Sure there's rationing and blackouts, but except for Pearl Harbor we've gotten off scot-free. When I think of those families in England sleeping in the underground—" He shook his head. "This is like being on another planet."

A shiver ran up her spine and she wrapped her arms around herself. "You sound almost angry."

"Do I?" He looked surprised. "I suppose in a way I am." He stubbed out his cigarette in a shell-shaped ashtray. "Not a real yuletide sentiment, is it?"

"No, but I think I understand. It's a private club, isn't it? All of you are in it together and the rest of us are outsiders." Johnny's reaction to Eddie Martin had been as simple as that.

His smile was without its old teasing big-brother edge. "You always were a smart girl, princess."

GIs like Mac and Johnny Danza had been places and seen things that most other Americans—God willing—would never know. Who wouldn't find the transition from blood-soaked battlegrounds to a festive yuletide table disconcerting? If Mac Weaver found it hard to break bread with his own family and friends, what on earth must Johnny be feeling?

She pushed back her chair and stood up. "Would you excuse me? I need to talk to someone."

Mac grinned at her. "Private Danza?"

She met his eyes. "Yes. I think I owe him an apology."

"Good for you, princess. That's the first step."

She didn't ask him about the second.

Chapter Nine

Johnny didn't look very happy to see her, but Catherine was determined not to let that stop her. Smiling brightly, she picked up the tray from the foot of her bed. "Finished?"

He nodded.

"How was it?"

"Swell."

She peeked under the covered plate. "You didn't eat much."

"Not because it wasn't swell."

"I think it's time for your medicine."

"I was afraid of that."

"I'll put the tray out in the hall and get it."

"Don't rush on my account. If I never see that brown swill again, it'll be too soon."

"You won't get better if you don't follow doctor's orders."

He looked at her for the first time since she'd entered the room. "Save the lecture for someone else, okay?"

She made it halfway out the door, then stopped in her tracks. Putting the tray down on top of her chifforobe, she cleared her throat and said, "I'm sorry."

His brows lifted. "What?"

"I said, I'm sorry."

A look of suspicion replaced the look of pique. "What for?"

"I was pretty hard on you before about Eddie. I didn't understand. Now I do, and I'm sorry."

"Your dad told me you talked first and thought second."

"Gee, thanks." She could just imagine what manner of family secrets Tom Wilson had passed on these past eighteen months. "What else did my father tell you?"

"That you could take it, as well as dish it out. Not too many people can."

She looked away, oddly pleased by the statement.

Johnny's expression softened. "He also said you can't take a compliment."

"Sounds like my father said an awful lot to you."

"Don't worry. Nothing bad." His eyes fluttered closed and she saw beads of sweat along his brow.

"Your medicine!" She dashed out to the hall bathroom and was back with it in a flash. "Sit up, Johnny."

He opened one eye, then groaned. "I was hoping you'd forget."

"No such luck." She poured the brown glop onto the spoon and held it out to him. "Open up, Private."

He did, then made a horrible face. "I'd rather be sick."

"Sorry. You landed on our doorstep for a reason. When you leave here, you'll leave here fit and healthy."

"You're a tough one, Cathy."

"My dad tell you that, too?"

He shook his head. "I figured that out for myself."

She sighed and recapped the bottle. "When my dad last saw me, I was anything but tough." Douglas's death had hit her hard. She remembered her father's pain at leaving her after such a traumatic loss. That was one of the few things she could recall from those dark weeks. "I've done a lot of growing up since he's been gone. You'd be surprised how fast you grow up when you're running a company."

He stifled a yawn. "The war won't last another year. Before you know it Tom'll be back and your life can go back to normal."

"Normal?" She looked at him and laughed. "I don't have any idea what normal is these days."

"You know what I mean."

"That I won't have to go to work?"

"That you won't have to run a company. You can go back to being a secretary." He paused an instant. "If you don't get married first."

A sigh built inside her chest. "Marriage isn't part of my plans, Johnny."

His eyebrows lifted. "No new boyfriend?"

She met his eyes. "You know I have no boyfriend."

They'd been writing to each other for more than a year and a half. He knew her daily schedule as well as she knew it herself.

"Don't worry," he said, echoing his words from a long-ago letter. "That won't last forever."

He looked away, his gaze drifting toward the window and the snow-covered street below. She thought she caught the ghost of a smile, but it might have been a trick played by the light filtering through the curtains—or the loneliness inside her heart.

CATHERINE WAS IN HER OFFICE bright and early the next morning, ready to work. Unfortunately she discovered that the entire tool-and-die department hadn't reported in. Pressing the intercom button, she called for Eddie to come to her office.

"What on earth is going on?" she exploded the second he stepped through the door. "We have six thousand units to do by New Year's Eve. We can't afford to lose a minute."

Eddie lingered in the doorway, head slightly turned. "They have a grievance," he said, his words a bit muddy. "Barnes is supposed to present it to you this afternoon."

"I can't wait for this afternoon!" She rose to her feet. "Time is precious. If we don't meet our commitments, our other contracts are in jeopardy. Would you talk to them?"

He shook his head. "I'm not talking to anyone today."

"Eddie?" She stepped closer to him. "What's the matter with your face?" He looked different somehow. Even in the shadows of the doorway she could see something was wrong.

He shrugged. "I got into a little scrape. Nothing serious."

She walked right up to him. "You have a black eye! Your lip's cut. Eddie, what on earth . . . ?"

Catherine touched his cheek and he winced. "Think it'll buy me points at the induction center?" He forced a smile. "The other guy looks a lot worse."

She shivered. "I can't imagine anyone looking worse. Have you seen a doctor?"

"I'll live, if that's what you mean."

"I'd feel better if you saw Dr. Bernstein."

"I'd feel better if you'd just let me get back to work."

"What time can I expect Barnes?"

"Around lunchtime."

She walked back and took her seat behind the desk. "I'll be ready for him."

HARRY BARNES was a brash forty-eight-year-old man who'd fought in the last war and sometimes didn't realize his side had won. He was argumentative, hotheaded and obviously one hundred percent right.

Catherine told him so. "I understand your feelings," she said, praying he wouldn't see the way her hands shook on her lap, "but there's nothing I can do. My father isn't in favor of unionization and I wouldn't do anything to cross him."

"Your father ain't here," Barnes pointed out in his belligerent way. "Who's running the ship, anyway?"

She sat up straighter and looked him square in the eye. "I am." She paused. "Temporarily, at least."

"You're gonna lose out, lady, if you don't wake up and smell the coffee. If you want good workers, you're going to have to give 'em what they want."

"Wilson Manufacturing has the highest pay scale in New York City, Harry, and you know that."

"And the unhappiest workers."

She couldn't hide her shock. "I don't believe that! Not for a minute."

"Don't you listen to what we been tellin' you? Don't get me wrong—we don't mind workin' for you, Miss Wilson. But the fact is, there's no security here."

"No security? How can you say that, Harry? We've been in business thirty-three years. Why, my grandfather founded the company and my dad's done a truly wonderful job making it grow."

"All of that's true," Harry conceded, "but none of it changes the fact that no one can promise your old man will be coming back to work."

"That's a terrible thing to say."

"Yeah, but it's true. Working with girls on the assembly line is one thing. Working for the boss's daughter is something else. I'm here to tell you that it ain't going to work over the long haul."

Her face flamed with anger and embarrassment. "I think I've done an excellent job," she said, her voice low and controlled. "I doubt if my dad would disapprove of the choices I've made."

Barnes shrugged. It was obvious he didn't give a fig for anything she had to say. His mind was made up and nothing she said or did would change that.

If she had been a man, she would have punched him right in the nose. But she wasn't a man, as he had so neatly pointed out, so she had to control her temper and use her mind instead.

"Why don't your men present me with a list of grievances in writing, and I'll deal with them on a case-by-case basis."

"Your old man would've gone down into the factory and talked to the guys face-to-face."

She took a deep breath and prayed for patience. "As you told me not five minutes ago, Harry, the men don't want to talk to the boss's daughter."

Barnes looked discomfited and Catherine took some pleasure from that. He agreed to put the problems on paper, but made it clear nothing would come from the exercise.

"Eddie Martin," she said. "Talk to him."

Harry shook his head. "Martin's a good egg, but all he can think about is getting into the army. First second he gets the nod, he'll be gone so fast your head'll spin." He got to his feet. "Darn fool wants to join Uncle Sam so bad he gets himself into a barroom brawl. No, Eddie ain't the one. You see what I mean? There's still no one we can talk to."

"I'll do my best for you, Harry," she promised, extending her hand to him.

He stuck his hands into the pockets of his work pants. "Like I said, what we need is someone who understands."

"You and me both, Harry," she muttered as he lumbered from the office. "What I need is someone I can talk to."

DOT AWOKE THAT MORNING with a renewed sense of purpose. Even before she opened her eyes, she knew everything was different. Tom was alive and well! His precious letter rested beneath her pillow—not that she needed to read it again, for every single golden word was etched in her heart.

The long months of waiting for news of Tom were drifting into memory, and for the first time in ages she believed the war wouldn't last forever.

The end wouldn't come tomorrow or the next day. It may not even come next month, but it would come. The day was approaching when her beloved husband would stride up the front walk, looking strong and handsome in his uniform, and all the empty places in her heart would be filled.

But that was still sometime in the future. Today she had something else to be grateful for. Johnny Danza, the wonderful young man who had saved Tom's life, slept soundly in Catherine's bedroom, and it was up to the Wilson women to make certain he grew stronger and healthier with every day that passed.

Dot washed and dressed swiftly, then hurried downstairs to the kitchen. The girls needed so little from her, and with Tom gone, she found it hard to find ways to fill her days. She cleaned the house and shopped for groceries and watched the clock, waiting for day to turn to evening and evening to turn into night.

At least now that Johnny was staying with them, she had a reason to get up in the morning. How wonderful it was to have a man to fuss over again.

The morning sped by. While she warmed turkey soup for Johnny's lunch, Dr. Bernstein popped by to check on his progress.

"Oh, to be young again." Sy Bernstein shook his head when Dot ushered him into the kitchen after his examination. As she reached for the percolator on the stove, he added, "That fever would've felled any one of us."

Dot poured coffee into two heavy mugs and placed them on the table next to a bottle of milk. "He's doing well, then?"

"He's doing well." Dr. Bernstein fixed his coffee. "I'd like to take credit for it, but I have a feeling your TLC has as much to do with his progress as any of the medicines I've prescribed."

Beaming, she took her seat opposite him. "You're giving me too much credit."

"Wish I could agree with you, Dorothy, but I have a feeling I'm not giving you and the girls enough." He took a long sip of coffee. "Delicious. I've told Betty time and again to ask you your secret."

"There's no secret, Dr. B. Just Eight O'Clock coffee from the A&P and my trusty old Silex."

They chatted awhile about Johnny. Dr. Bernstein explained something technical about the shrapnel wounds on Johnny's chest and how they had affected his fever, but all she could think about was the fact that they would have the boy's company for another few weeks. He was her link with Tom, and she welcomed a chance to repay his valor in some way, however small.

After Dr. Bernstein left, she bustled upstairs to Catherine's room with the turkey soup and soda crackers on her grandmother's silver tray.

Johnny was lying on his side, flipping through a stack of *Life* magazines. He glanced up when she entered the room, and her heart was gladdened by the look of pleased surprise on his face.

"Sit up," she ordered brightly. "Lunchtime!"

He tried to do as she asked. She noted that he had trouble pushing with his right arm. The effects of the shrapnel wounds must be more far-reaching then she had realized.

"Ouch!" he said, rolling back on his side. "I feel like a pincushion."

"No complaints, Johnny. According to Dr. B, you're doing splendidly. It won't be long before you're out there jitterbugging again."

"At least I'll be good for something."

She placed the tray on Catherine's dressing table and propped some pillows behind the soldier's back. "That's a gloomy statement. Dr B is so pleased." She settled the tray across his lap and sat at the foot of the bed. "Is there something he didn't tell me?"

He took a spoonful of soup before he spoke. "I'm doing great," he said after a while, "but not great enough for the army."

Maternal outrage filled her soul. "How dare they! Why, a body takes as long as it takes to recover from something as dreadful as the experience you went through. Who does the army think it is, forcing you out of your sickbed before your time?"

"That's not it, Mrs. Wilson. What I mean is, they don't think I'll recover enough to go back in." He explained that he'd been in the army since before Pearl Harbor, and his time in the service combined with the injury meant he was liable to be honorably discharged sometime in the next couple of months.

"Well, that's wonderful news, Johnny! You'll be safe and sound and you can pick up your life exactly where you left it years ago."

He fiddled with the silver soupspoon that had been her grandmother's and her grandmother's grandmother's before hers. She wanted to reach out and hug him the way she hugged her own children, but she knew men could be funny about things like that. If Johnny Danza knew she sensed his sorrow and loneliness, he'd back away from her quicker than a cat from a rocking chair.

"Yeah," he said finally, mustering a smile. "It's really wonderful."

She fussed with the dog tags and wallet and other items on the nightstand next to him. "Well, I'll be..." She shook her head and reached deep into the pocket of her apron. "How could I forget?" She placed a thin envelope next to his St. Christopher medal. "We found this with the letter from Tom. There was no name on it, so we figured..." She let her words drift delicately away.

"Thanks," Johnny mumbled, cheeks turning bright red. "It's nothing important."

You're as transparent as one of my own children, she thought, casting a glance at the soldier propped up in bed. *You're wearing your heart on your sleeve, Johnny Danza, but you're just too stubborn to admit it.*

She'd bet dollars to doughnuts the letter was meant for Cathy.

December 28, 1944

Dear Gerry,

This is my lunch hour but I thought it would be smarter to write a letter than to eat my peanut-butter-and-jelly sandwich. I'm still full from Christmas cookies.

I still can't get used to writing on these V-Mail sheets but they get to you so quickly it's worth a try. Isn't it hard to believe this letter will be put on microfilm and shipped across the Atlantic with a thousand other letters on the same film? I can't imagine how they turn the film back to letters again. Modern science!

We've settled into a nice routine at home. At first I thought having Johnny around would feel strange—it's been a long time since there's been a man in the house! But he's a really great guy and we like taking care of him. After what he did for Daddy, it's the least we can do.

The whole house seems to revolve around Johnny these days. Mom takes care of him during the day. She and Uncle Les bathe him and do all the things Mom thinks are too "personal" for Cathy and me to do. Of course there's still plenty for us, although Cathy seems determined to do the lion's share. I play cards with him and read him the funny papers and I've been doing my best to catch him up on all the scuttlebutt about the Yankees and the Dodgers, even though baseball hasn't been the same since the war started, with Joe DiMaggio and all the other heavy hitters in the army.

Nobody enjoys caring for Johnny the way Cathy does. He's only been here for four days now and already it's like she's become a different person. I can't tell you how long it's been since I've heard her laugh the way she does when she's with Johnny. Not that she has as much time as she'd like— there's some kind of problem at work and she doesn't get home until way after dinner. I've heard some talk along the assembly line that a union organizer is putting pressure on Cathy, but she won't talk about it with me.

Last night, however, I was stacking sheets and towels in the hallway linen closet and I heard her talking to Johnny. It wasn't hard to put two and two together and come up with trouble. The men at the plant don't want to talk to a girl and the fact that she's the "boss's daughter" makes it even worse. It hurts so much to see the look in her eyes when she walks into the cafeteria and the men ignore her. The women like her a lot. I guess they feel she's on their side, and having another girl in charge makes going out to work less scary.

But you know what hurts the most, Gerry? It's knowing that Cathy's really good at her job. The accountant told Mom that Wilson Manufacturing has had a banner year. Some of Cathy's decisions paid off in spades. She even gave everyone a little Christmas bonus, and do you think anybody thanked her?

Well, maybe in a few months this won't matter anymore. With the big success our troops had in the Ardennes forest, it seems it's just a matter of time. Daddy will come back home and Cathy can put all of these troubles behind her. Who knows? Maybe one day she'll even find someone to love.

Whoops! I just looked at my watch. It's almost twelve-thirty and I have to get back to work or Cathy'll have my head on a platter. I'll mail this on my way home and write you another letter tonight.

I love you so much, Gerry.

Nancy

CATHERINE WASN'T SURE if it was luck, skill or divine intervention, but the production quota of 6,000 units was made before work ended on December 31. Harry Barnes had given her a partial list of grievances, and she had gathered her courage and confronted the workers with her own partial list of remedies. That they hated talking to a mere woman was obvious; but also obvious was that, like it or not, she was the boss.

Wilson Manufacturing was ending 1944 in better fiscal shape than it had started the year, and Catherine Wilson was responsible. Unfortunately that didn't make facing New Year's Eve alone any easier.

She got home that evening in time to help Nancy primp for a party at her best friend Elaine's house; once Nancy was on her way, it was time to curl her mom's hair. The hospital where Dot volunteered was holding a social and her mother was in charge of entertainment.

"Have a great time," Catherine said, kissing her mother's cheek.

"Are you certain you won't change your mind, honey? We'd love to have you."

Catherine shook her head. "I'm exhausted, Mom. I think I'll stay home, listen to the radio, then go to bed early."

"Don't forget Johnny's medicine."

"I promise." The truth was, she intended to do everything she had to do as quickly as she could, then call it a night.

After her mother left she went upstairs to check on Johnny. He was sound asleep, still gripping the *Daily News*, and she smiled as she gently pried the newspaper from his hands and tucked the blanket around his torso. She placed the pitcher of water on the nightstand and rested the pill next to it. On a piece of notepaper she scribbled the words "Take this" and balanced it against the glass.

Dinner was soup and a sandwich by the fire. She listened to Edward R. Murrow's report and smiled at Jack Benny's New Year's Eve show. A light snow was falling outside and it was pleasant to sit there, curled up on the couch, watching the world go by.

"CATHY."

She burrowed her face more deeply into the sofa cushion.

"You're going to miss New Year's."

Johnny? She opened her eyes and found him sitting on the arm of the sofa. "What on earth...?" She yawned, then quickly ran her hands through her hair.

"Don't," he said. "I like it kind of mussed like that."

She sat up, tugging at the hem of her sweater. "I must have fallen asleep."

He grinned, his teeth flashing white in the darkened room. "Looks that way."

She stifled another yawn. "What are you doing up? You should be in bed."

"Got the all clear from Bernstein. Time I started getting my legs working again. Besides, I wasn't about to welcome in 1945 by myself."

"What time is it?"

"Ten to midnight."

She sank back against the sofa cushions. "This is a far cry from Times Square, isn't it?"

"Angie and I went there the year we got married. Too crowded, if you ask me."

"Angie?"

He stood up, tugging the belt on her father's old bathrobe. "My ex-wife."

"Oh." She swung her feet to the floor and felt around for her slippers. It was hard to remember Johnny had once been a married man. She'd never known a divorced person before. The notion of marriage being dissolved in a courtroom was as alien to her as the idea of space travel. "Why don't I get us some eggnog. I can't imagine welcoming in the New Year without a toast, can you?"

He rose to his feet and held out his hand to her.

She hesitated, then put her hand in his, rising to stand next to him. Again she was struck by how tall he was. His leanness only served to emphasize the natural power of his frame, the breadth of his shoulders, and she wondered how it was she had managed to forget what now seemed all too apparent.

Motioning for Johnny to follow, she led the way through the dimly lit hall to the kitchen. Why had she picked tonight to wear this foolish blue sweater? It pulled too snugly across her breasts and rode too high on her waist. Her hair spilled over her shoulders, and she wished she had a rubber band to tame it into a ponytail.

"Six minutes," said Johnny, pointing to the clock over the sink as she flicked on the overhead light.

"Sit down. I'll have it ready in two shakes."

Thank heaven for something to do. She found it so easy to talk to Johnny when he was lying beneath the covers in her bedroom, looking vulnerable and needy. These past few days she'd told him more about what was really going on at the plant than she'd told her mother in the past year. So why was she finding it almost impossible to breathe as she poured the eggnog into the heavy goblets? The only difference that she could see was that now Johnny was vertical instead of horizontal. But for some reason, that one little difference changed everything.

She handed him his goblet. "Three minutes," she said with a nod toward the clock. "Here or in the living room?"

"Living room."

Once again she led him through the hallway, conscious of the sway of her hips, the soft brush of her hair against her cheek, the idiotic way her heart was thudding in her chest. She switched on the table lamp in the far corner of the room, then tuned in the radio to a live report from Times Square. Johnny sat down on the sofa and motioned for her to join him. She felt as if she had lead inside her slippers; each step required an act of will.

She sat down on the cushion next to him. Her right knee brushed against the hem of his bathrobe and she blushed like a schoolgirl.

The radio announcer's voice filled the room: "...and as the clock approaches midnight, the world eagerly awaits the year of our Lord nineteen hundred and forty-five—a year we hope will bring an end to war..."

She lifted her glass. "To peace."

He lifted his glass in answer. "To your dad's safe return home."

"...eight...seven...six..."

"To your health," she said.

"To you."

"...three...two...one...Ha-a-ppy New Year, everybody!"

They clicked glasses. She raised the glass to her lips, but before she could take a sip, he took it from her and placed it with his on the coffee table.

"Johnny." Her voice was tremulous, low with both surprise and anticipation.

He took her hand. "Happy New Year, Cathy."

She looked down at their fingers, laced together. "Happy New Year," she whispered as the bittersweet strains of "Auld Lang Syne" crept into her heart.

He cupped her chin with his other hand and tilted her head slightly. Later on she marveled that she had recognised the inevitability of that kiss from the very beginning, yet when it happened it took her genuinely by surprise. He moved closer, closer, until his features blurred in front of her eyes. His lips against hers were tentative, his touch no more than a gentle sliding motion, but that gentle touch registered itself from her head to her feet.

And she knew it had to stop now, before everything changed and there could be no turning back. She placed her hand against his chest then remembered the shrapnel wounds and moved her hand to his shoulder.

But it felt so wonderful to be there in his arms, to feel his lips, to smell his scent. *Stop this now!* the logical side of her mind warned. *There's no point to this, no future in it. Don't start believing you can have the life you'd dreamed of when you were a girl....*

His eyes held hers, and for an instant she wished time would stop and she could sit there like that, with her hand in his, forever.

Johnny recognized the change in Catherine the moment it happened. Her lids lowered, her lashes casting smoky shadows on her flushed cheeks. Her lips curved upward into a shy smile that found its target deep inside his chest. And he couldn't help but notice the way her breasts rose and fell with the rapid tempo of her breathing.

He'd dreamed about this moment, wished for it a million times the past year and a half, but never for a minute had he believed he'd ever live it. But there she was, not more than a heartbeat away from him, beautiful and trembling and ready for his kiss.

He lowered his mouth firmly on hers. Her lips were soft as angel wings, her breath sweet as rose petals. Desire rose inside him, overriding injury and fatigue, and it took a heavy dose of conscience to keep from claiming more than he had a right to claim—except in his dreams.

Saint or sinner. Wise man or fool. Johnny didn't want to know. It took every ounce of willpower at his command to break the kiss.

Catherine didn't know whether to be relieved or disappointed. "We should drink the eggnog," she said once she found her voice.

"Yeah," he said. "We probably should."

Once again they raised their glasses in a toast. "To 1945," she said, meeting his gaze.

He nodded. "To 1945."

It was as good a place as any to begin.

Chapter Ten

The good news was, Johnny was getting better every day.

The bad news was, getting better meant he would have to say goodbye.

By the end of the second week in January, he knew that the time was almost there. He took long walks during the day, sometimes with Mrs. Wilson, sometimes on his own, as he tried to figure out what he would do with the rest of his life.

Today he was alone.

The morning mail had brought the news he'd been expecting. As of February 1, 1945, Private Johnny Danza would be a civilian. Any day now he'd be well enough to leave the shelter of the Wilson home and head out on his own again. What was that old saying? Oh yeah. The more things change, the more they stay the same.

He'd spent his entire life on the outside looking in. For a little while he'd glimpsed something different, something better, but the glimpse had been fleeting. He'd been born alone and alone he was going to stay.

There was no place for him in that strange new world called the American home front. It was a world inhabited by women and children and weak sisters like that Eddie Martin. Guys who were too soft or too scared to do their duty for their country.

But then again, how in hell was Johnny any better? Thanks to his injuries, he was about to become a civilian in a world where to be a civilian was to be less than a man.

He strolled the snow-covered streets, looking for answers in every street sign and shopkeeper's face. Did he stay in New York? Did he head out west to the wide-open spaces? Did he throw himself on Uncle Sam's mercy and beg his way back into the army, the only home he'd ever known?

Or would he stay right there in Forest Hills? The idea had its charm. The town was every bit as beautiful as Tom had told him during those dark nights of waiting for the enemy to strike. But the most beautiful thing of all about Forest Hills was Tom Wilson's daughter Catherine.

She had become a part of him, although he had yet to admit to himself, much less to her, how much he cared. During those long days and nights when he was coming back to the land of the living, it was Catherine's face he remembered, Catherine's voice that lingered in his head, Catherine's touch that made him burn.

"Damn," he muttered, his breath visible in curls of frost. He had no business thinking like this. The Wilsons had opened their home to him out of the goodness of their hearts. They talked endlessly of the unselfish act of courage that had saved their Tom's life, but to Johnny his act of courage paled by comparison to all they had done for him.

He'd made a hash out of his marriage, just as he'd made a hash out of his childhood and his teen years. He thought he'd found a home in the army, but that idea had gone the way of so many others dreams he'd had along the way. In these past few weeks with the Wilsons he'd found himself wanting things that were way beyond his grasp, things he had no experience dealing with. Home. Family. Permanence.

Catherine. Twice he'd almost given her the letter he'd carried with him all the way from that English hospital, but both times he'd plain lost his nerve. That brief New Year's Eve kiss had shaken him to his roots. The way she looked, the sound of her voice, the sweet smell of her hair—

"Forget it, Danza," he said into the wind as he turned back onto Hansen Street. "Just forget it."

"NO!" THE WORD BURST from Catherine's lips before she had a chance to think. "I mean, you're not well enough to leave yet, are you?" *Get a grip on yourself, girl! You sound like an idiot.*

Johnny looked at her across the dinner table. "I can't stay here forever."

"Now don't talk like that!" God bless her mother for adding her own two cents. "You know you're welcome to stay here for as long as you want."

"I appreciate that, Mrs. Wilson, but it's about time I got out of your hair."

Catherine found it impossible to keep her own counsel. "What about the army? Surely you'll be back with another squad or platoon or—"

"Forget it," said Johnny. "February first I'm a free man."

"Do you have a job yet?" Leave it to Nancy to jump right in with both feet.

Johnny shifted in his seat. "I, uh, haven't started to look yet, Nance."

"Don't be ridiculous!" Catherine glared at her younger sister. "The man is barely out of his sickbed. He has plenty of time."

"You'll need it," said Nancy with a knowing nod of her head. "Jobs are pretty easy to find but housing isn't. Believe me, I know. That boardinghouse I lived in this summer was awful."

"She's right," said Catherine, suddenly siding with her sister. "People are doubling and tripling up, and there still aren't enough apartments to go around." After Pearl Harbor, war-production plants had sprung up almost overnight, bringing large influxes of workers into areas ill prepared to house them.

Johnny stared down at his mashed potatoes and gravy. Nancy launched into a convoluted story about the assorted types she'd roomed with out in Long Island. Dot, oblivious to the undercurrent of tension in the room, bustled into the kitchen for more green beans and carrots to go with the roast chicken.

Catherine pretended to concentrate on her own dinner, but her mind was scattered in a million directions. Johnny was a grown man. He had the right to go wherever he wanted, whenever he wanted. Just because they owed him an enormous debt of gratitude was no reason to force the poor man to stay put while they paid off that debt.

And just because she could still feel the touch of his lips against hers was no reason to wish him anything but the best life had to offer, even if it meant moving on.

A FEW HOURS LATER Catherine knocked on the door to her room. "It's me," she called out, her voice deceptively bright and easy. "I need a few things from my closet."

Johnny swung open the door. He was dressed in a pair of army-issue trousers and a white cotton undershirt that emphasized the contours of his chest. Not that she was interested, of course, but it was difficult to concentrate on a man's eyes when there were other more fascinating places to look.

He stepped aside so she could enter the room.

"I'll get out of your way." He grabbed a shirt from the foot of the bed and slid his arms into it. "Promised your mom I'd take a look at the kitchen sink."

She positioned herself between Johnny and the bedroom door. "Mom went over to play bridge at the Weavers'. She won't be back until later."

"The sink's still there."

"Filled with dishes, Johnny. I'm afraid we're a sloppy group."

"Okay," he said, leaning against the chifforobe, "what's up?"

"You're very suspicious tonight." Casually she strolled over to her closet and flipped through the dresses hanging in neat rows inside. The sight of his trousers and shirts hanging side by side with her jumpers and frilly blouses affected her like a blow to the stomach.

"Do I have reason to be suspicious?"

She withdrew a navy wool jumper and a plain white cotton blouse with Joan Crawford shoulder pads to give it authority. "I'm not being very subtle, am I?"

He shook his head. "Not very."

"Okay," she said, draping the clothes over the back of a chair. "I'll give it to you straight." He folded his arms across his chest and looked her straight in the eye as she gathered both her courage and her words. "Now that you're going to be a civilian again it occurred to me... What I mean is, it seems you'll have a lot of time on your... The point is—"

"Are you offering me a job?"

Her breath rushed out in one relieved whoosh. "Yes!"

"At Wilson Manufacturing?"

"Of course."

"No, thanks."

"I haven't told you about the position." It had taken her two hours to work out a description enticing enough to mask the fact that her motives were less than pure.

"Doesn't matter. I don't take charity."

"Then you have nothing to worry about. I'm not in the habit of offering charity."

"Tell it to the marines, Cathy."

"Very original," she said, her tone frosty. "I'll have to remember that."

"Am I wrong?"

She hesitated a beat too long.

"That's what I thought. Nice idea but forget it. I'll find my own job."

"That might be harder than you realize, Johnny."

"I'll manage."

She took a step toward him. "We'd like to help."

"You've helped enough."

"Why don't you let me explain the job to you?"

"Why don't you give up?"

"Because I care about you."

Dear God, had she really said that? Her words echoed inside her head and she wished she could call them back, but it was too late. He turned away so she couldn't see his face. *Oh, yes,* she thought, *it was definitely too late for that now.*

"I can make it on my own," he said, his voice low and menacing. "I've never asked for anyone's help before and I'm not about to start now."

"Johnny, please listen to me." She crossed the room to where he stood with his back to her. Gently she placed her hand against his forearm. He remained still as a statue. She increased the pressure of her fingers against his arm. Still nothing. A chill began at the base of her spine, then worked its way upward to her scalp. *No...please, no...* she swallowed hard. "Why didn't you tell me?"

"Because it's none of your business."

She trailed her forefinger along the ridge of muscle that was as beautifully sculpted as marble—and as unfeeling. Her heart went out to him. "I'm so sorry."

He spun around, all rage and hurt. "Don't say that."

"But I mean it, Johnny. I wish you'd shared it with me— with us." She didn't have to ask how it had happened; she was certain it was a result of the heroic action that had saved her father's life. "I should have... I mean, I don't understand why we didn't notice—" She stopped cold at the look of anger on his face.

"Still have a job for me, Cathy? A little manual labor, maybe, something just right for a big strong guy like me?"

"Don't talk like that. Of course, I still have a job for you. This doesn't change anything." The loading dock. Assembly line. Everything she had thought of had been ruled out in that single instant of comprehension. But she'd come up with something else. She had to.

"You don't sound so sure of yourself, Cathy. Not so easy to find a job for a guy like me, is it?"

"It's not your arm that worries me, it's your attitude."

"Not grateful enough?"

Anger, towering and pure, soared through her and she lifted her hand to slap his face. "Damn you," she whispered as reason got the better of her. She had never cursed another person in her life, but her emotions were running so hot and fast that she couldn't control her tongue. "Don't you know when someone's trying to help?"

"Don't you know when it's not wanted?"

He pushed past her, and before she could say another word, he was down the stairs and gone.

"BAD NIGHT?" Eddie asked the next morning as Catherine slogged away at her desk.

She looked up from her latest stack of employee grievances, straight from the pen of Harry Barnes. "It shows?"

"It shows." Eddie sat on the edge of her desk. "Bad news from the front?"

"Bad news at home."

"Anything you feel like talking about?"

She shook her head. "Not this time, but thanks."

"I kind of miss our talks," he said, tapping a pencil against her desk. "Doesn't seem to be so much time since the war hero moved into your house."

She massaged her temples in an attempt to stave off the gathering headache. "Not today, Eddie. I'm not in the mood." She shifted her attention from the personal to the professional. "We have a new batch of complaints from Barnes."

"That's not the half of it. They're talking about a walk-out day after tomorrow."

Her mouth dropped open in shock. "Are you certain?"

"Certain as an outcast can get." Eddie's situation had been deteriorating in the past few weeks. When he wasn't fighting with some of his older coworkers, he was taking time off to visit draft boards from there to Boston and back.

She scribbled some thoughts down on a lined yellow pad. "Do me a favor. Go downstairs and make these proposals to Harry."

"Talk to those goons?" Eddie's laugh was short, bitter. "They'd have me for lunch."

"I need help, Eddie. This isn't something they want to hear from a woman."

"Yeah? Well, they'd rather hear it from a woman than a 4-F, I'll tell you that."

She started to tell him he was being oversensitive, but the memory of the latest in a series of black eyes gave her pause. "Don't worry about it," she said finally. "It's my problem."

Eddie stood up and went back to work, leaving Catherine with the nagging question: what on earth *wasn't* her problem these days? Everything from Eddie's situation to the stopped-up kitchen drain ended up on her shoulders. Something wrong? Call Catherine. She had all the answers. All you had to do was ask.

Trouble was, when it came to her own problems the answers weren't so easy to find. Eddie would probably never find his way into the army, no matter how she wished she could make it right for him. Harry Barnes would never listen to a word she had to say. The workers would stage the walkout they'd threatened and Wilson's productivity would stop cold. And, worst of all, Johnny would pack his duffel bag and disappear from her life forever.

"We've gotta talk."

Her head jerked up and she stared at the man in the doorway to her office. "Johnny?" It didn't seem possible.

He'd disappeared last night after their argument and, as far as she knew, hadn't come back home.

He motioned toward the chair adjacent to her desk. "Can I come in?"

"Of course." She swept the stack of grievances off to one side, then folded her hands primly atop her desk blotter. No more begging him to let her do him a favor. If he wanted to be a tough guy, the kind who needed nobody's help, she'd just let him stew alone. It would serve him right. "What can I do for you?"

"I'm sorry."

She blinked. "What was that?"

"I said, I'm sorry."

"You're kidding." She narrowed her eyes and looked at him. "You're *not* kidding."

He gestured, palms outward. "You think you got the market cornered on apologies?"

She smiled for the first time that day. "I guess not."

"I acted like a jerk last night."

"Yes, you did." She fiddled with the band of her watch, aware of how little she actually understood about him.

"You meant well."

"But?"

"But I can't take you up on it."

She nodded. "I understand."

He leaned forward, elbows resting on his knees. "I don't think so."

"Does it matter, Johnny? Your mind's made up. There's nothing I can do to change it. You told me that last night."

He broke eye contact, his gaze drifting toward the window. Any hope that he'd had a change of heart disappeared. Sighing, she was about to reach for the stack of papers she'd pushed aside when Eddie showed up in her doorway for the second time that morning.

"I think I blew it." He glanced over at Johnny, then, obviously decided to ignore him. "Barnes is on the warpath."

Catherine's stomach knotted. "What happened?"

Eddie stepped into the room, his back still to the other man. "Remember those grievances you wanted me to talk to him about? Well, I tried to deal with the men on their level but no dice. They told me—" He cast a quick glance over his shoulder at Johnny. "Let's just say I'm not the guy they want to talk to."

More than that, Eddie had infuriated the men, and Wilson Manufacturing now teetered on the brink of a major strike. She didn't know whether to cry or to grab Eddie and throttle him. Instead she sifted through the papers on her desk, searching for the key to avoid a work stoppage. "Like it nor not, they'll have to deal with me." She pushed her chair back and stood. "I'm going to—"

"I can do it."

Both Catherine and Eddie turned to stare at Johnny, who stared calmly back at them.

"You're kidding." Eddie's voice had a nasty tone.

Johnny ignored him. His eyes met and held Catherine's. "I've listened to what you have to say and I understand. Give me five minutes to look at your notes and I'll go down there and talk to the guys."

"I don't know..." Why on earth would Johnny think he could succeed where she and Eddie had failed?

"Look." Johnny rose to his feet. "I know these guys. I grew up with guys like that." He shot Eddie a look Catherine didn't particularly like, but Eddie kept his own gaze fastened on the view from the window. "I speak their language."

Catherine felt her resolve weaken. "Do you really think they'll listen?"

"I can't make any promises."

Eddie snorted. "Why is it that doesn't surprise me?"

"Eddie," she snapped. "Let's listen to what Johnny has to say." She focused her attention back on the soldier. "You're sure you want to do this? Last night you made your feelings very clear."

He brushed her words aside. "Last night was last night. I can do this for you, Cathy."

It didn't take more than a second for her to make up her mind. The situation was dire. She doubted if anything he did could make it any worse. Besides, she had a sneaking suspicion he just might be the ace up her sleeve.

"Okay." She extended her right hand. "You're on."

They shook on it while Eddie mumbled something ominous from the doorway. She handed Johnny the papers, gave him a brief rundown on the current situation.

"Am I missing anything, Eddie?"

Unfortunately Eddie was no longer there.

"He stormed out a few minutes ago," said Johnny.

"Oh." She couldn't waste time worrying about Eddie's fits of pique. There were more important issues at hand. "I'll take you into the factory and introduce you to Harry."

"No. If you do that, you'll ruin everything. This has to be clean or you don't stand a chance of smoothing the rough spots."

She told him where to find Harry Barnes, then sat down to wait.

SO ALL CATHERINE'S talk was a lie.

She'd said Wilson Manufacturing was like one big family and in a way she was right. It was one big family, all right. A loud and angry family, hell-bent on tearing itself apart from the inside. Catherine and that 4-F, Eddie Martin, might know how to deal with the government and suppliers, but they didn't know a damn thing about dealing with men who made a living working with their hands.

But Johnny did.

That afternoon he spoke to them from the heart, the Brooklyn kid still struggling to make good. Sure it helped that his story had preceded him. Tom Wilson was held in high esteem by his employees; his daughter was, as well, but not for the same reasons. They admired Cathy's spirit, the way she had jumped into the fray, determined to hold the company together—no matter the cost—until her dad came home and took over again. Harry Barnes and his pals didn't give a hang about the bottom line or productivity. What they cared about was a weekly paycheck big enough to keep a roof over their heads and food on their tables.

Johnny understood and it came across. Barnes backed off on the idea of a walkout. Cathy gave an inch or two on their demands. Johnny was able to walk between the two enemy camps and keep them talking to each other. The walkout was tabled for the time being, and it seemed apparent to everybody that it was all Johnny's doing.

When he returned to Catherine's office she was standing by the window, her delicate profile silhouetted against the winter sunlight that streamed through the panes of glass. She turned to face him, and for an instant he couldn't quite draw a steady breath.

"Well?" She sounded jittery, apprehensive.

His fingers flashed the victory sign, which Winston Churchill had made so popular on the home front. "They're going to keep working."

She exhaled slowly and he watched, mesmerized, as the apprehension on her face turned to pleasure. "Well, what do you know, Johnny Danza. We're in your debt again." There was an edge to both her voice and her smile that only an idiot would have missed. "Would you be offended if I bought you lunch?"

"Yes." What the heck, he might as well go for broke this time around. "If you're with me, I pay."

She nodded. "I thought you'd say that."

She wanted to offer him a job at Wilson, but was afraid he'd blow up at her the way he had the night before.

He wanted her to offer him a job at Wilson, but couldn't swallow his pride long enough to ask for one.

For an unsteady moment they watched each other, neither one sure what the other's next move would be.

"Johnny, would you—"

"Cathy, about last night—"

They laughed nervously.

"Ladies first," he said.

She had nothing to lose. "I'm in trouble here, Johnny. I need your help. They won't talk to a woman the way they'll talk to you. Would you reconsider working here at Wilson?"

"Yes."

"Yes, you'll reconsider?"

Quit being cute, Danza, he thought. *Don't let her get away from you.* "Yes, I'll take the job."

She put out her hand and they shook on it—maybe for an instant longer than necessary, but neither one acknowledged that fact. Though she felt funny talking about wages with Johnny, she threw out a number and he nodded.

"Sounds fair," he said.

She agreed, even though she knew there wasn't enough money in the world to repay him for all he'd done for the Wilson family. "You'll have to fill out some papers," she said, almost apologetically. "Quite a few of them actually."

"Can't be as many as I filled out for Uncle Sam."

"Miriam will get you started." She told him where to find the personnel manager.

"Sounds great," he said, meeting her eyes.

She ducked her head for an instant. "Well," she said, "I guess I'd better get back to work."

He opened his mouth to say something but thought better of it. "See you at home."

"Yes," she said smiling. "I'll see you at home."

Whistling, he headed down the hallway to find Miriam.

The factory was no place for a woman like Catherine, but it was the place where Johnny belonged.

March 1, 1945

Dear Gerry,

The newspapers are filled with the latest bombing of Tokyo. They say the Pacific Fleet's been attacking Japanese convoys. I couldn't sleep at all last night, worrying that you might be in danger.

Doesn't everything seem to be happening at once? Uncle Les isn't very happy about the meeting President Roosevelt had at Yalta with Churchill and Stalin. Uncle Les says we shouldn't trust the Russians, but I can't imagine that they would ever do anything to hurt us. If we can't trust our Allies, who can we trust?

Maybe I'm just getting nervous, Gerry. I don't understand a lot about battles and strategy, but even I can see that this time the end really is right around the corner. For three years almost you've lived right here inside my head. Your voice is *my* voice. I have that picture of you from your high-school graduation, from back before you joined the navy. I bet you don't even look that way anymore.

I'm scared, Gerry. I know I love you, the person you are deep inside, but what if I don't measure up to the me you've created inside your head? What if you decide you don't really like girls with red hair and freckles? What if I'm taller than you thought or uglier? What if you don't like my New York accent?

I know we agree on the big things, like being Catholic and having a houseful of children and loving each other forever and ever, but what about the little things? I want a dog, a big beautiful collie like Lassie. I want a house somewhere that isn't here. I can't imagine spending my whole life in Forest Hills when there's a great big world out there to discover. Mom loves knowing things will be the same day after day after day, and I know Cathy would be happy to spend her whole life right here, too. I want something more, Gerry. I want something that's all ours. Something that isn't like anything anyone has ever had before.

With all my love,
Nancy

Chapter Eleven

March 1945 brought with it more changes.

The marines won a bloody victory claiming Mount Suribachi on the island of Iwo Jima. The cost for Americans was high, but Old Glory once again flew on the mountaintop.

General MacArthur returned to a freed Manila, the "Pearl of the Orient," and swore that no enemy would ever displace the Stars and Stripes.

James Byrnes, head of the Office of War Mobilization, announced that 600,000 civilians had left the defense industry in 1944. Most had taken jobs in nonessential industries; some no longer worked at all. Byrnes declared they must return to war plants immediately. Now wasn't the time to ease the pressure on the enemy; now was the time to knuckle down and continue the fight. New signs joined the Loose Lips Sink Ships posters on the walls at Wilson Manufacturing. One was particularly effective in combating absenteeism: a picture of a well-scrubbed, wholesome young soldier in uniform and the words "This Soldier May Die— Unless You Man this Idle Machine."

A letter came from Tom. A letter filled with certainty that he'd be home before the year was over. "The Nazis are on the run," he wrote. "The good guys are going to come out on top, you'll see...." No one seemed to notice the air of desperation that permeated his words. Dot lived for her work at the hospital, for her family, and for the day when her beloved husband would come back home and life would get back to normal.

Nancy and Gerry continued their long-distance courtship. Of course nobody took her seriously, and her engagement to the young navy man was all but ignored. How could she possibly know what she was doing, falling in love with a boy she'd never even met? Once the war was over she'd come to her senses and fall in love with somebody she'd at least laid eyes on.

And then there was Catherine. Life at Wilson Manufacturing was as bumpy as a night flight over Tokyo. Eddie Martin's fruitless quest for acceptance into the military had taken its toll on him. More often than not he showed up for work on Monday mornings with a black eye and a brutal hangover. The bruises faded; his anger, unfortunately, did not.

The long hard hours necessary to keep a defense plant at maximum productivity no longer appealed to workers eager for some free time to spend the money they'd been making. You could almost smell victory in the wind. Before long it would be time to stop making metal parts for tanks and battleships and start gearing up for peacetime production in what promised to be a time of booming prosperity.

Oh yes, Catherine knew it was time to start thinking about the future.

And every time she did, it seemed her mind turned to thoughts of Johnny Danza.

Johnny had settled into life at the plant as easily as he had settled into life at home. The men liked him; the women adored him. Only Eddie seemed to find fault with his performance. Johnny knew when to roll up his sleeves and pitch in. He knew when to stand toe-to-toe with Barnes and lay down the law. And he certainly had no problem storming into Catherine's office when he felt she was being unfair to her employees.

His intentions to move out of the Wilson home had been honorable, but the housing shortage had conspired against him. When Dot offered him their finished basement, he had no choice but to accept. "I'll pay the going rate," he'd insisted, all male pride and bravado. "Not a cent less."

Cathy's heart had swelled with emotions she didn't dare put a name to. She couldn't imagine not having Johnny around the house. The sound of his voice, the sight of him across the dinner table at night, the touch of his hand against her elbow as he ushered her into the train as they rode to work in the morning... Had there even been a time when Johnny wasn't part of her life?

Sometimes late at night she'd lie awake in her narrow bed, restless, tangled in the sheets, painfully aware that his long sinewy body had once rested in that same spot. Now and again she could almost convince herself that his scent lingered in the pillow. The memory of how he had felt beneath her hands tormented her. Christmas Eve she had washed that broad chest, his muscled back, let her gaze linger over his flat abdomen...

She was a bundle of conflicting emotions, yearning toward what she knew she could never have. They were so different, she and Johnny, so impossibly different in every way you could possibly list. And yet the connection was there, the attraction.

Or was it?

That kiss on New Year's Eve had shattered her defenses. But apparently it had meant little to Johnny because not once had he attempted to kiss her again. And, God knew, she had given him ample opportunity!

The Weavers tossed themselves a thirtieth anniversary party on St. Patrick's Day. Catherine and Johnny didn't go to the party as a couple, but they did arrive at the same time and leave at the same time, and they did spend all the time in between talking and laughing together. But still no kiss.

Catherine stared in the mirror and experimented with new hairstyles and different shades of lipstick. But Johnny didn't seem to notice.

Or worse, maybe he didn't care.

Maybe she wasn't his type. The thought struck terror into her heart. Maybe all this time she'd been fooling herself into believing he cared for her as a woman, not as a little sister. The awful realization that he might care for her the same way he cared for Nancy brought tears to her eyes, and as March drew to a close, she struggled to keep her emotions safely locked inside her heart.

IT WAS THE FIRST SATURDAY in April, the kind of day you threw open the windows and let the gentle fragrant breezes clean house. Nancy had gone shopping at Macy's with her best friend. Dot was busy scrubbing the kitchen floor while she sang along with the radio. "My Dreams Are Getting Better All the Time" was her favorite song and it seemed to symbolize the wave of optimism she and most Americans were riding.

Catherine had awakened early, filled with energy. She'd slipped into a pair of dungarees and an old shirt of her father's, then headed out into the backyard, determined to get a head start on preparing the small plot of land they used for a Victory Garden. Last year she'd been drowning in a sea of sorrow, unable to look around and see the trees budding and hear the birds singing—all the clichéd and wonderful signs of the earth renewing itself once again.

She was wrist-deep in weeds when she heard a familiar voice behind her.

"Isn't it a little early in the year to plant?"

Shielding her eyes with the back of her hand, she turned and looked up at Johnny. "It's never too early to be prepared. There's a lot to be done before Mom plants her vegetable garden. I thought I'd pull my own weight this year for a change."

He nodded as if what she'd said made perfect sense to him.

She laughed and tossed a clump of dandelion at him. "You know you Brooklyn boys don't have a clue what I'm talking about. Where did you think all your canned vegetables came from?" Canned vegetables were shipped to the front while civilians turned to their Victory Gardens for fresh products.

He brushed the toe of his right shoe against the rake and hoe lying on the ground by her side. "I was stationed in Kansas before the war. Learned the world wasn't all glass and concrete."

"Nature boy, huh?" She grinned and motioned toward the gardening equipment next to her. "Grab yourself a rake and refresh your memory."

He hesitated and she instantly felt contrite.

"Look," she said, scrambling to her feet and brushing the dirt from her knees, "I don't mean to sound like I'm barking out orders. I guess it's a holdover from the factory."

"Good," he said, sticking his hands into his pants pockets. "So you don't have to stick around?"

She shook her head. What on earth was he driving at, anyway? "No. I just thought I'd get a head start on the Victory Garden."

"I was thinking we could take the train into Manhattan, walk around Central Park, maybe take in a show, dinner..." His words trailed off. "What do you say?"

"I says it's sounds absolutely wonderful."

The look of happiness on his face thrilled her. "Can you be ready around noon?"

"You bet!" She extended her hand and he helped her to her feet. "I'd better go change."

He made a show of inspecting her muddy jeans and threadbare shirt. "I think you look pretty cute the way you are."

"Very funny." She waggled her dusty gloves at him. "I'll meet you at noon in front of the house."

She burst into the kitchen in a whirl of excitement.

"What on earth?" Dot spun around from the icebox she was defrosting. Pans of hot water and soggy newspapers were piled up on her freshly washed floor. "Make a paste of baking soda and water. I'll pull out the stinger!"

Catherine, who was yanking off her soggy loafers, started to laugh. "I haven't been stung by a bee, Mother."

Dot's expression shifted from concern to blatant curiosity. "Then what's all this commotion about? You look like you've been shot out of a cannon."

It was impossible to contain her elation. "I'm going to spend the day in the city."

Dot arched on eyebrow. "Oh, really?"

"Yes. I'm going for a walk in Central Park, maybe take in a show, dinner..." She tried to keep a straight face but failed miserably. "I'm going out on a date, Mom," she said, bursting into laughter. "With Johnny!"

"You look beautiful, honey." Dot's eyes shone with pride ninety minutes later. "Like something out of a fashion magazine."

Catherine looked at her reflection in the bedroom mirror and frowned. "Are you certain this dress doesn't look its age?"

"Positive. With that belt it looks almost brand-new."

Catherine studied herself carefully. The white belt set off her narrow waist and emphasized the graceful lines of the gently flaring skirt that came just at the middle of her knee. The bodice fit snugly; the deep U-neckline bared her collarbone, while the short puffed sleeves narrowed in to a starched cuff a fraction above her elbow. It was the perfect springtime dress. Young and fresh and pastel pink with buttons shaped like rosebuds. With her white gloves and peekaboo hat, it could almost pass for something from *Vogue*!

"Well," she said, grabbing her purse from the dressing table, "I'm off."

Dot gave her a big hug. "You have a wonderful time, honey."

Catherine managed a nervous smile. "Are you sure I shouldn't pin my hair up?"

Dot laughed and pushed her out the door. "Positive. You look beautiful with it down around your shoulders. You're only young once, honey. Now go out and meet your young man."

Johnny was pacing the sidewalk in front of the house. His hair was neatly combed and he wore dark gray trousers, cuffless thanks to the war effort, a white shirt and tie, and a suit jacket. He had filled out considerably since his return home, and she noted the way his shoulders strained the seams of his jacket as he raised a cigarette to his mouth. She'd seen him every single day for the past three months, but suddenly she felt as if he was a stranger. He turned and grinned at her as she started down the steps. *An extremely handsome stranger . . .*

"You look swell," he said, stubbing out his cigarette on the sidewalk with the toe of his shoe.

"Thank you." Her own feet, in her open-toed pumps, looked so small next to his. "So do you."

He looked down at her. She looked up at him. He wouldn't kiss her right there in the middle of Hansen Street, would he? He moved closer. Her breath caught. Instead of kissing her, he reached for her hand and they started down the block for the subway station. Outwardly she looked cool, calm and collected. Inwardly she felt like a giddy high-school girl on her first date.

Les was sweeping his front stoop and they waved as they strolled past. He had a great big smile on his face and Catherine suspected he was going to toss down his broom and run inside to tell Edna the news the moment she and Johnny disappeared around the corner. Maybe she didn't look quite as cool and calm as she'd first thought.

The E train was noisy and crowded, and they amused themselves by reading the advertising placards that lined the walls of the car. "Lucky Strike Green Goes To War," "Don't be a public enemy! Be patriotic and smother sneezes with Kleenex to help keep colds from spreading to war workers" and AT&T's exhortation, "Joe needs long-distance lines tonight," warning civilians to use the telephone only when absolutely necessary. Photos of beauty-queen contestants claimed a fair amount of wall space, and they took turns guessing who the winner of this month's Miss Subways contest would be.

Every single day they rode this same train together, looked at the same advertisements without comment. Why did it all seem new today, new and wonderful and exciting?

They exited at Fifth Avenue and climbed the endless steps to street level where, to their amazement, they found flower vendors selling white gardenias and luscious purple orchids at "a special price just for you."

Johnny purchased a white gardenia. He reached up and removed her peekaboo hat, then tucked the fragrant flower behind her ear. "Thank you," she whispered, breathing deeply of the sweet smell. "It's beautiful."

He touched her cheek with the tip of his fingers. "So are you."

They fell into an embarrassed—and delighted—silence and headed up Fifth Avenue. A few big yellow Checker cabs glided by, and huge double-decker buses rumbled past, but much of the traffic she remembered from pre-War years had disappeared thanks to gas rationing. Other than that it was easy to pretend there wasn't a war going on, that this was the same graceful world that had existed before Pearl Harbor.

"Look at that beautiful dress," she sighed as a tall brunette in ivory silk drifted by. "I'll bet that cost thirty or forty dollars."

Johnny did a double take. "Thirty dollars for a dress?" He shook his head. "Looks like I've been away longer than I thought."

"She also had hose on," Catherine said. "Just goes to show you that if you're rich enough you can find anything you want."

Johnny looked at her sharply. "You noticed all of that in two seconds?"

"You'd be surprised what a woman notices." She was starved for fashion and feminine fripperies, more starved than even she had realized. "She was wearing a pearl choker, two circle pins, and the most cunning button earrings I've ever seen."

Johnny stared at her in amazement. "What color were her eyes?"

"I don't know, but her lipstick was Max Factor's medium red."

"She didn't look any better than you, Cathy."

Catherine started to tell him he was crazy, that she couldn't hold a candle to truly fashionable ladies, but she caught herself at the expression in his eyes. A warm feeling that had nothing to do with the balmy spring weather filled her heart. "Thank you," she said instead.

They angled across the street and into Central Park.

"Where to?" asked Johnny as they set off down the path. "The lake, the carousel, the zoo—"

"The zoo!" she exclaimed. "I haven't been to the zoo in years!"

The zoo was exactly as she remembered it, small and delightful and filled with memories of her childhood. The balloon vendors, whose wares had been sacrificed to wartime production, weren't around, but the peanut sellers still plied their treats along the pathways. Johnny bought two paper bags of the salted nuts, and Catherine stripped off her gloves and proceeded to feed the pigeons who flocked around them in obvious delight.

By the boating lake they sat together on a wrought-iron bench and watched the lovers in their rowboats and the little children whose paper and wood skiffs glided across the smooth water.

Johnny let go of her hand and her heart sank—until she realized he was about to drape his arm about her shoulders. She could feel his heat through the fabric of his suit. His fingers rested lightly across her shoulder, grazing her collarbone, tantalizing her with a thousand promises. She was aware of every breath he took, every movement of every muscle. Once she turned to watch a little girl run after her puppy and her breasts brushed against his side. The heat inside her body matched his own.

"Have you ever ridden the carousel?" he asked as a private nurse in her crisp white uniform and sleek navy blue cape walked by, pushing her tiny charge in an elegant English baby carriage.

"No," she managed, acutely aware of the picture they made as they sat there. *Lovers,* she thought. *People probably think we're lovers. . . .*

He grinned at her and she felt the pressure on her shoulder increase. "Feel like horseback riding?"

She grinned back, heart soaring. "I'd love it!"

The carousel was back near the entrance at Sixtieth Street and they raced down the path. Catherine was gasping for breath when they reached the elaborate and beautiful merry-go-round with its painted ponies straight out of a fairy tale. Johnny bought two tickets and the moment the carousel came to a stop, they went to claim their steeds.

Catherine fell in love with a glorious palomino with a mane of golden curls and eyes bluer than the April skies overhead. How to climb aboard her mount was the question of the moment, but Johnny came to her rescue. He put one hand on each side of her waist. She could feel the difference in strength on his right side, but he swept her up into the air and deposited her sidesaddle on her painted pony as if there was no problem at all.

He swung himself onto the horse next to her. The touch of his hands on her waist lingered, and she couldn't keep from anticipating the moment when the carousel stopped and he would sweep her into his arms again and help her dismount. Round and round went the carousel as the giddiness inside her heart grew. How hard it was to tear her gaze away from him. His neatly combed hair was tousled now by the breeze; she could almost feel its silkiness against her cheek, smell the fragrance of the hair tonic he used. How commanding his profile was, with his cheekbones high and pronounced, his straight nose and strong proud chin.

The carousel slowed to a stop. Her horse halted at the highest position off the ground and she waited, her breath caught, as Johnny jumped from his own horse and came to fetch her. Her skirt rode up an extra inch and she felt the heat of Johnny's gaze on her exposed flesh. His shoulder brushed her bare knees as he gripped her once again by the waist. The contact was intimate, as thrilling as it was unexpected. He swept her from the horse and held her, suspended, for a long and painfully sweet moment with his breath warm against her bare neck.

"We can ride again," he said, his voice low for her alone.

"We could," she said, her gaze lingering shamelessly on his mouth, the curve of his strong jaw.

"Or we could just stand here." His words were a caress, lingering, seductive.

"I'd like that, too."

She felt as if they were enclosed in a world of their own, a magical place that had never existed before that moment, a haven where—

"Hey! Whaddya doin'? Posin' for animal crackers?" A woman's Brooklynese voice shattered the spring air. "Either get on or get off. I got my eye on that horse."

There was nothing to do but laugh. Johnny set Catherine firmly on the ground. She resumed normal breathing. But that moment, that magical wondrous moment, still lingered.

They cut across the grass, past the skating rink, then again followed the footpath back to the Fifty-ninth Street exit. The Plaza Hotel, looking for all the world like an enormous French château, set down in the middle of Manhattan, bustled with activity as fashionably dressed men and women nodded their way past the liveried doorman.

They headed down Fifth Avenue, where beautiful women in elegant day wear carried parcels neatly tied in bright red ribbons. Men in suits vied for sidewalk space with boys in uniform, who stumbled over their own shoes as they gazed at the sights that only New York had to offer.

Not that Catherine or Johnny noticed any of it. Something magical had happened back at the carousel—their friendship had made the final, inevitable turn into romance. The city fell away from them, becoming only a backdrop to the enchantment that held them both in its thrall.

Johnny felt as if he were walking on air. For almost two years he'd dreamed about a day like this, never believing Lady Luck would smile on him.

Well, not only had Lady Luck smiled on him, she'd handed him the keys to heaven in the bargain!

Catherine was smart, compassionate, headstrong—and probably the loveliest girl he'd ever known. And she didn't seem to realize how beautiful she was. Heads turned as they strolled toward Times Square, and his chest swelled with pride as he saw the looks of envy on the faces of the guys they passed.

Funny thing, though. He used to think the best thing in the world was to have a beautiful girl on his arm, the kind of girl who caused a commotion everywhere she went. To his surprise, he'd discovered that while being with a beautiful girl was every bit as wonderful as he'd imagined, it was even better to be with a beautiful girl who had brains.

Who'd have thought it? War had changed him; that was a fact. He'd gone off a cocky hotshot with a failed marriage under his belt and a heckuva lot of bravado. He came home a cocky hotshot with a failed marriage under his belt and a different view of the way things were. He'd been put to the test and come out aces high. He'd never figured himself for the hero type, but when push came to shove, he'd found the courage and compassion to do the right thing. He'd paid a price—the partial paralysis of his arm was proof of that—but if he had it to do all over again, he'd save Tom Wilson's life even if it meant losing his own.

Whaddya know? Johnny Danza, the orphan kid from Brooklyn, was a better man than he'd figured. A nice thing to find out on the afternoon of your twenty-sixth birthday.

He looked down at Catherine, at her honey-colored hair sparkling in the sunshine. A swell way to spend the afternoon of your twenty-sixth birthday, walking hand in hand with the girl you loved.

Not that he was ready to say those words yet. They kind of scared him. Each time he thought he was ready to give Cathy the letter he'd written from his hospital bed, his feet turned cold as ice and he stuffed it back into the drawer of the nightstand. He'd made one mistake when he was young and lonely, and he wasn't about to make another one. Especially not if his mistake could hurt Catherine. That was the one thing he would never do.

Today, however, was nothing but blue skies and sunshine as they turned onto West Fifty-second Street. Fancy night spots that featured good food, good drink, and the best dance music in town lined both sides of the street. In a few hours the sounds of laughter and boogie woogie would spill from the windows and doors, bringing the entire neighborhood to life.

In his breast pocket were two tickets for *Oklahoma!*, burning a hole right through the fabric. He'd bought them a few weeks ago, meaning to ask Catherine to go with him. But the big war hero had trouble screwing up his nerve, and it wasn't until this morning, in a do-or-die moment, that he'd finally asked her to spend the day with him. She still didn't know about the tickets to the Broadway musical. He hoped she liked surprises.

CATHERINE loved surprises.

"We could see a movie," she suggested after a turkey dinner at Toffenetti's. "*A Tree Grows in Brooklyn* is playing right around the corner."

"I have a better idea."

Johnny slid the pair of tickets under her dessert plate, and when she saw the word *Oklahoma!* she almost swooned.

Thirty minutes later they made their way to the elegant old theater. "What wonderful seats," Catherine said as they settled down in the eighth row center. "How did you ever manage them?"

Johnny grinned and ducked his head. "It's not hard when you buy them two months ahead."

"Two months? You bought these tickets two months ago?"

"Yeah, well, it's kind of a special occasion." He met her eyes. "My birthday."

"Oh, Johnny!" Before she had a chance to consider her actions, she leaned close to him and planted a kiss on his cheek. The slight scratch of stubble against her lips sent a thrill of excitement up her spine. The soft brush of her mouth against his cheek made Johnny's head spin.

Finally the house lights dimmed and the theater went dark. Catherine held on to Johnny's hand as the orchestra launched into the overture. In no time they were swept up in the story. The romance of the land. The colorful characters battling the odds. But most of all, the love story of Laurie and Curly.

It was the way he looked at her as if she were a gift from heaven. The way she appeared so delicate and lovely in his brawny arms. The way they tried so hard to pretend that what was happening wasn't really happening at all. When Laurie and Curly sang "People Will Say We're in Love," the truth of their words pierced Catherine's heart and she had to avert her head to keep Johnny from seeing her tears.

But he knew. He felt the truth of the song in his own heart and he gently stroked her hand. The hand that had once worn another man's ring. *There's a chance for us now. Maybe this can be more than a dream....*

They didn't talk much on the way home. The meaningful lyrics still echoed in their heads, and they simply held hands and walked slowly down Hansen Street, happy to be together on such a beautiful night.

They went in the back door; the entrance to Johnny's basement apartment was off the mudroom near the kitchen. The house was quiet and the room was dark. Catherine fumbled for the light switch, but Johnny covered her hand with his.

"Wait a minute," he said, stepping close to her.

"I was going to make us some cof—"

"No." He touched his forefinger to her lips. "Not now."

His mouth covered hers, sweet and light as a springtime breeze. The pressure of his lips against hers was pleasurable, and she sighed as his hands slipped around her waist and held her close. She closed her eyes and placed her hands, palms flat, against his chest. The steady beating of his heart thudded against her fingers and she registered his heat.

She heard a creaking from the hallway, the squeak of footsteps on the stairs. "Johnny, I—"

He again touched her lips with the tip of his index finger. "Shh."

He kissed her again, more deeply this time. He slid his tongue along the place where her upper lip met her lower one, then slipped it inside her willing mouth. She opened her eyes for an instant, almost as if she had to reassure herself that this was really and truly happening, that she wasn't asleep in her bed and dreaming about what would never be. *This is real,* she thought, heart soaring. *Johnny feels the same way I do!*

The silky motion of his tongue against hers set off sparks in her, and it took every ounce of willpower at her command to break away.

"Someone's coming," she whispered, reaching for the light. Before she could flip the switch, he cupped her chin in his hand and whispered something low and tender. When she turned on the light, he was gone.

Chapter Twelve

As it turned out the interruption was a false alarm. Catherine stood motionless in the silent kitchen, aware only of the beating of her heart and the taste of Johnny on her lips.

The basement apartment. All she had to do was go downstairs and tap on the door and—

No. They were right to stop. Their responses to each other were so intense, so dangerous, that she dared not imagine where they might lead.

And so she did what she was supposed to do, what she had been brought up to do. She climbed the stairs to her room alone. The light was on under Nancy's door and Catherine tiptoed swiftly by and on down the hallway. She didn't want to see her sister or her mother. She didn't want to answer questions about her date with Johnny. She didn't want to say or do anything that would diminish the magic, turn the extraordinary into the mundane. The night belonged to her and to Johnny, and she wasn't ready to share it with anyone else.

She had a quick bath, brushed her teeth, then, wrapped in a cotton quilted robe, padded back to her room. Her bed was turned down, the quilt folded at the foot, her pillows fluffed and ready. A cup of hot chocolate sat on her nightstand, along with a note from her mother and an envelope addressed to her.

"Hope you had a wonderful evening, honey," said the note. "Thought you might enjoy this. Talk to you in the morning. Love, Mom. P.S. This letter came for you in the afternoon post."

She sat down on the edge of the bed and looked at the envelope. Johnny's unmistakable scrawl. Her heartbeat accelerated until she could scarcely breathe. Hands trembling, she opened it, then unfolded the two sheets of paper. They were separate letters. The first said:

I wrote this a long time ago. I didn't have the guts to send it to you. Didn't even have the guts to finish it. I still don't, but somehow that doesn't matter anymore. What matters is that you know how I feel about you.

A goodbye, that's what it was. *It's been nice but...* She took a deep breath and unfolded the second letter.

December 1, 1944

Dear Cathy,

I've written this letter over and over in my head for weeks now. For a while I didn't know if I'd ever have the chance to put these words on paper, but now that I do, I'm wondering if it's such a smart thing, after all. But by now I guess you know I'm not always the brightest guy around. I tend to shoot off my mouth first and think second, so why should this be any different?

I'm writing this from a hospital in England. How I got here isn't real important. I'm going to be fine. But being here has given me a chance to think—not something I've done a lot of in my life. You may not like what I've come up with, but here it goes: I think I'm in love with you, Cathy.

I know you're probably ready to throw this letter in the junk pile, but hear me out. I don't know what this means or if there could ever be any kind of future for us, but since the first moment I saw you in your blue dress, you've been part of me. I can tell you everything we said at the Stage Door Canteen. I can remember how you felt in my arms, the way your hair—

I'm not asking much, Cathy, just that you give me a chance. The war won't last forever. Someday soon I'll be back in New York and

That was all there was to the letter, but each word became part of Catherine's heart and soul, and when she finally fell asleep sometime near dawn, she believed there might be a future for them after all.

"WILL YOU LOOK at them?" Dot peeked out the back window the next afternoon and sighed. "I knew it. I knew it from that very first night."

Nancy mumbled something and continued pouring the cream off the top of the bottle of milk. She was as happy for Catherine and Johnny as her mother was, but must she hear about it nonstop? There were other things going on in the house on Hansen Street, other romances that nobody seemed interested in hearing about.

She sighed and patted the tiny bulge in the pocket of her linen skirt. What would they say if they knew Gerry had asked her to marry him? That he'd sent her his high-school ring as a pledge of commitment, to be replaced by the real thing the moment he stepped back on U.S. soil? Would anybody even care?

She poured the last of the cream into the pitcher then placed the paper lid back on the milk bottle. She put the pitcher and bottle into the icebox, then wandered upstairs to her room. Gerry's letters were tied with a red velvet ribbon and tucked in her lingerie drawer. So many hopes and dreams captured on paper and growing closer to coming true. Letters didn't lie. You couldn't write to someone every day for more than three years and not learn an awful lot about him. She bet she knew more about Gerry Sturdevant than most wives knew about their husbands after twenty years of marriage.

She'd been honest with him about herself, too—warts and all. She'd been vain and sweet and generous and selfish, scared and lonely and every other emotion in between, right there in black and white for him to read.

And he still loved her!

It would be nice if her mom and sister could be happy for her, too, but in the end it really didn't matter. All that mattered was Gerry and the future she knew they'd have together.

CATHERINE DIDN'T MENTION the love letter and Johnny didn't ask if she'd received it. She bumped into him on her way home from church the next morning, and in the light of day it was hard to believe she had been swept into the arms of such a handsome man.

Or been kissed by him . . .

"I like that," he said, tugging playfully at the brim of her best spring hat.

"I like your smile," she said.

Oh, God, what on earth had possessed her to say something as forward and silly as that? She blushed furiously, but the embarrassed yet pleased twinkle in his blue eyes made up for it.

"Had trouble sleeping last night," he said as they walked side by side down Hansen Street.

"Me, too." She hesitated. "I kept thinking about the play."

His glance thrilled her down to her toes. "Not me. I kept thinking about you."

Her lips still registered the sweet pressure of his mouth. She was acutely aware of his closeness, of the way his arm brushed against hers, of how deeply she wished he would link his strong fingers with hers.

"That was the best birthday I've ever had," he said as they passed the Weavers' house.

"You should have had a party," she said, looking up at him. "And a birthday cake."

He shrugged. "Never had either one."

"You're kidding!" She couldn't imagine having twenty-six birthdays without any acknowledgment.

"Not a lot of celebrating in orphanages, Cathy."

She touched his forearm. "I forgot, Johnny. I'm sorry." *Idiot! How can you be so insensitive?* Not everyone had been as lucky as she and Nancy.

"Doesn't matter. Yesterday made up for it."

Her breath caught as he took her hand in his. "I still think you need a birthday cake."

He grinned. "Yeah?"

"Definitely! And I'm going to see that you get one."

AT FIRST Johnny didn't believe it was happening. She'd said she was going to make him a birthday cake, but a lot of people say a lot of things and most of those things never happen.

He should have known Catherine was different. She'd disappeared for a few hours that afternoon and he'd heard all sorts of noises coming from the kitchen, accompanied by some tantalizing aromas.

Mrs. Wilson served the usual Sunday dinner of roast chicken, gravy, mashed potatoes and string beans, and he was about to get up and help clear the table when Catherine put her hands on his shoulders and pushed him back down into his seat. "You stay there," she cautioned, eyes dancing with mischief. "We'll bring dessert out."

He sat there listening to their laughter floating out from the kitchen. He knew it had to have something to do with his birthday, but he figured on rice pudding with a candle in the middle of it. Not for a minute did he expect the big beautiful chocolate cake with fluffy white frosting and a dozen skinny blue candles burning brightly around the edges.

Their off-key rendition of "Happy Birthday" sounded better to him than the voices he'd heard last night at the theater. Especially Catherine's.

She placed the cake down on the table in front of him. Her thick honey-colored hair was gathered in a ponytail and tied with a pink velvet ribbon. "Happy Birthday, Johnny," she said, her voice soft as summer rain.

A lump formed in his throat. Years and years of being alone, or wishing for things he could never have, and now... He struggled to maintain his composure.

"Make a wish!" Nancy cried as Mrs. Wilson set out the dessert plates and forks. "Make a wish, then blow out the candles."

He looked at the birthday cake, then at the women standing around the table. Make a wish...

He met Catherine's eyes. She smiled at him, a private smile. The kind of smile a man dreams about. He made his wish.

And then he blew out the candles.

CATHERINE AND JOHNNY did their best to keep their feelings a secret at Wilson Manufacturing, but trying to hide new love is an impossible task. They glowed with it, warming everyone who came near. It was a pleasure to have something new to talk about in a world that was sick to death of war, and everyone, even Harry Barnes and his ilk, couldn't help but be affected, if only for a moment.

Everyone, that was, except Eddie Martin. From the start he'd made it clear Johnny wasn't his favorite person, and to Catherine's regret, Johnny hadn't done anything to help change that situation. Johnny was many things, but tolerant wasn't one of them. Catherine had tried to explain Eddie's problem to him, but he couldn't—or wouldn't—understand. No matter that Eddie had spent the better part of three years trying to get into the army; all Johnny saw was the end result.

And that end result was the saddest thing of all. The war was winding down, and with it went Eddie's hopes of ever serving his country. There were so many things Catherine wanted to say to him, but Eddie had erected a wall of liquor around himself that she couldn't breach. He called in sick more times than she would tolerate from any other employee, but still she tried to look the other way. He was in pain and she wouldn't do anything to make that pain any worse.

There were times she felt that she'd somehow failed Eddie. Her life had changed drastically since Johnny exploded into it that Christmas Eve, and perhaps she'd been less of a friend to Eddie than she could have been. When she'd broached the topic with him a few days after her first real date with Johnny, Eddie had brushed off her attempt with a wave of his hand.

At least she'd tried, but it just didn't feel as if she'd done enough.

But of course there were many other things to think about those first days in April. Allied tanks were pushing toward Berlin while the British swept eastward across the Westphalian plain. The Russians took Danzig and invaded Austria while, in the Pacific, six task forces were operating off the Ryukyus.

And then there was Johnny. She made dinner for him twice, elaborate affairs made possible by the extra ration coupons she had begged and borrowed from friends and neighbors. They went to movies at the Forest Hills and the Elmwood cinemas, but rarely remembered what they saw. Kissing in the balcony was as much fun at twenty-three as it had been at sixteen.

Catherine worked an hour late on the second Thursday in April. Johnny was waiting for her at the front gate of the factory. He had long since run out of his army-issue Camel cigarettes and was smoking one of the roll-your-own brands most civilians had been reduced to.

He brushed a lock of hair back from her forehead. "You look tired."

She nodded. It had been a long day, one filled with personnel problems. "You didn't have to wait for me."

He grinned. "Sure I did."

"I'm so tired I'm asleep on my feet."

"I can take care of that."

He swept her up into his arms and she shrieked with laughter. "Johnny! Put me down! Someone might see us."

"Let them." He kissed her on the lips, right there in the middle of the street. "I missed you today." He'd spent most of it out on an excursion to western Long Island to talk with a Mr. Levitt who had some ideas for constructing housing in what were expansive potato fields.

She ducked her head as he went to kiss her again. "Johnny, please! What if one of the workers sees me?"

He put her down but he didn't let her go as they headed toward the subway. "Isn't it about time we went public?"

"I thought we agreed that wasn't a good idea—at least, not at the factory." Being the owner's daughter was difficult enough; being Johnny's girl would be impossible.

"You won't be at the factory forever."

Her heart bumped up against her rib cage. "I won't?" It was a struggle to keep the emotion from her voice.

He took her elbow and guided her down the subway stairs. "You hear what's happening out there," he said as he dropped a nickel into each of the two turnstiles. "The Nazis are practically done for, and it won't be long before the Japanese are in the same boat. Your dad's going to come home one day soon, Cathy, and want his office back."

She bit her lip and kept her gaze fastened on the steps as they hurried down another flight to the platform below. *You dope, Catherine*, she thought as she blinked back tears. Here she'd been imagining Johnny was about to propose marriage, and all he wanted to talk about was the war coming to an end. She didn't pay much attention to his words. All she knew was that he wasn't asking her to marry him—

and that she was more disappointed than she'd have ever imagined.

It was a little after six-thirty when the train slid into the station at Continental Avenue.

"Mom and Nancy are going to a church supper with Aunt Edna," Catherine said as they strolled toward home. "Maybe we should stop at the deli and get some bologna or something. I'll make us sandwiches." She stifled a yawn.

"I have a better idea." He steered her back toward Continental Avenue. "How does the T-Bone Diner sound to you?"

"Like the answer to a prayer." The thought of doing anything even as energetic as spreading mustard on a slice of rye was dreadful. "They have the best egg-salad sandwiches in town."

How splendid it was to stroll down the street with your best beau. She loved holding hands with him, walking proudly next to a man as tall and handsome as Johnny. People said they made a lovely couple. She tried to pretend that didn't matter one whit, but the truth was she wanted everyone in the world to notice them, to smile at them, to acknowledge just how perfect she and Johnny were together.

The diner was doing a brisk business these days, what with the wartime prosperity, and Catherine considered themselves fortunate to find a booth near the rear. She and Johnny made light conversation while they waited for their orders to be served, but the moment their triple-decker sandwiches arrived they got down to the business of eating.

"You should've ordered the BLT," Johnny said, reaching for his chocolate malted. He snitched a French fry from her plate.

She laughed and made a grab for his coleslaw when something at the counter caught her eye. She froze, her fork poised in midair. Maisie, the counter waitress, was crying into her apron, and from the expression on her customers' faces, she wasn't crying over her tips.

"Something terrible's happened." Catherine tore her gaze away from Maisie. "Look Johnny." She gestured toward the counter. "Look at their faces."

Johnny lowered his sandwich to his plate. "Maybe she got some bad news about her kid." Maisie had a son who flew bombers somewhere in the Pacific.

A cold sweat broke out at the back of Catherine's neck. "I don't think so." She grabbed Johnny's wrist. "You don't think we've lost the war, do you?" A hundred possibilities, all of them terrible, occurred to her. What if the Japanese had bombed Pearl Harbor again or—worse—what if they had somehow managed to bomb the California coast? There'd been talk of Japanese firebombs scattered throughout the Oregon forests.

A woman at a window table started to sob, while the man she was with lowered his head and began to cry openly. The cook came out of the kitchen with a radio, plugged it in, then placed it on top of the counter. He fiddled with the dial as static crackled through the diner. Johnny reached for Catherine's hand.

"... unexpected news. For those of you just joining our broadcast..." The radio announcer's voice trembled, then gathered strength. "For those of you just joining our broadcast, it is our sad, sad duty to announce that at 3:55 Eastern War Time our beloved President, Franklin Delano Roosevelt, died of a cerebral hemorrhage at the Little White House in Warm Springs, Georgia. His funeral cortege will be brought by railroad tonight to the capital. Sources close to Mrs. Roosevelt say—"

The cook clicked off the radio. The diner was silent save for the sound of crying. Catherine's tears flowed freely, and she looked across the table to see Johnny wiping away tears of his own.

Their meal was forgotten. By silent agreement they both rose and, after paying their tab at the cash register, started walking. They had no destination in mind, but it didn't matter. Motion was what was important. Maybe if they kept moving they could stay one step ahead of the terrible truth.

"It's so unfair," Catherine said as they walked past the Forest Hills Inn. "We're so close to winning the war. Why did he have to die now?"

"Who said life is fair?" Johnny stroked her hair. "Nothing about this whole stinking war has been fair." Extermination camps, he thought. Innocent children beaten and left for dead. Everything that was fine and good about the Old World turned to ashes and rubble.

They passed other dazed New Yorkers who gathered on street corners and on front stoops as they tried to make sense of the unthinkable.

"What's going to happen to us?" Catherine asked as they passed the Rego Park Synagogue. "President Roosevelt is— I mean, was—the heart of this country. Who's going to lead us now?" She laughed shrilly. "I can't even remember the name of the vice president."

"Truman," Johnny said, "but now he's *President* Truman."

She stopped walking and turned to him. "I'm scared, Johnny," she whispered. "What if our troops lose hope? What is this going to do to us?" Harry S Truman was a shopkeeper from Missouri. How on earth could he make the tough decisions necessary to bring about victory for the Allies? It was all too terrifying.

They turned back toward Forest Hills. Johnny tried to comfort her, explaining how the president's death would spur the troops on to win the war as quickly as possible as a tribute to their fallen leader, but Catherine wasn't buying it. "Fine for us," she said, "but what about the English and the French and everyone else? What if they feel that we can't fight without a leader? What if—"

"When you're out there, you fight for your commanding officer, Cathy. I didn't give two hangs about FDR when I was out there with your dad."

She started crying again, big graceless sobs against his shoulder. He waited patiently, patting her shoulder and back, until she managed to stop long enough to catch her breath.

"Come on," he said, leading her across Queens Boulevard toward a bar named Bill's Bus Stop. "You need a drink."

She didn't argue with him. Bill's was dark and crowded, exactly the kind of place where you could cry into your beer and nobody would notice or care. A group of guys in uniforms were shooting pool in the back, playing with a dark intensity sharply at odds with the brightly colored billiard balls shooting back and forth across the green felt table. Men in shirt-sleeves sat on bar stools, glumly listening to the endless reports drifting from the radio on the shelf behind the bartender.

"What can I get you, folks? Not exactly the greatest of days, is it?"

Johnny shook his head. "You got that right." He glanced at Catherine. "Beer?" She nodded. "Two Rheingolds."

The bartender looked at Catherine, who was struggling to keep from crying again. "Find the little lady a chair, why don't you, then come back for your beers. She looks like she needs to sit down."

It was wonderful to get off her feet, but the cold beer sat uneasily in her empty stomach.

"I don't feel too well, Johnny." She pushed her mug away and averted her eyes from a dish of greasy peanuts. "I think we should go home." The bar had gotten more crowded, and the combination of smells—beer and sweat and cigarette smoke—were making her stomach churn.

Johnny polished off his beer and extended a hand to Catherine. "Come on. Let's get some fresh air."

Gratefully she followed him as he threaded their way through the crowd in the bar. Some kind of ruckus had broken out near the pool table, and they were almost out the door when something—she would never know exactly what—made Catherine turn around and look.

"My God," she cried, stopping dead in her tracks. "That's Eddie back there."

Johnny cast a quick look over his shoulder. "Shooting pool?"

"No, Johnny. He's fighting! They've got him pushed up against the wall." She grabbed Johnny's arm. "Do something."

The look he gave her was cold and hard. "He's gotten himself out of scrapes before, Cathy." He pushed open the door, but she wouldn't budge. "Look, I admit I don't like the guy, but I don't want to see anything happen to him. He'll be fine."

"You have to help him."

"He's a man, Catherine. He has to fight his own battles."

"He's my friend." She pulled away from him and started toward the back of the bar. "If you won't help him, I will."

Johnny hesitated a fraction of an instant. She was easily the most pigheaded woman he'd ever known, but also the most loyal. Johnny would just as soon let Martin go toe-to-toe against the entire Luftwaffe, but there were Catherine's feelings to consider.

"Go outside and wait," he ordered her. "I'll see what the problem is."

Of course, the problem was easy to figure out. Eddie Martin was 4-F. The others weren't.

Martin and a lanky soldier were circling each other like prizefighters. From the look of the bruise blossoming on Eddie's cheekbone, he hadn't landed the first shot.

"What's going on?" he asked calmly.

"Mind your own damn business," growled one of the soldiers. "Andy's got a score to settle with this son of a bitch."

A second soldier started circling Eddie like a starving vulture. Johnny might not like Eddie, but he sure as hell wasn't going to let him go down in an unfair fight.

As she paced the sidewalk in front of the bar, Catherine thought, *He's going to take care of it.* Johnny would step in there and put an end to the nonsense. Eddie would realize what a wonderful guy Johnny was, while Johnny would finally understand how tough things had been for Eddie.

None of this could be happening. She didn't know the kind of man who got into barroom brawls. What on earth was the world coming to? The president dead. A new leader already on his way to the White House. Her dear friend Eddie battling street toughs as if he didn't care what became of him.

Johnny will take care of it, she whispered silently. *Johnny will take care of everything.* She'd almost convinced herself of that when the door burst open and the two men in question were unceremoniously kicked out. Johnny's shirt was ripped and he was massaging his bad hand, but other than that he looked fine. Eddie was another story. He looked as if he'd fought the Battle of the Bulge alone and lost.

She ran to Johnny's side. "What happened?"

"I didn't like the odds," Johnny said.

"Son of a bitch."

She jumped at the ugly sound of Eddie's words. She'd heard language like that occasionally in the factory, but most men did their best to shield women from profanity. Swallowing her apprehension, she approached her friend. "Your chin, Eddie. Let me see—"

He pushed her away roughly. Johnny made to step in, but Catherine motioned him to stop.

"Eddie, please. I asked Johnny to—"

"Keep that son of a bitch away from me," Eddie said, glaring in Johnny's direction. She cringed at the harsh words. "I can fight my own damn battles. I don't need some half-assed war hero doing it for me." Eddie swayed on his feet.

"You've had too much to drink, Eddie." Catherine linked her arm through Eddie's as he struggled to regain his balance. Johnny's jaw was set in granite. "Let us take you home."

"Not him." Eddie tilted his head toward Johnny. "Don't want him near me."

"I'm afraid you don't have too much choice, pal." Johnny swung the drunken man over his shoulder as if he were a pile of laundry. "Which way?"

"He lives on Dexter."

"Go to hell," Eddie mumbled. "Go to..."

"He'll feel better tomorrow," Catherine said, looking at her now unconscious friend. "Won't he?"

"No." Johnny met her eyes over Eddie's battered body. "I don't think he will."

IT WAS AT LEAST a mile to Eddie's house. Johnny never complained during the walk, nor did he stop. Twice Catherine asked him if perhaps they should take Eddie to her house because it was closer, but Johnny shook his head and kept on walking. A shiner was blossoming under his left eye, and blood was caked on the torn cuff of his shirt.

They dropped Eddie off at his parents', and Johnny did some neat sidestepping when they asked what had happened to their son.

"Had a retirement party at the factory," he said easily while Catherine nodded in agreement. "Afraid it turned into a wake after the news came over the radio."

The Martins, who had been glued to their Philco listening to the reports about FDR's death, thanked them profusely, then set out to make Eddie comfortable.

"That was nice of you," Catherine said as they left the Martins'. "You didn't have to protect him like that." It was a touch of grace coming in the middle of an evening of pain.

Johnny shrugged and started down the street. He seemed far away, as if he was still in that barroom with Eddie.

"Thank you." She reached for his hand and kissed the bruised knuckles. "Eddie needs all the help he can get."

"I did it for you," he said. "That's the only reason."

She linked her arm in his and they walked the rest of the way home in silence, just as the country settled down to mourn her fallen leader.

EDDIE DIDN'T RETURN to work the next day or the day after. On the third day Catherine called his home, but his mother fumbled with excuses, then finally burst into tears and hung up. "You can't save the world," Johnny said as they sat on the front stoop after dinner. "He's a grown man. He's going to do what he wants to do."

"You know, I don't understand you, Johnny. Why do you find it so hard to admit you have a good heart?"

He puffed on his cigarette as he watched the Bellamy grandchildren playing hopscotch in the middle of the street. "No evidence."

Her own heart ached in response. How could he think such a thing? This wonderful brave man who had saved her father's life and brought such happiness to hers. "Sorry, Johnny," she said lightly. "I can't buy that. I have some pretty good evidence to the contrary."

He looked over at her, a half smile lifting his mouth. "After a few years go by, you might need some more. I can be pretty tough to get along with."

Her body resonated with his words. The future! He was talking about the future! Not just tomorrow or next month. She forced herself to keep her tone easy, unconcerned, as if her heart wasn't racing with excitement. "Oh, I think the evidence is good for another twenty or thirty years." *Do you know what you're saying, Johnny? Am I really hearing this? Do you want the same thing for the future as I do?*

He met her eyes. "Written evidence is the best kind."

"I know." She swallowed hard. "I keep it tucked under my pillow."

"The letter?" His voice was low, uncertain.

"The letter."

His mouth curved into a swift smile that was gone before she could be sure it had been there in the first place.

He gestured toward the newspaper tucked under his arm. "We're practically in Berlin. I think this thing is finally winding down."

The change of topic threw her. Had it not been for the look in his eyes, a look of such appealing vulnerability, she might have believed she'd imagined the letter and all it implied. "I know," she said carefully. "With a little luck, Daddy'll be home before too long."

Johnny lit a cigarette. He offered her one but she shook her head. "He probably can't wait to get back to work at Wilson." He met her eyes. "The company means a lot to him."

"And well it should. He's worked hard for it." *And so have I.*

"It'll be good to see things get back to normal."

"I can't wait," she answered. "I have a thousand ideas for Wilson. If our deal with Mr. Levitt pans out, we can soar into construction the minute peace is declared." She beamed at him. "It will be so wonderful to work with you and my father." There was no limit to how far Wilson Manufacturing could go with both her and her father at the helm and Johnny at their side.

JOHNNY LEANED BACK against the stoop and listened as she waxed enthusiastic about her plans for the future. *Okay, so it isn't the right time to ask her.* She was so filled with energy, so optimistic about the world after the war, that he couldn't bring himself to burst her bubble. Not that a proposal of marriage was a bad thing, but somehow the conversation didn't lend itself to romantic proclamations.

She'd done well by Tom. The company she would be handing back to him was vigorous and strong. Now it was her turn. She was a woman. She needed a life of her own, a family to nurture, the way she had nurtured Wilson Manufacturing.

She needed a man who loved her more than he'd believed he could ever love someone.

Oh, hell—she needed him.

April 28, 1945

My dearest Tommy,
At last, a moment to sit down and write. So many soldiers arrived at the hospital today that they had to ask the volunteers to help out in the operating room. I was terrified I would faint, but I managed to help out during two operations to set broken legs. I wouldn't say I'd be the best nurse in the world, but I held my own and I'm quite proud of myself.

We are finally getting back to normal. The stores draped black bunting over the doors to commemorate FDR's death, and there was such a feeling of sadness in the air that you couldn't help but wonder how all of you overseas were feeling. What on earth was God thinking when He called the president home with the war so close to an end? Eleanor has been so strong and brave—oh, I can just hear you now, Tommy! "That big-mouth woman—why doesn't she just stay home where she belongs and let her husband run the country?" Remember how we used to argue about her many trips? It all seems such a long time ago, almost as if it were another lifetime. How my heart goes out to her now.

I feel so lucky to have my family around me and the knowledge that my beloved husband is alive and well. With so many families grieving, God has truly seen fit to bless us and I'll be forever grateful. A young corporal who'd served with Patton told me the feeling is that the war in Europe will be over in the next few weeks. The plan is that most of the soldiers will be sent home for a thirty-day furlough before being reassigned to the Pacific. He mentioned a new points-system program (I think he called it 85 and Out) that will muster out some very lucky soldiers. I lit a candle tonight on my way home and prayed that young corporal was right. Can you imagine, darling? Home to stay!

Last night I couldn't sleep. I'd had supper with Edna and Les, and Edna asked me what it was I wanted to do when you came home. A vacation in the mountains? A trip to the seashore? Kick up our heels in a different nightclub every night? Darling, do you know something funny? All I could think of was the way things used to be. All I want is for everything to be exactly the way it was. I'd never ask for anything else.

Nancy is still writing to Gerry. She says she loves him. I try to tell her that it's just an infatuation—wartime romances are quite appealing. Especially long-distance romances like this. So many times I've tried to encourage her to go out and meet people, but she shakes her head and looks at me with those sad eyes of hers and I just give up. I'm afraid our little girl is in for a letdown when the war is over and her Gerry just disappears.

As for Cathy, well, there's no doubt about it. Cathy and Johnny are in love. They're two headstrong individuals and there are days when you can actually see the fireworks going back and forth between them. Johnny loves our girl and he'll make a good life for her. I just wish they'd declare themselves. She deserves a life of her own, a husband and children. It's what every woman wants and, God knows, I so want it for our daughter.

Oh, Tommy, we'll have so much to celebrate when you come home! The day is almost here...

Your Doro

Chapter Thirteen

When the end came in Europe, it came swiftly.

Adolf Hitler and his mistress committed suicide on April 30, and the Reich that was to live a thousand years drew to a close. V-E Day was proclaimed the very next day and joyous thanksgiving filled the land. It was easy to believe the war was over, that not one more American boy would lose his life fighting for freedom.

Of course, the war wasn't over, and no one understood that better than Nancy. She was overjoyed that her father would be coming home soon, but that joy was tempered by the fact that, for her and Gerry, the war still raged. Her mother danced through her days, singing at the top of her lungs while she scrubbed every inch of the house in anticipation of the day her beloved Tom came home.

The Weavers were planning a block party for V-E Day. Their son, Mac, would be heading home from the front just as Tom Wilson would be, but no one had any doubt that Mac would be sent over to the Pacific in the first wave of reassigned troops.

Catherine tossed a lunch-hour celebration at Wilson, but warned her employees that the job was only half-over. There was still a war to be won against Japan, and their efforts would have to double the moment the celebration ended.

"So what do you want to do?" asked Johnny that evening as the employees flooded through the gates on their way home. "The block party? Dancing at the Inn? You name it."

Catherine looked up at him and grinned. "Let's go into the city. I want to be right there in the middle of the excitement."

He threw back his head and laughed. "Times Square? It'll be a zoo. You heard how jammed it was yesterday."

She nodded. "I know, but this is a once-in-a-lifetime event, Johnny. I want to remember it for as long as I live."

Johnny hoped she was right as he felt for the small box in his shirt pocket. It was there, same as it had been for the past four days. Hard to believe such a tiny ring could make such a huge difference in the way a man felt about life. *It's time,* he thought as he waited for her to gather her things. It was more than time. He wasn't the man he used to be, closed up, with his feelings locked tight behind the bars around his heart. He'd made mistakes with Angie, lots of them. He knew that now. Marriage was more than saying some words in front of a judge then setting up house together. You had to share a part of yourself, expose the light and the dark, give even when there was nothing to be gained from giving.

He could do all that with Catherine. He'd already done it, time and time again. They knew how to fight, but they also understood how to stop fighting and get on with it. More than anything he wanted to give her time to slow down, time to rest and recover that part of herself that had been lost in the war years.

He wanted to give her a home of her own and a life of her own. And he wanted to give her children. Lots of them.

"What are you smiling about?" she asked as they headed toward the subway. "You look like the cat that ate the canary."

"Just thinking."

She squeezed his hand. "Good thoughts?"

Cathy waiting at the door when he got home...a hot meal on the stove... their children doing their homework by the fireplace ... his Cathy—his wife—turning down the blankets and welcoming him into their bed ...

"The best," he said, patting the ring box one more time. "The very best."

Johnny was right. Times Square *was* a zoo. Young men in uniform danced with even younger girls in front of the replica of the Statue of Liberty, and Catherine and Johnny each bought a fistful of Liberty Bonds from the USO workers near a fifty-foot-high cash register that totaled the sales. They joined in a conga line that snaked up and down the Square and laughed uproariously.

Soon, however, the din became too much even for Cathy, and they went on to Longchamps where they dined on sautéed filet mignon and shrimp cocktail, definitely a special dinner. Catherine was in ecstasy. "Beef!" she said with a sigh. "I can't remember when I've enjoyed a meal more."

Johnny couldn't concentrate on his dinner. She devoured an enormous strawberry shortcake while he smoked cigarette after cigarette, waiting for the right moment. Finally she finished eating and he paid the bill.

"Want to walk for a while?" he asked.

Catherine groaned. "I'd better, or I'll have to let out my seams tomorrow."

They strolled through the gathering twilight. From Times Square they heard the faint sounds of music and cheers. Cathy chattered on about the delicious meal and he could only nod and pat his jacket pocket. He felt jumpier than he had in a foxhole with Nazi fire exploding all around him.

The carousel, he thought. Or the little bench near the lake ... There had to be one perfect place, one *lucky* place, where a man could propose to the girl he loved.

And then he saw it. A hansom cab waited near the fountain in front of the Plaza. "Come on," he said, swooping her up into his arms. "Let's go for a ride."

Giggling, Cathy found herself carried across the street and deposited in the back seat of the elegant carriage before she could muster a protest. Not that she wanted to protest.

Riding through the park in a hansom cab was probably the most romantic adventure she could possible imagine!

The gentle clip-clop of the horse's hooves lulled her into a wondrous romantic blur. Birds chirped softly high in the trees, and now and again you could hear murmurs and whispers from lovers sitting together on the park benches, hidden now by the blue light of dusk.

Johnny recognized the perfect moment when he saw it. He casually reached into his jacket.

"I have cigarettes in my purse," Catherine said.

"That's not what I'm looking for." He pulled the tiny box out of his shirt pocket and placed it in her hand.

Her eyes widened, then her gaze lowered to the box with its shiny white ribbons.

"Johnny?" Her voice was soft, her tone both puzzled and cautiously delighted.

He closed her fingers around it. His heart hammered the way it had in combat. He wasn't very good with words. "Open it," he said, knowing he sounded gruff, but when your heart was in your throat it was tough to sound any other way.

Calm down! Catherine thought. *Don't go setting yourself up for disappointment!* A pair of pearl earrings, maybe. A shiny gold locket on a slender chain. A carousel charm for her bracelet. She opened the box.

"Oh, Johnny!" Her breath rushed from her body.

"I'd drop to my knee," he said, "but there's no room." He looked jittery and uncertain, hopeful and terrified, and she loved him more in that instant than she had ever loved anyone.

"Marry me, Cathy," he said, plucking the sparkling diamond ring from its bed of black velvet.

Her left hand trembled as she extended it toward him.

"I love you, Cathy." How beautiful the words were! How beautiful they made her feel. She'd never expected to hear them again. "I want to spend the rest of my life with you."

Tears spilled down her cheeks and she didn't bother to wipe them away. She was certain her smile was brighter than a full moon in August.

"Yes," she said as he slipped the ring onto her finger. "Oh, yes!"

The driver let out a cheer, and Catherine giggled and buried her face against Johnny's shoulder. "I love you," she said for him alone. "I'll love you forever."

We'll work side by side, Johnny. Things will be the same as they've always been, only better.

Johnny felt as if he'd captured the stars with his bare hands. *A brand-new life, Cathy. Before long, you won't have to work for a living. You can concentrate on being my wife.*

"A toast to the happy couple," said the driver, passing back a bottle of champagne and paper cups he kept on hand for occasions like this. "May you have a long and happy life together!"

The happy couple clinked glasses and drank to two entirely different futures.

THE LIGHTS WERE ON late that night at the Wilson house. Dot burst into happy tears and ran across the street to bring Edna and Les Weaver and their other neighbors over for an impromptu celebration. The block party had just ended and now an engagement party was about to begin. Even Nancy seemed genuinely glad for the two of them, and she raised a glass of blackberry wine and said, "To the two luckiest people in the entire world—may you have a hundred years of joy together!"

Catherine's tears were tears of joy when Aunt Edna and Uncle Les kissed her and hugged Johnny and wished them both everything wonderful that life had to offer.

If only her father had been there with them, the evening would have been picture perfect.

The next day it was back to business as usual at Wilson. Well, as usual as business could be the day after your engagement. Oh, yes—there was also the small matter of victory in Europe. There were an awful lot of hangovers at the factory that morning and a lot of smiling faces.

Of course, the biggest smiles of all belonged to Catherine and Johnny. Johnny was doing a good job of keeping business and pleasure separate, but Catherine was finding it difficult to tear her gaze from the diamond ring glittering on her left hand. Engaged. She and Johnny were engaged. Out of the most difficult years of her life had come her greatest happiness. The man she loved. Work that mattered.

The memory of another man, another engagement ring, wasn't far from her mind. *I'll always love you, Douglas,* she thought, gazing out the window. *You'll always be a part of me.* Love wasn't the finite quantity she had once believed. It bent with the wind; it grew in barren soil; it lived even after you'd given up hope.

"You wanted to see me?" Eddie Martin, hands thrust in the pockets of his brown trousers, stood in the doorway.

She motioned him inside. "We need to talk."

"Sounds serious." He smiled, but the smile didn't reach his eyes. This intense, angry young man seemed almost a stranger to Catherine.

"I've been reviewing attendance records, Eddie, and I'm afraid yours isn't the greatest." He said nothing. "Is there a problem?" she continued. "If there's something wrong you have to tell me so we can do something about it."

"Nothing you could do, Catherine, even if you wanted to." *Catherine.* Had it come to that? She'd always been Cath or Wilson or some other crazy nickname to Eddie.

"The war's over, Eddie, at least in Europe. We're going to have to consider the future."

He leaned back in his chair. "I hear you've been considering your own future."

She laughed nervously. "The grapevine is in fine shape." Shyly she showed him her ring. "It just happened last night."

"Congratulations."

Her smile wavered. "That's all? Just 'congratulations'?"

"What do you want me to say? I'd be lying if I said I think you've found a great guy."

"I know you and Johnny have had a rough patch or two, but he's a wonderful man. I think you'll get to like him."

"So when do you quit work?"

"Quit work! Where'd you get an idea like that?"

"It's what you do when you get married, isn't it?"

"Well, yes, it is—I mean, it *was*. I've done a good job here, Eddie. I can do even more once we go back to civilian production."

"Don't try to convince me. Convince your future husband."

"I don't have to convince Johnny of anything," she said hotly. "He knows how important this company is to me."

She did her best to bring the conversation back to Eddie's absenteeism, but his lack of interest was like a splash of icy water in her face.

"I've made my position clear," she said in exasperation. "Things have to change, Eddie. It's time to put the past behind us and look ahead." *Talk to me, Eddie. We used to be friends. Don't let it slip away from us like this....*

"You're right," he said as he rose to his feet. "I quit."

"Eddie, please. You don't mean this—"

"It's over, Cathy. Face it. I don't have a place here anymore."

"We can work it out. We can—"

He shook his head. "No, we can't. Everything's changed, whether you want to believe it or not. It's over. All of it." He turned and left the office and for an instant she wondered if she would ever see him again.

"Don't be ridiculous," she said out loud as his footsteps disappeared down the hallway. "He'll be back."

But the weeks went by and finally Catherine had to admit Eddie Martin was gone for good.

ONE MONTH LATER Dot stood on the dock, craning her neck to see over the crowd.

"Calm down, Mom." Catherine laughed and winked at Nancy. "I don't think the *Queen Mary* will get lost in the crowd."

"Look at all those tugboats," Nancy said, pointing toward the flotilla of escorts heralding the arrival of the world's most famous troopship as it entered the narrows. "I'll bet Daddy's up there on deck directing traffic."

Her two daughters laughed, but Dot was so nervous she was afraid she'd fall apart if she uttered a sound. Johnny patted her on the shoulder and she gave him a quick smile, grateful for his solid presence. *This is it,* she thought, hugging herself to stem her trembling. *Any moment now the ship will dock and my husband will walk down that gangplank and I'll—*

Dear God, what? Would she run to him and fling herself into his arms? Would she stand rooted to the spot while he strode proudly across the dock to her waiting embrace? Why hadn't she taken more pains with her hair, pinning it up or brushing it loose or rolling the top into the pompadour he'd always loved. Would he like her new pink lipstick, or should she have rummaged around for the bright red that she'd always worn?

Later on she would ask herself exactly how she and Tom found each other in the teeming crowd of humanity jamming the pier that day in June. She remembered Nancy's tears and Catherine's look of joy and the way Tom and Johnny met each other's eyes, then embraced like father and son, but how it was that she and Tom had found their way to each other—well, only God had the answer to that wonderful mystery.

The weeks and the months and the years without him vanished, and she found herself looking into the eyes of the man she loved, the boy she'd married, the father of her children, as if they'd never been parted, not even for an instant.

She cradled his beloved face between her hands and kissed him soundly. "Oh, Tommy," she whispered. "Don't you ever go away again, you hear me?"

"I'm back, Doro." He held her close and she felt his tears against the side of her neck. "I'm back."

June 21, 1945

Dear Gerry,

Well, my dad is home at last. He arrived safe and sound yesterday on the *Queen Mary*. Can you believe 14,526 soldiers all came back together! I don't have to tell you that my mother is beside herself with happiness. She's fussing over him constantly, making certain he has lemonade and clean shirts and all the back issues of *Reader's Digest* that he missed. I don't think I've ever seen her so happy in my entire life.

I almost hate to write this, but I have to say it to somebody—Daddy isn't the same. And it's not the gray hairs or the weight he's lost—it's something a lot more complicated and scary. The look in his eyes is different. Gerry, it's almost like he's not really there, you know? Last night everyone on the block came over and Mom put together an impromptu party and even though my father said and did all the right things, you didn't have to be a genius to see he wasn't enjoying himself at all. Cathy tried to tell him all about the company and how well things are going and he just said, "That's nice, princess," and continued thumbing through the June 1944 *Reader's Digest*.

Well, I guess it really doesn't matter, does it? Come Monday, Daddy'll be back at work and everything will settle down the way it used to be. At least I hope so.

All my love forever,
Nancy

"YOU OLD FOOL," Dot whispered to her reflection in the

mirror as she struggled with the ribbon tie on her brand-new peignoir set. "Married almost twenty-five years and you're trembling like a bride on her wedding night."

Which, of course, in a way it was. How strange the slither of lace felt against her bare skin. How powerful and seductive her thoughts. Tom had been home for two nights now. Each night she had come to bed, giddy with anticipation, to find him snoring deeply. He was tired, she knew, but it was time.

She glanced at herself in the revealing—and terribly foreign—negligee. "Don't go losing your nerve, Dorothy," she warned herself. "This is your husband. Go to him."

He was standing near the bedroom window, smoking. He was thinner than she'd remembered, and older, but then time had wrought changes in her, as well. Her heart ached as she thought of the years they had lost, at the thatch of gray hair that salted the brown.

"Tommy." She stood near the foot of the bed, arms at her sides.

He turned slowly, almost reluctantly. No! She wouldn't think thoughts like that. Foolish ideas had been popping into her head all day. *Something's wrong,* her mind would say. *He isn't the same Tom who went to war,* but she pushed these thoughts firmly aside and would allow them no quarter. She noticed that his hand trembled. Her heart went out to him.

"You look beautiful, Doro."

She lowered her eyes. "Thank you." *We're acting like strangers, Tommy. Sweep me into your arms and make love to me the way you used to.* The memory of their last night together had warmed her throughout the intervening years, but it was time to create new memories. She sat down on the edge of the bed and patted the spot next to her. "Come here."

He stubbed out his cigarette and slowly crossed the room. He eased his body onto the bed as if he were settling onto a mattress of nails.

She met his eyes. "I've missed you, Tommy."

He said nothing, but she could see his Adam's apple working convulsively. She touched his cheek, his jaw, the bristly GI haircut that felt so strange. Tears welled in her eyes.

"Please say something, Tommy. You're scaring me." She paused, swallowing hard. "Is there someone else?"

He shook his head. "Never. There's only you, Doro. Always."

"Then what?" She took his hand and placed it against her heart. "Its been so long, darling. So very long..."

And then her heart broke as the man she loved let her see inside his soul. "Hold me, Doro," he said, his voice cracking. "Just hold me close."

She did as he asked. She held her husband close through the long summer night, and when the sun came up the next morning, she knew that things would be different between them for a long time to come.

But it didn't matter. He was her husband and he was home to stay.

TOM WILSON DID GO BACK to work on Monday, but not quite the way anyone expected.

After two hours of nonstop "Great to see you...so happy you're home, Mr. Wilson..." he stepped into his office and called both Johnny and Catherine in.

Johnny came directly from working on a problem with one of the machines down in assembly. His hands were stained with grease and he waved off Tom's handshake with a quick laugh and the remark, "I wouldn't do it to you, Tom."

Catherine smiled. Her dad was seated behind the desk that she'd called her own these past twenty-four months. How odd it felt to see someone in the seat she'd come to consider her own.

How odd it felt to see that empty look in her father's eyes. She watched as he glanced around the small office as if he had never seen it before—nor cared to see again.

Since he'd been home, the only time her dad had come to life was when she and Johnny broke the news of their engagement. His blue eyes had sparkled and he'd hugged her tight, then clapped Johnny on the back and welcomed him into the family.

"Be patient," Johnny had said to her this morning. "Remember what it was like for me? Coming home is like being dropped on the moon. It takes some getting used to."

She looked over at her dad and smiled at him. He was still her father, still Tom Wilson, president of the company. It would just take time for things to return to normal, that's all.

Ten minutes later, all of her hopes were shattered.

"No!" The word burst from her lips. "You can't mean that, Daddy. Wilson wouldn't be the same without you."

His smile was weary. "These figures don't lie, princess. Wilson did just fine without me and it'll continue to do fine."

"But I don't understand. Why on earth would you want to retire? What will you do?" He was only forty-four, not some doddering old goat ready to be put out to pasture.

"Nothing," said Tom. "I just want to do nothing."

Panic snaked its way through her chest. He'd gone crazy, that was what. Absolutely, totally crazy. She'd heard stories about battle fatigue, but it never occurred to her that her own father would fall victim.

Johnny leaned forward, his handsome face creased with concern. "You planning on selling the firm, Tom? Not much call for transactions like that these days. You might want to—"

Her father leaned back in his chair and laced his fingers together. "Don't worry. I'm not looking to sell. I'm just looking for a rest."

Catherine's heartbeat returned to something one step closer to normal. But the whole situation still didn't set right with her. "A vacation," she said, glancing over at Johnny. "Now that the travel restrictions are gone, you and Mom should take a nice long trip. I'll hold the fort while you're gone."

Johnny met her eyes and nodded. "No problem, Tom. Do a little sight-seeing, then come back and take the reins after you're rested."

"You're not listening to me, either one of you. I'm talking about a permanent change."

Catherine held her breath, palms wet and clammy.

"You've done a wonderful job here, princess. I don't think I could have done better."

She thanked him. "Johnny made all the difference," she said honestly. "If he hadn't come aboard to help handle the employees, we wouldn't be in the good shape we're in today."

"I know," said her father. "That's why I'm handing the reins over to him."

She leapt to her feet, not even noticing the cup of coffee that went sloshing to the floor. "No! You can't do that!"

Her dad's astonishment mirrored Johnny's. "Why not?" asked Tom. "The war's over. You're not going to want to come to work every day to do a man's job. Johnny's the logical choice."

Johnny started to say something, but Catherine couldn't control her tongue. "How can you do that to me, Daddy?"

"He saved my life," Tom said calmly. "Now I owe him."

"What about me?" cried Catherine. "I'm your daughter. I saved your company. Don't you owe me anything?"

How could her own father take away the one good thing to come of her years of loneliness and fear? How could he not see all she had done for him?

"Look, Tom," said Johnny. "I don't want to get in the middle of a family argument." He stood and headed for the door, but her father stopped him.

"You're family now, too, Johnny. You have every right to be here. If you're going to take my job, you need to hear Cathy's objections."

She turned to the man she loved, her heart and soul on her sleeve. "Tell him, Johnny. Tell him he's wrong. Tell him I should have the job."

"Don't go making any mistake about it," said Johnny, looking from Catherine to her father and back again. "I want the job, but not this way."

Her heart swelled with emotion. *Oh, Johnny! I love you so much.*

But Johnny wasn't finished talking. "If I take the job, there has to be something here for Cathy, too."

"Yes," she snapped. "*Your* job."

He took her hand and drew her attention to the engagement ring. "You have a job, Cathy. You're going to be my wife."

"But that doesn't mean I can't run Wilson. Married women work, Johnny. Have you looked at the women on the assembly line? They manage to do both."

"They've done both because they had to," he pointed out as her father nodded in agreement. "Don't you think they'd be happier at home?"

"Ask them!" She pulled her hand away from his. "It's not like I'm taking a job away from a veteran." She turned to her father. "I'm your flesh and blood, Daddy. How can you do this to me?"

"You're overwrought," said her father. "When you calm down, you'll thank me."

"Thank you? For what? For slapping me in the face after I've put everything I have into working to make you proud of me?"

"What about a family?" Johnny asked, his voice growing louder. "You'll take this job and two months after we get married, you'll have to quit."

"Why?" she tossed back at him. "Does pregnancy destroy brain cells?"

Her father inhaled sharply. "Watch your tongue, Catherine Anne."

"Pregnant," she said. "Pregnant, pregnant, pregnant. Sandra Mihalik worked until her sixth month. Miriam, the personnel manager, worked right up until she had David, then came back six weeks later. It can be done, Johnny."

And then the ax fell. "Not by my wife."

She stared at him. "What was that?"

Johnny kicked back his chair and got to his feet. His expression was a picture of pure male rage. "I said, not by my wife."

"Meaning what?"

"You understand English. Figure it out."

That was her father's cue to slip out of the office. Neither combatant noticed.

"I'm just a woman," she said sweetly. "Maybe you should explain it to me."

"My wife doesn't work."

"Your girlfriend did and that didn't bother you."

"You were doing what you had to do, Cathy. You did it for your father."

"Yes," she conceded, "that's how it started, but hasn't it occurred to you that it's come to mean something more to me?"

"No."

Her anger and hurt were so intense she could scarcely breathe. "How can you say that, Johnny? You've worked next to me for almost six months now. Don't you know anything about me at all?"

"It isn't right for a married woman to work. It's up to the husband to take care of the family."

"Did your first wife work?"

The look on his face was murderous as he shook his head. "Like I said, my wife stays home."

Her laugh was triumphant. "And then you were divorced. So much for that theory."

"Don't push me, Cathy."

"What'll you do?" she asked, her temper out of control. "Steal my job out from under me?" She brushed away angry, powerless tears. "Oh, excuse me. How could I forget? You've already done that."

"What the hell do you want from me?" he exploded. "I didn't ask for the job, Cathy. Your dad offered it to me. He's damn sure not going to give it to you. Would you rather it go to a stranger?"

"I'd rather you'd given me the choice before you said yes."

"I'm a man. If I'm going to support us, I need the best job I can find."

"So do I."

His voice was low, deadly. "You're not going to support the family. Not while I'm alive."

"Don't you hear a word I'm saying, Johnny? I don't want to be the only breadwinner in the family, but I do want to contribute."

"Are you telling me that taking care of a family isn't contributing?"

"Are you telling me that I'm good enough to run a company when there's a war on, but once peace is declared, I'm just a helpless woman?"

"Yes."

"You can't mean that." All of her illusions about the man she loved were crumbling right in front of her eyes. How could she have been so blind?

"Stop fighting things you can't change, Cathy." His look was sharp, angry. "I didn't see you kicking up a storm to risk your life on the front line with us men."

"That's different."

"Damn right it is."

"I've worked hard to see Wilson get where it is. Don't I deserve to see the rest of my plans through? There's so much to accomplish with the war ending." *Johnny, let me get through to you, please, before it's too late!*

For a brief moment she thought that she had, that her words had reached the stubborn part of him that refused to see her point, but then his expression hardened. "I want what your parents have," he said at last. "I want a wife who lives for her husband."

"Then there's nothing more to talk about." She yanked the engagement ring off her finger and threw it at him. It bounced off his chest and fell with a clink to the floor. "Enjoy your new job, Johnny." She turned and ran from the office.

What hurt more than anything was the fact that he didn't follow her.

IT WASN'T THAT Johnny didn't want to run after Catherine, pull her into his arms and promise her the moon. He did. He really did. But there was his pride to consider. What she was asking of him was so far beyond the pale that he didn't know how to deal with it. Sure, she'd done a hell of a job at Wilson Manufacturing. All you had to do was look at the bottom line and you'd see how successful she'd been. But there was more to that bottom line than met the eye. He knew—and she admitted—that if he hadn't come along when he did, she would've had a full-blown strike on her hands and Wilson Manufacturing's bottom line would've been shot all to hell within two weeks.

She was smart but he was shrewd. She understood books and numbers, while he was better with the intangibles. Like a man's pride. She'd failed miserably with Harry Barnes and his workers. No man wanted to take orders from a woman. No man wanted to crawl to a woman and ask for a raise.

It was a man's world. Always was, always would be. Her dad would've handed his company over to Eddie Martin quicker than he'd have laid that burden on his daughter.

He retrieved the ring from where it had rolled under the desk; it nestled cold against his palm. It had been nice while it lasted, thinking he could buy into the dream of a family of his own, but he'd learned early on that most dreams never come true. And this dream was no exception.

CATHERINE RAN PAST her father, who was talking to some of his cronies near the lunchroom, then burst out the front door. Chest heaving, she looked around the barren factory landscape for a rock, a brick, anything she could pick up and fling through the office window. She gasped for air while righteous anger made her heart thud crazily. She felt powerless, helpless, worthless. *A woman.*

Her laugh was wild, out of control. That was it. She felt like a *woman.* Everything she had achieved, all of the accomplishments of the past two years had been brushed aside by her father as if they were an underdone chocolate cake or a soggy apple pie.

She'd been good enough to run the company when nobody else was available, but now her dad was pushing her aside. It was unfair, so horribly unfair, and there was not one blessed thing she could do to change it.

How could she have ever been so stupid as to believe Johnny was special? That they could be both a couple and a team? She'd never done anything to make him feel uncomfortable working for her. Had he been biding his time, waiting for the first opportunity to throw it all back in her face?

She stormed down the steps and headed toward the subway. "I don't need you, Johnny Danza," she said out loud. The pain in her heart was horrible, but she would live. She was stronger than heartbreak; she'd proved that to herself when Douglas died.

Johnny Danza was stubborn and headstrong, but he had met his match in her. He would never see her cry again.

Chapter Fourteen

July 4, 1945

Dear Gerry,

Well, the war in Europe may be over, but the war at the Wilsons' is going strong. I can't believe how everything has changed in just one week. My father just put Johnny in charge of the business. Daddy still owns Wilson Manufacturing, but he doesn't even want to go into the office. He says he's taking a sabbatical (whatever that is) but it looks a lot like giving up to me.

Even worse, Cathy gave Johnny back the engagement ring, and Johnny moved out of the basement and is living at the factory. Mom is trying to make peace between Cathy and my father but Cathy's having none of it. I begged her to make up with Johnny, but she pushed me off her bed and slammed the door in my face.

And worst of all my dad just sits there in the rumpus room all by himself with "Sentimental Journey" playing over and over again on the Victrola. It's gotten so if I met Doris Day in person I'd put a sock in her mouth.

We'll never have these problems, Gerry. I don't want anything more than to be your wife. I can't imagine a more beautiful life than taking care of our home and raising our children. How could any woman ask for more?

All my love,
Nancy

IF JOHNNY EXPECTED Catherine to come around, he was sorely mistaken.

If Catherine expected Johnny to admit he was unfair, she was in for a surprise.

As the days slowly passed, their positions grew more intractable. Catherine tried to talk to her father, but her arguments fell on deaf ears.

"You're taking this too much to heart," her mother said one morning as Catherine stared out the window at other women rushing off to work. "You can always find another job."

"I don't want another job, Mother," she said with a long sigh. "I want the one I had." A job wasn't the issue. She wanted what was rightfully hers.

Her mother patted her on the shoulder. "Be patient with your father, honey. It's a long road back home."

"Sure," said Catherine dispiritedly. "I have all the time in the world."

Johnny felt caught between a rock and a hard place. The one thing he was certain of was that Tom wasn't coming back to work any time soon. It wasn't the same at the factory without Catherine. He hadn't realized how hard she'd worked until he sat down behind the desk and started looking at the pile of paperwork for disposition. He wasn't an office type. He was better out there with people, thinking on his feet, mediating problems. This kind of fancy paper shuffling made him itchy. He'd seen her working on monthly reports, her pencil whizzing across the ledger sheets like a German rocket. He could sit there behind the desk for the rest of his life and never make sense of any of it.

Or like it, for that matter.

He'd gone over to the Wilson house one night when he knew from Nancy that she and Catherine were going to the movies. Dot had hugged him and kissed his cheek. "Give her time," she'd said about her headstrong daughter. "She'll come around. She's just confused."

Johnny nodded and said the right things, but in his heart of hearts he knew the only way Catherine would come around was if he gave in. And that wasn't about to happen.

Tom didn't want to hear much of anything Johnny had to say. They talked about the Dodgers and the Yankees and touched briefly on what was happening in the Pacific, then Johnny said good night and went back to his makeshift accommodations at the factory, more despondent than before.

He'd spent his whole life alone, but he had never felt this lonely before. Catherine had filled all the corners of his heart and soul. Seeing her, hearing her voice, sharing the days with her had made him feel hopeful, that his life could amount to more than counting down the days.

But, all of that was gone now and he was damned if he could see a way to get it back.

ONE WEEK after Catherine stormed out of Wilson Manufacturing, she returned to get her final paycheck. It was early on Monday morning and she hurried into personnel, hoping she could get in and out before too many people noticed her. Miriam was filled with chatter and Catherine kept glancing over her shoulder to make certain Johnny was nowhere to be seen.

"Don't be a stranger," said Miriam as she gave Catherine a hug. "Just because you're a lady of leisure these days doesn't mean you've got to forget the rest of us."

"I won't forget you, Miriam," she said, kissing the older woman's cheek. "I couldn't forget any of you."

Walking out that door was even harder the second time around. The first time she'd been fueled by outrage. This time she was fueled only by regret. She was halfway to the gate, immersed in dark thoughts, when she realized she was walking behind a familiar figure.

"Eddie?" She increased her pace. "Eddie, wait up."

Eddie stopped but didn't turn around. When she caught up to him she saw why.

"Oh, God, Eddie..." She went to touch him, but he moved away. "What on earth happened?"

His face was a mass of cuts and bruises, including a vicious black eye and split lip. He tried to smile, but the effect bordered on the grotesque. "Would you believe I walked into a door?"

She couldn't smile back. "What are you doing here?"

"A little unfinished business with personnel. I forgot to give back a locker key."

It was difficult to concentrate on anything but his poor battered face. "Did you...do you know my dad's back home?"

"Yeah. Grapevine's still pretty good."

"Then you must—" She stopped. She couldn't bring herself to mention her and Johnny's breakup.

"I know that, too." A touch of the old Eddie was in his bittersweet smile. "I could say I told you so."

"Yes," she said after a moment, "but you won't, will you?"

"Not if you don't ask me what happened to me."

She sighed. "Looks like we both have our secrets now, Eddie. Times have certainly changed."

"It was good to see you again."

She touched his forearm. "Take care of yourself."

"Yeah," he said, with a mock salute. "Anything you say, boss."

It was the last time she saw Eddie Martin alive.

SOME PEOPLE SAY bad news travels faster than the speed of light, but in the case of the death of Eddie Martin, that old saw didn't hold water. Two days after she bumped into Eddie at the plant, he was killed in a barroom brawl in Long Island City. Nancy brought home the news on Friday night.

"The funeral's tomorrow morning," she said, blotting her tears with a pink tissue.

Dot and Tom came in the back door from tending the garden. "Are you talking about poor Eddie Martin?" her mother asked.

Nancy nodded. "Miriam said he—"

Catherine pushed back her chair and stood up. "Excuse me," she said, then hurried upstairs to her room where she locked the door behind her. If only she could lock out her thoughts as easily.

She kicked off her shoes and curled up on the window seat overlooking Hansen Street. Edna's roses were still in bloom, their scarlet and blush and snow-white blossoms dazzling against the deep green of early summer. She'd sat like this, watching the world beyond her window, that June evening two years ago, looking out at Edna pruning her rosebushes and wondering what her future would hold. How well she remembered that night, laughing with Nancy about leg makeup while she hurried to dress for the Stage Door Canteen. It seemed like another life, and she marveled that she'd ever been so young and hopeful.

Oh, yes, she remembered that night. She would always remember it. That was the night she lost Douglas.

And the night she met Johnny.

Past, present and future had all come together then in a dizzying whirl of sorrow and rebirth. God had taken from her with one hand but been generous enough to hold her close in His other. But now that thought no longer comforted her.

"Lucky you," she whispered into the evening breeze that ruffled her curtains. "You've loved two men and lost them both." One to death, the other to circumstance. There was nothing she could have done to save Douglas's life, just as Eddie's fate had been beyond her control.

But as she sat there and watched dusk settle over Forest Hills, she wondered why it couldn't have been different with Johnny.

Few things in life lasted. Her love for Douglas hadn't ended with his death. Her love for Johnny wouldn't end simply because she said it must. Her heart had a will of its own—and that night she was afraid her heart would break.

MORNING DIDN'T COME a minute too soon.

Catherine hadn't slept well at all. She'd sat in the window seat until well after midnight, trying to make sense of the emotions at war inside her chest. Guilt over Eddie's death. Regret that she hadn't tried harder to help him, even if that help had been unwelcome.

Her thoughts were jumbled and bleak as she walked with her family to St. Mary's for the funeral. She'd stuck to her principles, and see where it had gotten her? She'd lost her position at Wilson, and more important, she'd lost the man she loved. How arrogant she was to throw away a gift like that for something as insignificant as the right to sit behind that scarred oak desk.

How foolish she was to still wish there was a way she could be Johnny's wife and her own woman, both at the same time.

But there wasn't, so why even think about it? The moment the war in Japan ended, America's female work force would trade their soldering irons for lace-trimmed aprons and march en masse back to hearth and home. The returning soldiers would take their places again in the factories and the office buildings, and life would go back to normal. Everyone would be happy.

Why don't you stop tilting at windmills? she thought as she took her seat in the half-empty church. She tried very hard not to look at Eddie's casket resting near the main altar, but its presence compelled her. Life was precious; Eddie's premature death was proof that the war would continue to take casualties even though much of the fighting had stopped. Any day, any moment, could be your last. Did it make any sense at all to turn away from love if you were lucky enough to find it a second time?

The funeral mass was unbearably poignant. Catherine cried through the brief eulogy. What could you say, after all, when a young man died of a broken spirit?

"Requiescat in pace," prayed Father O'Herlihy, and she sent her own prayers heavenward that Eddie would find the happiness with the Almighty that had been denied him on earth.

You missed so much, Eddie, she thought. *Love and marriage…a home and children…the chance to grow old with someone who loves you....*

All the things she'd turned her back on when she'd walked out the door on Johnny.

But that was different, her mind argued. *You were right to toss that ring back at him. What kind of life could you have with a man like that?*

But I love him, said her heart. *Nobody said loving a man like Johnny would be easy.* When did anything in life that mattered ever come easy?

The church emptied. Still Catherine sat in the pew. "Honey?" Her mother touched her arm. "Should we wait for you?"

She shook her head. "I need to be here for a while." Her father patted her on the head the way he used to when she was a little girl. She wished she could run to him with her problems and have him make those problems disappear, but those days were over. Her father was a different man now, and it was his decision that had changed her life and Johnny's.

What a hopeless complicated tangle her life had become. If only she could sit down with Johnny now that the first passion of anger had cooled and tell him what was in her heart. But it was pointless even to think about it. Someone had to make the first move and she knew her stubborn pride would keep her from being the one. And when it came to stubborn pride, Johnny was her equal.

Gathering her purse and gloves, she rose to leave the church. She was halfway up the aisle when she saw him.

Johnny, standing at the back of the church. His hands were clasped behind his back, and his countenance was sober, as the occasion warranted.

She was oddly touched that he had chosen to acknowledge Eddie's passing, and she nodded briefly, eyes averted, as she walked by. It was only fitting, after all, that the man in charge of Wilson Manufacturing pay his respects to a former employee. It had nothing to do with her.

She pushed open the heavy doors and stepped outside, pausing a moment to let her eyes adjust to the bright summer sunshine. Johnny was right behind her. She started down the steps. So did he. He paused with her at the corner, then crossed the street when she did. His steps sounded behind her, steady, unrelenting. *Leave me alone, Johnny! It's over...it's all over....* But he didn't. Every step she took was matched by one of his. Finally, a half block away from the railroad station, she whirled about and confronted him.

"Stop following me," she snapped, nerves at the breaking point. "Walk on the other side of the street."

"The hell I will. In case you've forgotten, this is a free country. That's what all the fighting's been about."

"I don't need a lecture on why we went to war." She unceremoniously yanked the tiny black hat from her head and tucked it under her arm. "If you don't quit following me, I'll call the police."

She hurried down the street with Johnny a half step behind her. *Say something, you idiot!* her heart screamed. *This is the man you love, not a stranger. Don't give up without a fight.* She slowed her step at the start of Hansen Street. He bumped into her, almost knocking her off her feet.

"Damn!" She grabbed for her right ankle. Tears spilled down her cheeks and she angrily brushed them away with the back of her gloved hand. "Can't you watch where you're going?"

She remembered how it had felt to be held in his arms, to feel his lips on hers, to know the future was as bright as the sun shining overhead. He steadied her with an arm about her waist, and that simple touch released a flood of other memories.

"You stopped short." His hand brushed her cheek. "I'm sorry."

She had never felt more forlorn in her entire life. "Please go away," she said, voice breaking. "I just don't have the heart to fight you today." *Hold me, Johnny. Let's start again. Happiness is too precious to let it slip away....*

"I don't want to fight you, Cathy."

She looked up at him, into those beautiful blue eyes. "Let me go, Johnny," she said, glancing away. "There's no future for us."

She looked so desolate, so sorrowful, that hope leaped to life in Johnny's battle-scarred heart. She didn't grieve only for Eddie Martin; she grieved for what they'd lost between them. He knew it in his gut, his bones, his soul, and that knowledge gave him the courage.

"I think there's a way," he said, picking a path carefully through a mine field of emotions. "I think we can make it work."

Her laughter was shrill and high. "The United Nations couldn't make this work, Johnny. We're two different people. We'll never agree on the way to live our lives."

He grabbed her by the elbows and spun her around, forcing her to meet his eyes. *I love you,* she'd said the night he asked her to marry him. *I'll love you forever.* It couldn't be over. He wouldn't let it be. He drew a deep breath. "There's one thing we agree on—we can't be happy without each other."

"That's just too bad, isn't it?" she shot back, the fiery, opinionated woman he loved. "Because we also know we can't be happy *with* each other, either."

"Maybe we can."

She narrowed her eyes. "Are you going to give me back my job at Wilson?"

"No, but—"

She broke away from his grip. For a moment he thought she was going to take a swing at him, but she got a handle on her anger and glared at him instead. "I'm not going to be your secretary, Johnny. I'm not going to be your wife. I'm not going to be your friend."

"Would you be my partner?"

Her jaw sagged comically. He wanted to laugh, but knew he'd be risking dismemberment if he did. "What?" she said.

"My partner."

"You're kidding."

"No. I'm not kidding at all."

"Equal partners?"

"I wouldn't ask anything less of you, Cathy."

"I—I don't understand. If this is some kind of charity, Johnny, so help me, I'll—"

"Listen, woman." He grabbed her again and pulled her close. She smelled of softness and flowers. "Don't give me credit for being charitable. Your dad made a mistake. The company needs you." He swallowed hard and took a deep breath. "Who am I kidding? *I* need you."

Was he crazy or did he see a twinkle in her eyes? "All that paperwork getting you down, Johnny?"

Pride had gotten them into the trouble they were in. It was time to put his pride aside and speak from the heart. "I can't do the job, Cathy, not all of it. Wilson'll be in debt up to its eyeballs if I'm the one making the financial decisions."

She closed her eyes against a wave of hope that flooded through her body. *Forget your idiotic pride,* her heart begged. *Listen to him. This is the man you love, the man you want to spend your life with.*

"I'm not very good dealing with the workers," she said, voice low. "If I had to deal with them on a daily basis, I'd end up with an empty factory." *There, Catherine Anne. That didn't hurt so much, did it?*

He pulled her closer, so close she could feel his breath against her cheek, the warmth of his body.

"Looks like we're not much good alone, are we?"

She breathed deeply of his scent, then touched his cheek. His skin was smooth; only the slightest scratch of beard rasped against her fingertips. She longed to press her lips against the curve of his jaw, feel his lips against hers.

"Are you sure you can share responsibilities with a *woman*?"

He thrust a hand through his hair. She noticed again the way the last few fingers were rigid, his permanent legacy of war. "Want the truth?"

She nodded. "Nothing less."

"I want a wife, Cathy. I want kids to carry on my name. I've spent most of my life alone. That's not the way to live. I want a home of my own, a family of my own. But…" This was going to be harder than he'd thought. He struggled for the right words. "But I want you to be happy. I want that glow in your eyes to be there until the day I die, and if that means we work together at Wilson, well, I'll have to learn to live with it."

"That's not exactly a vote of confidence," she said, although she knew how much the admission had cost him.

"I love you. It's the best I can do."

And Catherine was a child of her times. "I want to make a home for you," she said slowly. "I want children, and grandchildren, and I want to grow old beside you. But there's a part of me I never knew was there." She laughed again, but this time her laugh was soft and almost sad. "I'm smart and I'm capable and I can make a difference. No," she corrected herself, "I *have* made a difference at the factory, and I deserve a chance to continue what I've started."

"I'm willing to give it a try."

"People won't like it," she said, her heart swelling with emotion. "My father won't understand."

"He'll learn," said Johnny, reaching inside his pocket. "We all will."

Neither one understood why such a simple solution would make everyone so uncomfortable, but there it was. In a country trying desperately to return to normal, Catherine and Johnny had discovered that the old roles didn't fit quite the way they had before. Like it or not, change was in the air, and there were tough times ahead for men and women in love.

He held out his hand to her and in his palm she saw the glitter of her engagement ring.

"I shouldn't have thrown it at you."

"I shouldn't have let you walk out that door."

"We can make it work," she said, her voice fierce with love and hope. "We *will* make it work."

"I love you, Catherine Wilson." He slipped the ring on her finger. "That's one thing that will never change."

She looked down at the diamond ring, the beautiful symbol of the future they would share together. She wanted to shout her happiness to the world, fling wide her arms and dance for joy that she'd been lucky enough to find love in a dangerous world. But more than anything she wanted Johnny to know just how very much she would always love him.

So there, right in the middle of the street, Catherine raised herself on tiptoe and pressed her lips to Johnny's ear. "I love you," she whispered. "Forever and ever."

And then, in full view of everybody, Johnny kissed the woman he loved.

DOWN THE BLOCK, Dot Wilson and Edna Weaver watched as Johnny swept Catherine into his arms.

"Well, well," said Edna, dabbing her eyes with the cuffs of her gardening gloves. "What do you think of that, Dot?"

Dot Wilson thought about the war, about love and separation, about second chances and happier days ahead. And then she threw back her head and her laughter floated up into the summer air. "Edna, I'd say it's about time."

Epilogue

"Nancy! They're going to cut the cake."

Nancy stuck her head back inside the front door. "In a minute, Mom." The Wilson house was so noisy and smoky and crowded, she could barely hear herself think. Catherine and Johnny had wanted a small and private wedding, but they hadn't counted on Dot's indomitable will. Somehow Dot had conjured up a long white dress, Edna Weaver's red roses, champagne and fifty happy guests waiting to taste the spun-sugar wedding cake and see who would catch the bridal bouquet on that beautiful Saturday in October.

The past two months had been a blur of excitement and upheaval. Japan had surrendered on August 14, and New York City had erupted in ecstasy as the electric sign of the Times Tower flashed the words: "Official—Truman announces Japanese surrender." By the time V-J Day arrived on September 2, Nancy had already sipped more champagne in two weeks than she had in her entire life.

The war was over. The bloodshed, the sorrow, the years of wondering if life would ever be the same as it was before Pearl Harbor.

Of course, everybody knew the answer to that one. Nothing was the same as it had been. President Truman's decision to drop the A-bomb on Hiroshima and Nagasaki had ushered in a new era of warfare—deadlier, more costly, more frightening than anything a Hollywood scriptwriter had ever imagined.

But nobody on Hansen Street was thinking of such things that Saturday afternoon. Catherine and Johnny had finally taken their vows at St. Mary's in a beautiful, tearful ceremony, and now the entire neighborhood was gathered at the Wilsons' for a celebration.

Everyone, that was, except Nancy. Oh, she was happy for Cathy and Johnny. She couldn't imagine any two people more right for each other than her sister and the handsome young man. It had been a rocky road to the altar, but somehow they had worked things out and their future seemed as bright as the lights of Manhattan.

And she was happy for her parents, too. Her dad still wasn't the same self-confident man who had marched off to war so long ago, but if the sparkle in her mother's eyes was any indication, it just didn't matter. Dot Wilson had her husband back at home and all was right with their world.

Aunt Edna and Uncle Les were in seventh heaven because Mac had come home on furlough—safe and sound— two weeks ago, and he and a date were inside toasting the newlyweds with everyone else.

It seemed there were happy endings all around—for everyone except her.

"Quit feeling sorry for yourself," she said out loud, hugging herself against the brisk autumn air. "He'll be here. He promised."

She glanced down at his high-school ring dangling from a chain around her neck. *I'm going to replace that with a diamond, Nance,* his last letter had said. *The first second I get back to the States . . .*

"Things change," her mother had said, trying to cushion her probable disappointment. "I'm sure the boy meant what he said, honey, but you know that war makes people say and do a lot of things they'd never do otherwise."

Foolish little Nancy, believing that her pen pal really loved her. Wasn't that a hoot? Falling in love through the U.S.

Mail. That Nancy, always cooking up some damn fool scheme to get attention—

"Nancy!" Her father's voice this time, louder and more insistent. "Get in here now or else."

"I'm coming," she called back. "I'm—"

She stopped, her gaze riveted on a lone figure at the head of the block. Bell-bottom trousers, a jaunty strut, a duffel bag slung over one shoulder.

"Gerry?" She placed her hand on her chest, as if to control the crazy pounding of her heart. "Gerry!"

He stopped in front of the Bellamy house. That wonderful, beloved face lit up with a smile so joyous she would remember it for the rest of her life. He tossed the duffel bag to the ground and opened his arms wide.

Lifting the skirts of her long, pale blue dress, she flew down the steps toward her future.

Take 4 bestselling love stories FREE

Plus get a FREE surprise gift!

PASSPORT TO ROMANCE
SWEEPSTAKES RULES

1. **HOW TO ENTER:** To enter, you must be the age of majority and complete the official entry form, or print your name, address, telephone number and age on a plain piece of paper and mail to: Passport to Romance, P.O. Box 9056, Buffalo NY 14269-9056. No mechanically reproduced entries accepted.

2. All entries must be received by the CONTEST CLOSING DATE DECEMBER 31 1990 TO BE ELIGIBLE.

3. **THE PRIZES:** There will be ten (10) Grand Prizes awarded, each consisting of a choice of a trip for two people from the following list:
    i)   London, England (approximate retail value $5,050 U.S.)
    ii) England, Wales and Scotland (approximate retail value $6,400 U.S.)
    iii) Carribean Cruise (approximate retail value $7,300 U.S.)
    iv) Hawaii (approximate retail value $9,550 U.S.)
    v)   Greek Island Cruise in the Mediterranean (approximate retail value $12,250 U.S.)
    vi) France (approximate retail value $7,300 U.S.)

4. Any winner may choose to receive any trip or a cash alternative prize of $5,000.00 U.S. in lieu of the trip.

5. **GENERAL RULES:** Odds of winning depend on number of entries received.

6. A random draw will be made by Nielsen Promotion Services, an independent judging organization, on January 29, 1991, in Buffalo, NY, at 11.30 a.m. from all eligible entries received on or before the Contest Closing Date.

7. Any Canadian entrants who are selected must correctly answer a time-limited, mathematical skill-testing question in order to win.

8. Full contest rules may be obtained by sending a stamped, self-addressed envelope to: "Passport to Romance Rules Request", P.O. Box 9998, Saint John, New Brunswick, Canada E2L 4N4.

9. Quebec residents may submit any litigation respecting the conduct and awarding of a prize in this contest to the Régie des loteries et courses du Québec.

10. Payment of taxes other than air and hotel taxes is the sole responsibility of the winner.

11. Void where prohibited by law.

COUPON BOOKLET OFFER TERMS

To receive your Free travel-savings coupon booklets, complete the mail-in Offer Certificate on the preceeding page, including the necessary number of proofs-of-purchase, and mail to: Passport to Romance, P.O. Box 9057, Buffalo, NY 14269-9057 The coupon booklets include savings on travel-related products such as car rentals, hotels, cruises, flowers and restaurants. Some restrictions apply. The offer is available in the United States and Canada. Requests must be postmarked by January 25, 1991 Only proofs-of-purchase from specially marked "Passport to Romance" Harlequin® or Silhouette® books will be accepted. The offer certificate must accompany your request and may not be reproduced in any manner. Offer void where prohibited or restricted by law. LIMIT FOUR COUPON BOOKLETS PER NAME, FAMILY, GROUP, ORGANIZATION OR ADDRESS. Please allow up to 8 weeks after receipt of order for shipment Enter quickly as quantities are limited. Unfulfilled mail-in offer requests will receive free Harlequin® or Silhouette® books (not previously available in retail stores), in quantities equal to the number of proofs-of-purchase required for Levels One to Four, as applicable.

PR-SWPS

OFFICIAL SWEEPSTAKES
ENTRY FORM

Complete and return this Entry Form immediately—the more Entry Forms you submit, the better your chances of winning!
- Entry Forms must be received by **December 31, 1990**
- A random draw will take place on **January 29, 1991**
- Trip must be taken by **December 31, 1991**

3-HAR-3-SW

YES, I want to win a PASSPORT TO ROMANCE vacation for two! I understand the prize includes round-trip air fare, accommodation and a daily spending allowance.

Name_____

Address_____

City_____ State_____ Zip_____

Telephone Number_____ Age_____

Return entries to: **PASSPORT TO ROMANCE**, P.O. Box 9056, Buffalo, NY 14269-9056

© 1990 Harlequin Enterprises Limited

COUPON BOOKLET/OFFER CERTIFICATE

Item	LEVEL ONE Booklet 1	LEVEL TWO Booklet 1 & 2	LEVEL THREE Booklet 1, 2 & 3	LEVEL FOUR Booklet 1, 2, 3 & 4
Booklet 1 = $100+	$100+	$100+	$100+	$100+
Booklet 2 = $200+		$200+	$200+	$200+
Booklet 3 = $300+			$300+	$300+
Booklet 4 = $400+				$400+
Approximate Total Value of Savings	$100+	$300+	$600+	$1,000+
# of Proofs of Purchase Required	4	6	12	18
Check One				

Name_____

Address_____

City_____ State_____ Zip_____

Return Offer Certificates to: **PASSPORT TO ROMANCE**, P.O. Box 9057, Buffalo, NY 14269-9057

Requests must be postmarked by **January 25, 1991**

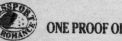

ONE PROOF OF PURCHASE

3-HAR-3

To collect your free coupon booklet you must include the necessary number of proofs-of-purchase with a properly completed Offer Certificate

© 1990 Harlequin Enterprises Limited

See previous page for details